Brian Amos was born and raised in Stapleford, a small town between Derby and Nottingham in the East Midlands.

He attended Albany Junior School, then Bramcote Hills Grammar before moving to Devon in 1982, to study Fishery Science at Plymouth polytechnic.

His first job after gaining a BSc. (Hons) degree was on a fish farm in Inveraray, a beautiful little village on Loch Fyne, in the west of Scotland. Here he met his future wife, Jacqui.

Dave and Jacqui moved back down to Nottingham where they live today. They have three grown-up children, Stephen, Leigh and Kayleigh, and one grandchild, Daniel Jack.

(

t
b

The Ferret, The Donkey and Snakesbelly

Brian Amos

The Ferret, The Donkey and Snakesbelly

Vanguard Press

To my dear wife Jacqui, thank you for having faith in me.

Prologue

The Subaru sat in the car park at the side of the river. Its sole occupant had the seat slightly tilted back and rested his head on the restraint. His eyes were shut as he listened to the police sirens getting closer and closer. He knew deep down that they were coming for him. How had it come to this?

It was strange really – he felt no regret, no anxiety, just a little numbness and maybe a little sickness. His mind was clear, his heartbeat remained the same. He wondered to himself why his heart wasn't racing. Surely his body should be pumping enough adrenaline around to be jizzing up his beat somewhat. He opened his eyes slightly and somewhere in the distance sensed a blue flashing light as the sirens continued to close in. He shut them again.

His thoughts wandered. What made people like him do such stupid things? He thought of the middle aged man on the dole, or jobseekers allowance, or whatever it was called these days, made redundant from his 'job for life'. He walked the streets during the day out of pure boredom. His life a mess, he lived on benefits in his council house with his wife and three kids. His wife has a job in the local petrol station putting in as many hours as she could to supplement the household income. He couldn't get a job in any capacity – well and truly on life's scrap heap. He'd known the good times and lost them. He now had no future and no hope. Surely he was a candidate for meltdown?

The rock star or business magnate who had earned millions in his lifetime, but now had fallen on harder times. No more Range

Rovers, fast women and social drugs. He'd geared up his lifestyle to expect and demand so much. He'd had hundreds of friends and parties were thrown every night, in his big, expensive mansion. Most of his friends had now gone, the parties fewer, the house smaller. Could this man crack up? – Of course; you often saw famous, wealthy people dropping off the 'social radar' and ending up hooked on booze or drugs.

Dean Muxlowe was none of these. He was a sensible bloke in his mid-forties, well educated, well respected and well liked. He had been married to Molly, a little blonde Scottish lady, for over twenty five happy years. He'd brought up three children, the two lads had finished university and now had moved out of the family home to plough their own way in life. His daughter, Rose, still lived at home, she was nineteen. Dean had his own finance brokering business in Nottingham, and it had become a very trusted and successful business. Why was he now sitting in his car at the side of a river waiting to be arrested?

The answer – severe clinical depression. Dean could never accept depression as a real condition – more of an excuse for people to have a few weeks off work. Depression sneaks up on you, forcing you to do things that you don't want to do – you are subliminally looking for an escape from some aspect of your life. You are trapped in an uncomfortable situation with no way out. Something has to change, but you can't consciously bring yourself to do it. Is it because by changing something you might upset someone else? You can't do that. You're too weak.

The pressure builds up and up and up. Your body starts producing all sorts of chemicals and hormones that send you crazy. You can't confront others so you argue with yourself, appearing fine to everyone who sees you from the outside. As time goes by and the pressure builds even more, you argue with your wife or husband, as a pressure release valve. Always the one closest to you.

Eventually you crack. 'Cracking' can take various forms. Some people commit crime, anything from shoplifting to murder, others take a lover. Some put all of their savings into a sports car or fast motorbike and rag it round at ridiculously high speed. Some even commit suicide as an escape. The 'strong' ones manage to do none of these things and conceal their feelings until they finally have a full blown nervous breakdown and spend the rest of their life on anti-depressants or in some institution somewhere.

Dean had been under pressure for longer than he had realised. His wife, Molly, had known full well that he was on the edge, but he would never admit it. He preferred to drink himself stupid most nights to forget – this just led to more arguments and compounded the situation. The waking up in the morning was never a pleasant experience – more headaches, more arguments, more stress, and back to reality.

Yes, Dean was in trouble but didn't appreciate it. He had been at his most vulnerable when a cruel blackmailer had approached him, anonymously, and forced him to commit a heinous crime. Dean was threatened with damage to his wife, daughter and dogs if he did not do as he was told. He did not go to the police or ignore the threats. He did as the blackmailer demanded. If the real truth be known he welcomed the distraction from his shitty life and it gave him a little excitement even.

This was the culmination of this episode in his life. He was waiting for the police sirens to cease as the cars pulled up beside him. He could now see the flashing blue lights even though his eyes were still shut. The sirens stopped as Dean anticipated the knock on his roof from the copper asking him to get out of the car. He smiled – his heart rate had still not increased.

This was it. This is what he needed. At last an escape route. Some say that arrest and prison are a punishment. Dean, even though he had no experience of the like, at this present moment in time, felt as though he was about to be set free. Not so much a punishment as a cure.

Yes, his wife, family and friends may be put through hell. Yes, he would be treated like shit. Yes, he may lose his house, his car, his business – a real life changing event. But, hey, it was better than some of the alternatives; suicide, nervous breakdown or, God forbid, carrying on as if nothing was wrong.

It would certainly test many things to breaking point – his marriage, friendships, and relationships with his family. It may even strengthen some of them. Molly would certainly have to be strong; either that or she'd turn away and go back up to her mother's in Scotland. A new chapter in the life of Dean and Molly Muxlowe and everyone who knows them. Just what the doctor ordered.

This is the story of how and why this man did what he did, who was responsible, and what effects, good and bad, it had on himself and others. Yes, good things do come from such situations. From the bad things we must learn, and in learning come to appreciate the good things. If we can't appreciate the good things then they may as well not be good. What if it was Christmas day every day? What if it was never cold outside?

One thing that Dean Muxlowe came to appreciate above all others was that old saying; 'everything happens for a reason.' By looking back on your life you can only truly understand this. Hindsight is indeed the only exact science, and by using it you can form yourself a better future.

So let's meet the characters and see how they play.

Chapter 1
Snakesbelly

Ernest Selwyn Gerrity was the sort of guy that you would willingly go out drinking with, but would not dare get too drunk with for fear of getting photographed in some compromising position with a high class prostitute, and then be offered the photographs at an extortionate price by Ernest Gerrity himself so that they didn't get into the 'wrong hands'. Trustworthiness was certainly not one of his attributes.

At forty years old, he stood six foot tall with a full head of black hair on a once handsome 'young Harrison Ford' type face. In his early years he had been quite slim and healthy looking but years of good living had piled on the pounds, adding more fat around his belly and flesh around the cheeks and chins.

He was originally from Newcastle but had moved to Nottingham back in 1990 at the age of twenty. He still retained his Geordie accent. He got married to Cilla shortly after making the journey south and had two lovely children, Paul and Victoria, now aged twelve and fourteen.

When he arrived in Nottingham he took up a position as a car salesman for a large motor retail group, Reynolds UK, selling new and used Citroens. He took to it straight away and, to be fair, became a fantastic salesman. Very soon he was selling the most cars and making the most profit. The boss, Joe Reynolds, was over the moon with his natural ability and hunger to earn a lot of money. The only thing that let Ernest down was his atrocious paperwork and false promises to his customers. Many of the new Citroen owners complained that things they had been offered in the deal had not materialised. When the 'squealers' did come in Ernest was nowhere to be seen, leaving all the problems for someone else to sort.

After a couple of years, Mr Reynolds did start getting a little pissed off with Ernest's failings in certain areas. When the sales slowed down a little, whether due to boredom on Ernest's part or loss of reputation due to his customer satisfaction policy, Reynolds started showing his displeasure. A combination of this and a particular invoicing inconsistency that came to light at that time caused a mutual split and Ernest decided not to work elsewhere but set up his own business trading cars from home.

Now whatever bad things you could say about Ernest Gerrity, he did have a knack of getting people to do what he wanted them to do. The definition, I suppose, of a good salesman – he was likeable, believable, eloquent, relatively handsome, extremely ruthless, and completely untrustworthy. Combine all this with his totally selfish side and you have a very dangerous animal.

Over the years, the nineties and early noughties he built up a very profitable business, and became a well-known face to all the Nottingham and Derby 'Gliterazzi'. He dealt with most of the local motor traders and became close friends with many 'high flyers', supplying them with their prestige Land Rovers, BMW's, Mercedes-Benz, Porsche or whatever – they trusted him, they believed his lies and they swallowed his bullshit.

His main line of business was to 'capture' a Sales Manager or person responsible for the buying and selling of stock vehicles, at local car dealers. Over a period of time he would befriend them and build their trust, often buying their trade cars off them at good prices and ideally overpaying on the odd occasion for a car that the dealership had overpaid for and risked losing money on themselves.

By overpaying himself Ernest would save the Sales Manager from getting into trouble and the embarrassment of explaining to the boss that they'd valued a car wrongly. Ernest was then owed one.

After a period of time, as the 'friendship' blossomed, the relationship would progress to a new level. "Fancy a quick pint after work?" was the first toe in the water. "…I'm paying."

At the public house the business relationship would be discussed. If the Sales Manager sold all of his part exchange cars to Ernest, Ernest would pay cash or part cheque, part cash. The invoice to Ernest would show a price less than Ernest would be paying, as long as the actual value of the car was higher than the price paid. For example, let's say the dealership took in a part-exchange, a nice little four year old Volkswagen Golf with a market value of £5000. They would either give the customer less for it than its value (known as 'nicking the swapper'), or write profit out of the new car that they were selling in the form of a discount. This would allow the dealer to show the car on their books at a lower value, let's say in our example, £4500. The Sales Manager would sell the car to Ernest for £4750, which he would pay in cash or part cash. The invoice to Ernest would show £4500 so that it would not show a loss on the sale and draw unwanted attention from the upper echelons. Ernest then had a car £250 less than its trade value and the Sales Manager would pocket the £250 cash that had been paid over the invoice price.

On the other side of the coin, if Ernest could get a used car dealership to overpay for the car his profit would be maximised. In our example if he sold the VW Golf to another dealership for £5250 – £250 too much – giving the used car Sales Manager a 'cash back bonus' of £100, he would have paid £4750 at one garage, driven it down the road and sold it straight to another dealer for £5150 (taking out the £100 he gives to the buyer) – that's a very quick, very easy £400 profit. Both Sales Managers would be happy, the only losers being the dealerships and their customers. Once the Sales Managers 'took the bung', they were captured.

If you can imagine ten to fifteen dealerships all doing this, you can see that Mr Gerrity was making quite a killing. If he didn't have a buyer for the car he would send it to the auction, chances were it would still make a profit as it was bought under market value. All he needed was enough casual drivers to pick up and deliver these cars, usually old blokes that had retired and were bored and willing to work for peanuts. It wasn't unknown on the odd occasion for Ernest to pick up a batch of cars on a twelve car transporter (12 X £400 = £4800!)

Around the early noughties he came up with a rather ingenious, if not totally moral or legal scam to supply new prestige cars to his more wealthy customers. He concentrated on Land Rover, Mercedes-Benz, Lexus and Porsche.

The Government introduced a scheme to help severely disabled drivers buy a new car. In simple terms the scheme allowed a disabled driver, if in receipt of the higher rate Disabled Living Allowance, to purchase a new car free of the VAT, at that time a saving of 17.5%. The car must be 'substantially and irreversibly' adapted to the requirements of the driver – adaptions such as wheelchair hoists, ramps and the like were considered to be 'substantial and irreversible', however no such guidelines were in writing as such.

The basis of Ernest's scheme was that the forms required to confirm that the vehicle had been substantially and irreversibly adapted, and hence exempt from VAT on the Government's scheme, were signed by the Sales Manager of the car dealership. Oh, dear! There was no restriction on the type of car available on the scheme or its value.

Ernest's first task was to set up a network of disabled people who qualified for the exemption. For signing a few forms and allowing money to be moved through their bank accounts, they would be paid £250 a time. To a disabled person living on benefits this was a very tempting offer. Ernest would complete all the paperwork for them and transfer all the money. If any correspondence came through the post he would call by and collect it, even stopping for a chat and a cup of tea. Ernest found these people very trusting and malleable. The £250 a time helped.

Ernest then set up a network of new car Sales Managers that would supply the cars and sign all the necessary forms. They usually had no problem with this as the cars all made profit, they all counted as new car registrations for the dealership and each signature on the right form attracted a cash 'facilitators fee' paid by Ernest. Most were blinded by the benefits and believed what they were doing was totally legal. "It's a loophole, mate, perfectly legal. Just don't tell anyone or they'll all want some." Ernest often referred to his 'team' as 'coin operated.' "The only loser is the VAT man." The trouble is though, as we all know, the VAT man doesn't like to lose.

The major fraud that was being committed was that the 'substantial and irreversible' adaptation carried out on the car was usually a small knob fastened to the steering wheel that could be removed with a screwdriver by the new owner.

Ernest started by selling cars to his friends. He'd sell them a new car with a bit of a discount. If he sold them, as he tended to specialize in, the new prestige models that were difficult to get hold of, he would leapfrog to the top of the waiting list and supply the car at full-up list price, plus maybe a cheeky £1000 cash fee to get to the top of the list. Who controlled the waiting lists? – The Sales Managers!

Ernest would buy the £40-50-60000 car with a discount of up to 10% depending on the model and availability, plus, of course the 17.5% VAT off by registering it in the name of one of his network of disabled drivers. He would then sell it to the end user showing them a little saving on the new list price – if he had to. Usually it was just enough to get them to the top of the list on the latest model. Sometimes he'd charge them the £1000 premium on top. The profits were phenomenal – as they say in the US of A –'you do the math.'

Logistically all that Ernest would do was transfer the money to the disabled persons bank account plus the £250 fee, get a draft from their bank to pay the dealership the full amount for the car, pick up the car and drive it to the real end user. On most occasions he got the real buyer to transfer the money he'd charged them to his account before he paid it into the disabled persons, creating a positive cash flow situation.

The only further thing that Ernest had to do was call round to the disabled person's house after a few days to pick up the newly arrived V5 registration document from the DVLA. He would then re-tax the car in the real owner's name to change the ownership. There was no minimum time that the disabled person had to own the car before they 'sold' it. He even got round the insurance to tax the new car – he'd get a cover note in the name of his man, give it to the dealer to tax the car, then cancel the policy within the fourteen day cancellation period – he'd tell them the deal had fell through or he'd had a cheaper quote or something.

The profits as I already mentioned were extreme and Ernest, being Ernest, got used to it. He geared up to a £500,000 barn conversion on the right side of the river Trent, big cars, big expensive holidays, the lot.

Ernest had one Land Rover dealership so under his spell that he was 'buying' many of their new Range Rover Sports. These cars at the time had a huge waiting list of customers. So much so that new cars that were registered and sold as 'used' were fetching thousands of pounds over the list price of a brand new car, as the dealer cannot sell a vehicle above the manufacturers list price when new. People were prepared to pay over the odds for a car now rather than have to wait for it for six to twelve months. The dealers had to pay lots of money for good used Range Rover Sports.

Ernest would buy the cars new from the dealer, register them to the disabled person on the scheme, and then sell them back to the dealer as a registered used car with no miles on at full list price. The profit margin would be the 17.5% VAT, so on a £50000 car Ernest would earn about £8000 – plenty to be able to lubricate a few palms along the way. The car dealer makes full up profit margin on the car plus he then has the car back to sell as a used vehicle over the odds. The Sales Manager gets his usual £500 'facilitator fee' and again everybody but the VAT man is happy. Sometimes the cars never moved from the dealerships new car compound until they were taken to the used car pitch.

As the money rolled in Ernest became more and more extravagant. He was out every night, pissed, always with a different woman flashing his wad – poor Cilla was always left at home with the two kids – she became very sad and depressed, even with the money sloshing about. Although she wasn't kept short, Ernest didn't like giving her too much, just what she needed.

With money comes image and status – or at least the desire for its portrayal. Also comes temptation – drink, cocaine, and prostitutes – whatever is on offer. Ernest started on the road to ruin. At the time he was unbeatable, untouchable but unaware. You don't want to think, you daren't think 'what if?'

In June 2006 Cilla threw Ernest out of the house. She could be quite a terror when pushed and had finally given up on him. To be fair she had given him many chances, too many chances, but he just couldn't 'keep it in his trousers' as she kept barking at him.

Anyway, he left and shacked up with another woman, one of his latest conquests.

Stella was a divorced woman in her mid-twenties (Ernest was now thirty-six). She was professional, own house, own car, no kids, you would like to be able to add 'plenty of common sense' …but no. She was very attractive, long dark hair, green eyes, fair skin, five feet nine tall and a slim but shapely nine stone.

Cilla was relentless and took Ernest for everything, and then some. Then some more. Ernest Gerrity the so-called 'big business brain' was totally outclassed and outflanked in the divorce courts. Cilla moved into a smaller house, bought out of the equity in the barn sale, and Ernest ended up with absolutely fuck all.

Over the next couple of years Ernest saw many more changes in his life, although his new woman stuck with him through thick, thin and thinner.

The thinner started when many of the sales managers that he had 'in his pocket' started to falter. A lot of the smaller garages were sold to the bigger groups, who had a policy of sending all cars taken in part exchange to the auction to ensure a fair market price. They also employed Group Buyers who bought cars for the whole group of dealerships – this allowed one man to buy a lot of cars and get them cheaper – bulk buying power.

This, of course, cut out the sales managers in many dealerships from buying and selling cars. This had the knock on effect of cutting out much of Ernest Gerrity's income. Every month seemed to see another small 'owner driver' swallowed up by the big groups and lost as a meal ticket.

Ernest, in an attempt to retain his income level, pushed more and more for the VAT free Motability scheme cars. Unfortunately the scam became too widely known as sales managers moved around and got a bit greedy, trying to set up their own 'little earners' with other traders.

As the scheme grew it inevitably came onto the VAT man's radar. The revenue people had to step in. Millions and millions of pounds worth of VAT were being lost. It was reported at one stage in a local paper that a disabled car trader from Liverpool had alone made over one million pounds out of the job. Investigations were launched, police were involved, and dealership officials were sacked. As you can imagine, particularly with the upsurge of large dealership groups, the scheme was scrutinised as every application was made. Adaptations to the cars were checked as being 'substantial and irreversible' and in some cases the disabled customers were actually being watched on CCTV as they picked up their new car. Bank accounts were checked and questions asked – 'where is the money coming from to buy the car?'

It was disaster on a number of fronts for Gerrity. How things change in the motor trade, eh? One thing that did remain constant was his appetite to spend money. He was addicted to sunshine holidays, cold champagne, and more worryingly, had become quite a fan of crack cocaine.

Money ran low. He'd hidden some but it wasn't a vast stash. Come November 2008 he was getting desperate – he knew he only had 6 months, maybe a year if he stopped eating out at restaurants and doing crack. SHIT! The clock was ticking...he needed a plan.

An ode to Ernest Gerrity – Snakesbelly

Ernest Gerrity esquire
Cannot lie straight in bed
His greed for money, wine and song
So fills his crooked head

The need to lie is like a drug
To cheat, to graft, to steal
There is no equal he can see
Just how it makes him feel

He'd rather not waste too much time
Working is not funny
No, there is a better way
To earn a lot of money

One quick hit, good and hard
Some unsuspecting loser
Take his dough and slap his arse
Then off down to the boozer

Chapter 2

The Donkey

Dean Muxlowe was a plodder. Nothing more, nothing less. Seemingly he was satisfied with his lot in life. Satisfied, not necessarily happy. He was forty-eight years old, five feet eight tall, with a bit of a paunch, round face, small features, and ginger hair just starting to go grey at the edges and very thin on top.

He was married to Molly and had been for the past twenty-five years. Three children: Alan, twenty-five; Ronnie, twenty-three; and Rose, nineteen. The two boys had done the university thing, done the travelling thing and had now moved out of the family home in an effort to plough their own way. Rose was still at home in their four bedroomed detached property in Lenton, a leafy suburb on the outskirts of Nottingham. The three of them shared the house with their two cocker spaniels called Guinness (a black one) and Gilbert (a white one).

Dean had been to University many moons ago before carving a career in the motor trade as had Ernest Gerrity. Indeed he had worked with Gerrity in the early nineties for a short period at Reynolds UK, the Citroen dealer.

Dean was a specialist in the finance department of the selling process, getting the customers the necessary funding and selling them add-on products such as payment protection insurance, extended warranties and service contracts. He'd proven very successful.

Unlike Gerrity, Dean had remained working for car dealerships up until 2006. He'd had spells with Vauxhall, Ford, Land Rover, Porsche, Mercedes-Benz, and Toyota. Although he didn't deal with Gerrity on any basis, he would periodically bump into him and pass the time of day.

It was 2006 that he got fed up of working for someone else. The time had come, he thought, to channel all of his acquired knowledge, experience and skill into creating a business of his own. Something to build and to be proud of. The time was right. The economy was buoyant and he'd reached that point where he realised his career was heading on a downward slide towards retirement (the bit of your life just before death). He needed a new challenge.

He wasn't alone in his thoughts. His wife, Molly was very supportive of course, but one of his colleagues at the Land Rover dealership that he currently worked for in Nottingham was very keen to join the quest. At first Dean was a little wary and intended to do it all on his own, but after sitting down and talking it through with James Hunter-Browne, he decided that there were benefits to having a partner. After all it was a huge step into the unknown, and maybe quite a lonely one.

Hunter-Browne was younger than Dean at thirty-eight years old (Dean was forty-five at this point). He was also married, to Michelle and had a little daughter called Penny, aged three. He had only been married for four years but been with Michelle for twelve years. At six feet two and thirteen stone, James Hunter-Browne was quite slim, with short, jet black hair, chiselled features and glasses – the ones with thin rectangular lenses trying to give the impression of intelligence and aggression. Always shaved, always smart.

The business that they set up they called 'MHB Finance Ltd.' The MHB relating to the initials of their surnames. They would basically act as a finance broker arranging loans for customers to buy cars or vans from dealerships or privately. Both Dean and James had accumulated, over the years, a large pool of wealthy customers that they could approach to drum up some business. They would contact all of these people with the message that next time they looked for a car to give them a call rather than accept what finance the supplier had to offer. By using their suite of lenders they could shop around and find a better deal for them and do all the legwork. It would piss off the motor dealers because finance commission was a big source of income for them. They weren't in it to make friends, just money.

So in September 2006 they both handed in their notice to Land Rover and on 1st October 2006 moved into a small office in the middle of Nottingham to start trading. They'd both taken out loans of £20,000 to live on for a few months with no income, and invest in the necessities such as laptops and office furniture, telephones, printers, photocopier, a car each.

The office was a bit of a windfall. One of James' old customers had shown an interest in the business and let MHB have one of his offices for free for six months. After that they would pay a minimal rent when they were, hopefully, on their feet.

Initially the prospect of going alone was very daunting. No back-up from an employer. If anything happened or broke down you had nobody to ask. You were on your own. You set up the printers, phone system, fax machine and computers. You need furniture – you fetch it and build it. You get a bill – you pay it.

The immediate priority, once the office was set up, was to get the finance companies to agree to lend their customers money. With the experience and reputation that both Dean and James had, they were quite confident of success in this area, but nothing now was a given. They contacted many of the big banks and recognised finance companies. Some were quite interested (or was it just polite?), some would not deal with brokers, and some wanted to wait until MHB

Finance Ltd. became a little more established. However, meetings and appointments were set up and the two of them pushed hard at contacting literally hundreds of their past customers by telephone, by letter and by email. Initially the response was very slow, and although they did expect it to be so, there was a little nervous energy in the air – verging on panic.

Then after a fortnight of trading, or rather trying, there came a breakthrough. They had arranged a meeting at their office with the local NatWest bank, who were located just 200 yards down the hill, in the centre of Nottingham. The meeting went great – the local representative, Shaun, and his boss both knew Dean by reputation and had, indeed crossed swords in the past when the bank was trying to finance cars bought through the dealership that Dean was working at. He had talked to the customer and basically provided finance through the dealership for the funding, which pissed off the bank in a big and special way. Still that was in the past. The result of the meeting was that the bank would take finance proposals from MHB Finance Ltd. and fund their customers, subject to status, paying the advances to the dealerships supplying the cars and paying a commission to them for introducing the business. This was what they needed and the same day a business customer, Midlands Engineering Co. Ltd. from Ilkeston contacted them to help finance a Range Rover that they were buying locally. The first deal was done. The proposal was accepted by the bank. The car was invoiced by the dealer to the NatWest and they paid the money to the dealer and £1,500 finance commission appeared in MHB's bank account. It all seemed very easy. After the first deal came the second, then another, then another. Before long Dean and James were in no doubt that they had done the right thing.

Other finance companies wanted to be involved once they could see MHB trading and no longer desperate for their help – Barclays,

Yorkshire Bank, Santander, ING. This gave MHB the ability to play one off against the other and if the NatWest didn't accept the deal they had somewhere else to try – another bite at the cherry, so to speak.

The business went from strength to strength and in their first year MHB Finance Ltd arranged over £3million of loans for people and businesses, earning over £150,000 finance commission. Happy days.

It was near the end of this first year of trading that Dean heard some warning bells in his head. Everything was going very well, almost too well, and as a result his partner, James, started acting strangely. He seemed to be possessed by the demon money, wanting more and more.

Dean couldn't put an exact date on it but around May/June time, 2007, James was spending less time prospecting customers and more time looking at estate agent websites, showing an unhealthy interest in big expensive houses. Over the weeks this behaviour progressed from casual interest, to general enquiry, to tentative viewing, to 'having another look', to 'toe in the water' offer, to firm offer. Eventually, despite Dean's strong and vocal advice not to, James and Michelle had an offer of £545,000 accepted on a barn conversion in the middle of the countryside. The house was OK – the middle property in a complex of three – Molly described it as 'the world's most expensive terraced house' – she shared Dean's concerns. James and Michelle were obviously looking for the status symbol, the bragging factor. James needed to impress his wife, family and friends. He needed to show people how successful he was and what a shrewd businessman he had become. He wanted to give his wife a house she could hold parties in and invite all the 'right people'. What he didn't realise was that most of his so called friends were laughing behind his back and taking the piss out of his lavish lifestyle. He

27

came to be known as *Brewster* after the character in the film, 'Brewster's Millions.' Whenever Dean spoke to people, almost unanimously they warned him and advised him to dump James Hunter-Browne as he was a business liability. There was only one place he was heading – down the tubes, and he would take Dean and MHB Finance with him. He would not, or could not appreciate the 'what if' factor.

At that time the mortgage marketplace was full of crooked brokers who could arrange, without too much trouble, a huge mortgage based on a person's self-assessment of their income if they were self-employed or a company director. Whether this assessment was a true reflection of reality or a pipe dream seemed to be irrelevant at the time and so with only a small deposit coming from the equity in his current house he organised a £2,000 per month interest only loan to buy the house. Again Dean protested but Hunter-Brown ploughed on regardless. Looking back Dean saw this as the beginning of the end.

Anyway, business for the time being continued to roll along nicely, the only downside in Dean's mind was that, due to a high level of personal commitments, most of the profit was being taken out of the business as dividends. Nothing was being saved to build up a 'what if' fund – a parachute in case of problems.

The business was joined by two of Dean's old colleagues – Michael O'Dell and Bernard Johnson – Mike and Bernie, as in 'Winters'. They were employed as finance reps to go out and be a bit more pro-active in getting business.

With the big house and gardens, James was now into ride-on lawnmowers, quad bikes, landscape gardening contractors, a Range Rover for the parasitic non-earning wife, and even talks of a horse for Penny. 'Ridiculous,' Dean kept telling him, even to the point of conflict, but all to no avail. 'Lord of the Manor' syndrome was well and truly installed into the head of James Hunter-Browne.

'A recipe for disaster'. Dean's friends, Dean's wife, Dean's customers, Dean's business colleagues – all continued to warn him of the inevitable huge pitfall. Everyone had an opinion. Everyone was a fucking expert. James himself would openly brag and shout from the highest rooftop to anyone who was twat enough to listen, about how much he paid for his house and how much it cost to run and maintain. How all the décor had to be 'in-keeping' and thus ridiculously overpriced.

Dean, who deep down knew all these people were right, refused to agree with them to their faces. They continued to tell him to get out and start again on his own, but no, he didn't – he would stand by and stick with it – what a twat, what a mistake. But that was the way he was.

Early 2008 saw a downturn in business, or rather good business. There was a trend towards global recession and banks getting into problems. Talk was of Northern Rock going bust, to be probably followed by others. Government bail outs, quantative easing (printing more money), house repossessions up, unemployment up, exports down. In general the country was fucked and the banks and finance companies became more and more frightened to lend money. Bad debt was rising and the knock-on effect down the line was affecting virtually all businesses to varying extents. Dean and James noticed a marked reluctance of their finance companies to lend money to their customers, even the good, clean, creditworthy ones.

The problems were from both sides – not only did banks not want to lend, the customers couldn't afford to borrow. Those that had borrowed heavily on cars in the past couldn't afford their repayments and had to hand the cars back to the bank. Because so many were being handed back the auctions were flooded with cars, particularly big lumpy cars, and thus the market values were brutally cut – usually to a lot less than the customer owed to the finance company. They would sometimes try and sue for the difference but very rarely did they have any joy. Millions had to be written off due to this negative equity. Many people ended up with county court judgements and bankruptcy orders.

Car finance was the area that most money was lost and so it was inevitable that the finance companies started pulling out of the market. First Barclays, then NatWest and Yorkshire Bank. It was very soon the case that MHB Finance Ltd. were on the verge of closing down due to lack of both creditworthy customers and, just as importantly, willing lenders. Customers could be found with a little hard work, but if you had no money to lend them there was little point looking.

Of course this caused major panic for James and Dean, particularly James who would find it very difficult to find a job in a dealership that would fund his £4,000 per month lifestyle. Good God – what would the 'Gliterazzi' make of Lord Hunter-Browne selling cars for a living? The problem was that the only big wages in the motor trade came from selling big prestige cars – cars that nobody could afford to buy outright and were unable to finance (except, of course, premiership footballers).

As good fortune would have it, just as very little hope was left, two finance companies approached MHB with offers of deals. They were only small companies and didn't pay much commission but the offer was there. The embers of hope still had a faint glow. Both Winston Brothers Finance and Alpine Funding were there to try and mop up some of the better brokers. They were backed by wealthy individuals who wanted to move in and take advantage of the general financial decline. As rates were reduced by the government these two saw the opportunity to lend money to customers at higher rates paying less commission to brokers – a highly profitable situation.

They could also be fussy as to who they lent their money to i.e. low risk only. It meant a lifeline to MHB though, but a much reduced income. Still, the company would survive. Could Hunter-Brown?

'No', was the answer.

The two had to work harder to earn less money. James could not survive on the reduction so had to set up a supplementary company he would supposedly operate in his spare time called 'Hunter-Brown Specialist Cars' – the 'own time' bit was the grey area. Dean became less and less happy as James spent more and more of his time buying and selling cars for his own benefit, leaving the finance side to him. Dean was doing more work for the business, still having to split the profit 50/50 at the end of the month, whilst James supplemented his own income buying and selling cars for himself, not splitting his profit at the end of the month. Why was Dean such a pushover? Deep down all he wanted was for everyone to be happy and successful and have what they wanted in life. More and more people were laughing at him and telling him what a mug he was. Dean still refused to accept that he was wrong.

As Hunter-Brown Specialist Cars did quite well and got busier, James spent even less time with MHB Finance. Dean was starting to wobble.

It was now November 2009, every month was seeing an increased frustration in Dean Muxlowe. Over the last six months he had continually argued with Molly over the business, had more ridicule than he could stand off his friends about the business, spent significantly more time and energy working for the business, and as, he believed, a consequence of his shit life in general, had started to heavily drink every night to escape from, and forget about, the fucking business.

What the fuck could Dean Muxlowe do to change his life? Then it happened…

An ode to Dean Muxlowe – The Donkey

Dean Muxlowe plods on like a mule
His life is in the drain
What must he do to be reborn?
And get his demons slain

He's 48, he's tired, he's bored
He drinks like Moby Dick
His wife, his mates, they all can see
Something must happen quick.

Along comes a beast, so foul and cruel
Life's so unfair sometime
This little bloke, such easy meat
Forced to a life of crime

Yes, he's drifted from the path
So straight and so well paved
But after all his pain and grief
He knows that he's been saved

Chapter 3

The Ferret

Paul Milford was not a very nice man. He was the sort of person that didn't seem to have any personal attributes or skills, but was particularly lucky in some of the things he did.

He was quite arrogant, quite ignorant, and not too bright but he thought that he was, and not much liked, but thought that he was. He had no sense of humour and very little empathy with anyone. In appearance he very much resembled the caricature of a ferret. At the time there was a kid's program on the TV that was very popular that starred a pair of puppets who were supposed to be ferrets. Paul Milford bore a striking resemblance to one of them which led to the entire crowd at the local pub calling him Wee Ferris – the character's name.

At five feet four tall he weighed nine stone 'wet through'. Sixty years old, short spikey grey hair, constant stubble and thick rimmed, thick lensed glasses. The spikey hair and stubble was his attempt at 'rugged youth'.

Because of his luck in life he had managed to accumulate quite a substantial wealth. With this wealth he 'bought' his friends. He was always visiting his local pub, 'The George and Dragon', always getting the drinks in for the locals. The only price they had to pay was to put up with his company – his grating little voice squawking on about his construction business and how successful it was, how much money he was earning, and how he was spending it. Most locals would rather have bought their own drinks.

Paul was brought up in Fenton, a small village on the outskirts of Nottingham. His father had started up a bricklaying business with his partner. The business was called 'Milford Park Construction Services (John Park being his partner). It started in June 1960 when Paul was ten years old.

The business became very successful in the provision of skilled labour to local projects, and the Milford family became very wealthy. John Park, in 1970, decided to jack his share in and retire. He was quite a bit older than Paul's father, who bought him out for a pittance; nowhere near what it was worth, which left room for the twenty-year-old Paul to become part of the business.

Throughout the '70s and '80s Paul led a playboy lifestyle, sustained by the business being run by his father, who retired officially at the age of sixty-five in 1985, although he was still very active for several years after that because Paul wasn't really capable of running the job. However, Paul was his only son and he didn't have much choice.

Paul's father made sure before he let go completely of the reigns that he created a company that 'ran itself', with good staff and management so that Paul didn't have to get too involved. He just owned most of the company and took his dividends.

The guy who effectively ran the business, and did it properly, was Paul Fairchild. He joined the company in July 1980, at the age of thirty-five. He was a lawyer by trade, and a very aggressive businessman. He developed a new side to the business that Paul really warmed to.

Basically, they would take on a contract to build houses, subcontracting out the windows, electrics, painting, plumbing etc. to other, small companies and tradesmen. They would then take the money from the developer and find any excuse at all not to pay the subcontractor – sub-standard work, time penalties – any excuse. If the subcontractor squealed too much or came on heavy, then Fairchild would direct them to their lawyers, or they would get a visit from their 'quote adjusters'. The 'quote adjusters' were really price adjusters – thugs who would visit the subcontractor mob-handed and offer a pitiful amount of money to settle the disagreement once and for all. The subcontractor usually had labour and materials waiting to be paid so that they could complete the job. They were put under so much pressure that they usually capitulated and took the money, leaving Milford Park very profitable.

Milford Park, because of this reputation became the people not to do a job for and expect to be paid fairly. However as the recession bit there were still more contractors than jobs and there was always somebody prepared to take the risk.

In March 2009, Paul had a bit of good luck. The business was doing OK, and he still wasn't really needed, just a figurehead to be brought out and dusted down at certain occasions to make the right guffawing noises, shoot the odd pheasant and munch the odd canapé, washed down with a drop of fizz.

On his way back from The George and Dragon on the first Thursday in March he called into the local Tesco fuel station to fill up his car – a new white Range Rover Sport HSE Diesel. After a good hundred pounds worth he wandered over to the kiosk to join the queue. It was packed that night for some reason and sod's law had it that only one till was in use. Apparently one of the cashiers had had an accident and had to be sent to the Queens Medical Centre for treatment. Only two people on, one of which was busy sorting a problem on the forecourt.

After fifteen minutes queuing, Paul was one customer away from the till. He was hopping up and down with rage, and after his five and drive of Stella at The George and Dragon, was dying for a piss. The guy in front handed over his card and asked for a number three, £5 lottery scratch card – the ones with the £250,000 jackpot.

"Of course, Sir, I've just got to wait for my colleague to come in as the cards have slipped forward and I need the key to get one out." The male assistant was overly friendly. 'Employee of the Month' material.

"No problem," said the man, pleasantly. "I'm in no rush."

"I fucking am." Muttered Paul, in a voice that he hoped would not be heard, but was.

"Sorry, sir," chirped the assistant. "My colleague won't be many minutes." Paul turned crimson.

"Whilst I'm here," continued the guy, "I'll have a Mars bar, two plain crisps, and a sausage roll."

"OK, sir, I'll take the money and get your ticket very shortly."

"Fine," agreed the customer.

Paul's bladder was now about to burst. Of course there was a problem with the customers PIN. The forecourt assistant came in having sorted her problem, opened the cabinet and took out the appropriate card for him, putting it next to his Mars bar, crisps and sausage roll.

"Thank you," sang the cashier. Paul was sure he was gay.

After rubbing the debit card several times and it not working the customer was getting hot and flustered. Eventually he tried another card. The queue behind him was now a huge line of scowling faces. Bingo! It worked. The customer picked up his stuff and virtually sprinted out of the shop, running the gauntlet of the angry crowd, smiling pathetically.

"Pump seven," Paul squawked, shoving his card at the cashier who would not be rushed. The card went through fine.

"Thank you kindly," the cashier replied gaily, handing Paul his card back. "Shit!" he exclaimed. "That guy has forgotten his scratch card."

"Don't worry," said Paul, picking up the number 3 card. "I'll catch him with it; he's still out there look."

He grabbed the ticket and took off. The cashier tried to protest but the next punter's card was being shoved in his face. "Pump 4."

Paul had every intention of handing the card over but he just missed the guy as he drove off, "Shit," muttered Paul under his breath. There was no way he was chasing the guy or even going back to the kiosk to hand the card in. His only thought at that time was "Piss."

He pushed the lottery scratch card in his pocket and raced home to relieve himself.

Such ecstasy. His piss was so needed. The relief, he thought, was better than sex – and he didn't even have to cuddle the piss afterwards.

He walked into the kitchen to greet Heather, his partner, with a kiss, removing his coat and remembering the scratch card in his pocket. "Fuck it." He thought, taking it out.

"Have you got a coin handy, sweetheart?"

"Yes, sure," replied Heather, handing him a fifty pence bit. "I didn't think you liked scratch cards."

"Well, I thought I'd have a punt." He replied, rubbing off the silver coating. He didn't really know what he was looking for – a little like an old codger in a modern pub trying to play the fruit machine.

When he finished he studied the card. To him, he thought he'd won. Three horseshoes. "What do three horseshoes mean, Heather?"

"Let's have a look." She snatched the card off him. She studied it. "It means you've won a prize," she smiled. "Probably five quid. You've got to remove the 'prize box'. Here, let me do it."

Paul said nothing, just handed back the 50p coin so she could continue.

Off came the silver coating. Her face turned to stone. Her heart was in her mouth. She felt sick.

"Fuck me pink!" she tried to say, her mouth as dry as a camels piss-flaps. "You've won a quarter of a million quid."

"Fuck off," replied Paul. "You're as bad as them twats down the George and Dragon always taking the piss out of me."

Heather just stood there open-mouthed, checking it over and over again. After a few minutes silence she confirmed. "No joking. You have just won two hundred and fifty thousand fucking quid." She paused. Paul felt his heart travel to his throat. "A quarter of a million fucking quid." Heather confirmed again.

It was true; the card that Paul had stolen had been a £250,000 jackpot winner. He realised he was grinning like a Cheshire cat. "Best keep my gob shut." He thought.

After jumping around a bit and 'yahooing' a bit, Paul declared, "I'll go and get some champers; you call the take-away and get some grub in. Don't tell anyone yet, we'll enjoy it on our own for a while."

"Oh, no Paul," screamed Heather, "you can't not let me tell anybody."

"Not just yet," affirmed Paul, quite sternly. Do as I've said. We'll keep it to ourselves until it's all confirmed. Please do not tell anyone yet. OK?"

"If you insist," She conceded

"I do." He said.

Well they did have a good night in; Loads of champagne and loads of Indian food. Paul had to wrench the phone off Heather several times to stop her bleating about the win.

The following day Paul visited the same Tesco petrol station to buy a few bits, including a number 3 scratch card, after first making sure it was a different cashier on duty. He made a point of being overly chatty to the young guy behind the counter. He took everything home. On the way he removed the silver off the scratch card – it was a £5 winner – he threw it out of the window with a smile on his face.

"OK," he beamed as he walked through the front door. "You can tell people now." Everyone would now think that the ticket he'd just bought and thrown away was the winner, and so rightfully his. The CCTV would show him entering the shop and the cashier would hopefully remember him if there was any doubt.

Paul made it public knowledge very quickly, telling all his cronies at The George and Dragon, The Nottingham Echo, and all his staff at Milford Park. Everybody lied about how pleased they were for him.

So came November 2009, Paul was in a very good position. A successful business that he didn't have to work at, big house (paid for), and £250,000 in the bank.

He spent most of his days down at the gym, at The George and Dragon, on the golf course, or at some country hotel with Heather. They'd had a few foreign holidays but this was restricted as Heather didn't like to travel far.

What could go wrong…?

An ode to Paul Milford – The Ferret

Paul Milford is an odd old man
Not got much fun or cheer
He likes to think he's loads of mates
But he must buy the beer

The brain power of a tiny wasp
The charisma of a bear
How did he build up so much dough?
Life really is unfair

He doesn't like to pay his bills
A fact that's so well known
He ducks and dives and runs away
His heart is made of stone

His luck in life's beyond compare
He's such a jammy wee soul
I'm sure those million's he'd give up
To not look like a weasel

Chapter 4

The Scratch card 'winner'

Rocco Salatti was a painter and decorator by trade. He was forty-five years old, five feet ten tall, fourteen stone, and stocky build, a bit like Phil Mitchell off EastEnders but with a shock of short cropped white hair. He was born in England off Italian immigrant parents and had grown up all his life in Halesford, Nottingham, the next village to Fenton along the A52.

He had married at twenty-five and now had three children; two boys and a girl. He was self-employed and had a good, average life, although moneywise he was always skint, always on the edge. His large mortgage took up most of his income – he had been in his current house for ten years and had fifteen years left to pay, taking him up to sixty.

He didn't go out much, mainly due to money restraints, although he did have a couple of lads that worked for him and they tended to all drop into their local for a couple of pints on a Thursday and Friday night after a busy day. The first Thursday in March 2009 was no exception. They called into The Jolly Cobbler to discuss how the current job was going and relax a bit before facing the missus. Rocco's missus was out with her mother so the dinner would be late anyway.

It was around six p.m. and Rocco decided to fill his car up with petrol. He didn't drive his van home. He had a yard a couple of miles away. He'd always preferred to drop the van off with all the work stuff in and drive home in his little 'toy'. His car was an old Nissan

Skyline – lovely thing to drive and sounded great, but very, very thirsty for fuel.

He called in this night to the local Tesco service station and filled her up. He'd never seen it this busy here before but didn't mind too much as he was in no rush and had, fortunately, dropped in for a piss just before he left the pub.

There were very few staff on that night – just David, serving, and Shaz, who was fannying around with someone on the forecourt who'd let a load of unleaded onto the ground without realising it. The guy had a Smart car, one of those little plastic things with two seats. The fuel filler pipe had somehow become detached from the fuel tank and the guy had stood at the pump daydreaming whilst all the fuel passed directly from the pump to the forecourt.

Rocco had to smile. He used the fuel station regularly and knew that Shaz would be mocking and taking the piss for weeks on the back of this. Still, it left David on his own in the kiosk. Apparently there were supposed to be four of them on at any one time, but Rocco later found out that Andrew had taken Phillip to The Queens Medical Centre because he'd cut his thumb whilst opening a box of crisps with a Stanley knife.

After filling up, Rocco queued up to pay for his fuel. Behind him stood a rather disagreeable little man, fidgeting and sighing, commenting at the lack of staff and how much of a hurry he was in. His face was bright red and he gave Rocco the impression that he was half pissed.

David, to his credit, and the little man's obvious annoyance, remained cool. He had worked there for many years. He was one of those that had been doing that very same job from before he left school, and was now, Rocco thought, mid-twenties. He was always there and all the regulars knew him by name. He was one of those that was always up for overtime, always covered for illness and was never ill himself. The petrol station was his life, bless his little cotton socks. He was very thin, quite effeminate, dirty blonde hair, thin spotty face, around six feet tall. Really he should have moved on and got a proper job elsewhere, but he was well fixed in his comfort zone. Some people get to a point and just can't bear to change out of fear of the unknown.

Rocco finally got served, paid for his fuel and got a sausage roll, crisps and a Mars bar as he remembered that his wife, Pauline, wouldn't be making tea until later as she was out with her mother. Oh, yes and the usual number 3 scratch card.

The guy behind Rocco was becoming increasingly annoying. The sighs were getting deeper and he kept grumbling to himself. "Twat." Rocco thought. The idiot's mood didn't improve firstly when the lottery ticket dispenser had to be unlocked by Shaz, who they had to wait for to come in from the forecourt, and then Rocco's debit card wouldn't work.

Eventually he got sorted. He used another card. He picked up his crisps, Mars bar and sausage roll and left wondering why his card wasn't working. He was sure he'd got money in the account; maybe he'd damaged the card or something. He gave a pathetic smile to the guy behind him whose red face had an expression like thunder. Rocco was reminded of an angry little ferret.

Rocco jumped in his car and drove away, the non-working debit card still on his mind. Had he any money left in the account? He could now start to feel the effects of the two pints he'd had at the Jolly Cobbler. The traffic was still busy but as he approached the exit some kind soul left a gap for him to jump into. As he pulled onto the main road he looked into his rear-view mirror and thought he saw the ferret man waving at him. It was too late to go back, he was in the line of traffic now and was more concerned about not spilling his opened bag of crisps in his car.

When Rocco got home he parked up, went into the house and sat back in his favourite chair, TV remote in hand. He'd invested recently in cable TV so spent the next ten minutes looking through the guide for something decent to watch. He came across 'River Monsters' with Jeremy Wade. He liked that but didn't agree that the Wels catfish could possibly be classed as a 'ferocious predator.' The kids were all upstairs in their rooms playing on computer games or communicating with their friends on Facebook. His two boys, Dino and Shane, were fourteen and seventeen years old respectively. Victoria was his 'baby' at 11. He expected Pauline back at eightish, she would probably bring in fish and chips. Until then he polished off his sausage roll and Mars bar with a can of Stella Artois. "Bollocks." He thought as he realised that he'd not picked up his scratch card. He couldn't be arsed to go back now, and he would surely be over the limit anyway. Still, David would probably realise what he'd done and keep it for him until the next time he went in.

The lottery scratch card went out of Rocco's mind until the following Tuesday. He'd not been back to the fuel station, partly because he'd had a busy weekend, partly because he didn't feel it was that important – over the last few years he'd probably had two or three cards per week and never won more than a tenner at any one time.

That Tuesday he had finished work and went straight home. He didn't need fuel yet. Pauline had bought a copy of the Nottingham Echo and threw it at him as he walked in, opened at page three. "I see some jammy fucker from up the road in Fenton has just netted £250,000 on a lottery scratch card. Bastard. I wondered if you know him; Paul Milford. A bricklayer or something."

"Never heard of him," replied Rocco studying the paper. There was a picture of Milford and Heather popping a bottle of Champagne. 'There's money in bricks and mortar', was the headline.

Rocco looked at the picture, immediately realising that he knew the face but couldn't quite place it. "I know that guy," he frowned.

"Well, see if you can tap him up for a loan then. It reckons he's loaded anyway; 'successful businessman' it says; Money to fucking money, eh?"

Rocco's frown was suddenly replaced by a look of shock when he grasped who he was looking at. "Fuck, me. It's ferret man."

"Ferret man?" quizzed Pauline.

"Yes," Rocco went on. "Last Thursday I called in to fill the Skyline up down the road at Tesco and this guy was behind me in the queue. I remember because he was irritating me, obviously in a rush he kept moaning and sighing." Rocco read through the story. His heart started to flutter as a thought came into his head. He was gabbling with excitement now. "This bloke won £250,000 on a scratch card on Friday morning which he bought from Tesco garage. It just so happens that on Thursday night I bought a scratch card with a £250,000 jackpot prize and like a twat forgot to pick it up. I thought I saw this little ferret man waving at me as I drove off into the traffic. I hope it wasn't to give me the card that I'd left behind." He looked up at Pauline. Pauline was staring back at him open mouthed.

"Well it's one hell of a fucking co-incidence if it's not your scratch card. What can we do about it?"

"I don't know," answered Rocco. "I'm going down to see David at the garage. He'll remember."

"Why didn't you stop and see what he wanted when you saw him waving?" Pauline was starting to shout now as panic set in.

"I was on my way into the line of traffic by then and couldn't turn around."

"Fucking brilliant! Fucking brilliant! You've just given away quarter of a million quid because you couldn't be arsed to turn around and get your ticket. What was up? Had you been to the fucking pub again and were busting for a piss? Is that why you didn't turn round?" Pauline was now screaming. This argument would go on and on.

Rocco raced to the fuel station, sweat pissing from every pore. Every traffic light was on red and every dawdling old twat in the world was on the road to try and delay him. As he pulled in and parked up close to the kiosk next to the big 'every little help's' sign. He was relieved to see that David was on duty. He raced in through the automatic doors that wouldn't open fast enough, the paper in his hand.

"David." He called. "How are you?"

"Fine Rocco," chirped David as he span round. "What's up? You look like you've seen a ghost."

"Just have a look at this will you." He thrust the paper under David's nose.

"Yes," said David, "I've not seen the article but I'd heard we'd had a big winner. Andrew sold the guy the ticket on Friday morning."

"Doesn't that face look familiar?"

"Yes, a bit," confirmed David. "I can't place him though. Do you know him?"

"It's that guy you served last Thursday night. The guy that stood behind me huffing and puffing. You apologised to him about the delay." David was frowning, trying to think. "The night I forgot to pick up my number 3 scratch card."

"Of course," David remembered now. "Yes, yes, yes. I gave your card to this guy to give you as I was in the middle of serving the next customer and couldn't leave the till. He snatched it up and said he could give it to you as you were still out there. He was quite insistent. He seemed honest enough"

"You gave it to him?" Rocco was incredulous. "You're fucking joking?"

"No." David was on the defensive now realising where Rocco was coming from. "It was too busy. I was on my own." His lip started quivering.

"Right, OK." Rocco was thinking what to do. "Have you ever seen this guy here before?"

"No, never." Tears were welling up in David's eyes.

"OK. Thanks David." Rocco left the kiosk not really knowing what he would do, only that he must do something. Did he try to find Milford? Did he call the police? Or did he just give up on £250,000, his £250,000 that had been stolen from him? No fucking chance.

On careful examination of the photo in the Nottingham Echo it was obvious that it had been taken outside of The George and Dragon at Fenton. Rocco thought he'd pay a visit to see if anyone knew Milford. It was maybe his local; the article had said he was from Fenton. He felt sick and his head was in a haze. He'd been robbed, he was convinced. He was getting grief from his wife as she was blaming him. He couldn't have felt worse if his house had been broken into. It was the first day's work he was going to miss in ten years of being self- employed, but he couldn't work. He couldn't think straight. The George and Dragon opened at noon. He would be their first customer.

The first person he saw as he walked into the pub was George Popolopodis; a big, fat Greek bloke, friendly face, not far off retirement. "A pint of lager, please," Rocco requested.

"Certainly, sir. Not seen you in here before." George spoke very good English with only a slight hint of an accent.

"No," replied Rocco. "I don't get out much." A little false laugh. "I'm looking for a friend of mine." He showed George the picture from the Echo.

"Are you a journalist?" asked George.

"No, no. He's just a guy I've lost touch with over the years." Just a little lie from Rocco. "I see he had his photo took here. Is he a regular?"

"Yes," said George. "It's no secret I suppose. He's in here most days lately. He'll be here later today, probably around four 'o'clock. A few of them come in for an 'early doors'. They leave around sevenish." George finished pouring the pint. "That's £2.95, please."

"Thanks." Rocco paid for the pint and sat down at a table not far from the bar. He drank his pint then left to return later. He still didn't have much of a plan.

Rocco decided to leave it until about four-thirty p.m. If the guy had nicked his scratch card he might see Rocco at the bar and know he'd been rumbled. He certainly would remember his face.

As Rocco walked through the door he immediately saw Milford sitting at a table in the corner sharing a joke with a woman. Heather it was, the same woman in the photograph in the paper. Rocco ordered a pint.

"Hello chaps." Rocco approached the table where the two were sitting. Milford stopped laughing and turned white as he looked up and recognised him. The expression on Milford's face was all that Rocco needed to know the truth. The pure fear he saw in the eyes told him that the ferret man had stolen his money.

"Hi," said Heather, the smile remaining on her face, not picking up on her partner's terror. "Do we know you?" She looked across at Milford and instantly knew there was a problem. The smile faded.

"You don't know me, darling," answered Rocco. "But myself and Mr Milford have met. Isn't that right, Paul?" He looked straight in Milford's eyes and laid his hand gently on his shoulder. He felt him physically retract.

"I don't think so," stuttered Milford, as he looked away trying to avoid any more eye contact.

"I think so," pressed Rocco. "Last Thursday night in the Petrol Station; Tesco. Remember?" He waited a few seconds in silence for a reply. There wasn't one. Milford had gone from pure white to bright red as he was on the verge of being exposed. Rocco carried on. "I left my lottery ticket on the counter. You took it off David, the cashier, and were supposed to bring it out to me... You didn't." A long silence.

"Of course... Yes," stumbled Milford. "I missed you so I went back in and put it back on the counter. David must have it."

"He says not," countered Rocco. More silence.

"Well that's how it was," insisted Milford, getting over somewhat the initial shock, and starting to compose himself. "I bought my scratch card Friday morning. Ask Andrew, he sold it to me."

"Is that right?" Rocco's grip tightened on Milford's shoulder. He visibly flinched. At that time another figure approached the table. Ernest Gerrity stepped in.

"Listen mate, he won his money fair and square, now..."

"Don't 'listen mate' me," snapped Rocco. "This guy is a fucking lying, thieving little ferret faced bastard." The voice was now raised in aggression. He put his pint down on the table as if to free his hand to punch Milford. George was on his way from behind the bar, sensing trouble.

In one movement Rocco grabbed hold of the front of Milford's polo shirt, half lifting and half dragging him off his chair, across the bar and pinning him up against one of the pillars. "Now listen here to me you snivelling little bastard; you know what you did and you now need to face the music." Rocco's hate filled eyes bored into Milford's through his thick lensed glasses.

"Put him down." It was the authoritative voice of George, trying to conceal his joy. "Now."

Heather was on her feet. Rocco did not move an inch. Liz, the barmaid was lifting the phone to call the police. Seconds passed in silence.

"Well?" shouted Rocco. They were all looking at Milford who remained speechless.

"Look, mate." George was trying to remove the heat. He did not get far.

"Shut it you." Rocco's eyes were fixed on Milford, shouting at George. "This little shite has stolen from me."

"No, I've not," whimpered Milford.

"You lying twat. I can't believe that anyone can be such a wanker. You know that was my ticket you stole that won all the money." His grip on Milford's shirt remained tight.

"I bought my ticket on Friday." Milford's voice was shaky but insistent.

"Fucking liar." Rocco raised his fist as if getting ready to punch him. "I'm not going to give up." George stood gobsmacked. Heather started to cry. She'd obviously realised now what Paul had done but wasn't going to give up £250,000.

"OK, sir. That'll do Please put the gentleman down." Officer Gareth Moore was just passing The George and Dragon when he got the call about a disturbance. The call from Liz. He and his colleague, Alice Dew, were now stood in the bar.

Rocco looked across. "Officer, this man has stolen £250,000 off me. I want him arrested."

"Just put him down, sir and we'll talk about it. Do it now." The voice of authority. Rocco pulled his hand away and turned his back on Milford as if he couldn't bear to look at him.

Officer Moore asked Milford; "Are you OK, Sir?"

"Yes," replied Milford straightening his shirt. The last thing Rocco wanted was to be arrested so he moved away from the scene a little. Moore and Dew spent a few minutes having a little talk to Milford, Heather and George. They then moved onto Rocco who had taken a seat at another table. Moore was still the mouthpiece.

"I understand that you have a complaint."

"Yes I do," answered Rocco. "That guy has just won £250,000 on a lottery scratch card. I bought the card but left it on the counter at Tesco fuel station. He snatched it up telling the cashier he was bringing it out to me. He didn't. He played the card himself and it won the jackpot. It won a quarter of a million quid. Is that fair? It's theft."

"Have you got any proof, sir?" asked Moore.

"Well I don't know. CCTV? David at the petrol station will back me up. I don't know. Can't you guys do something?"

"Look, sir." It was Alice Dew's turn to speak. "Mr Milford has just told us his side of the story. Now if you want to continue to make a complaint then you need to do so down the station. I, personally, do not think that you have much of a case."

"What?" Rocco's anger level was increasing from hateful to murderous.

"Well." She continued in her level condescending tone. "He says that he bought the winning card on Friday morning. He has a witness – the guy that sold it to him. His partner, Heather, has confirmed this. He went public on Friday and the papers have printed the story. The article also features an interview with the guy who sold the ticket – on Friday morning. Unless you have some concrete evidence to the contrary, then I'm sorry, sir, I just don't think anyone will listen."

"What about CCTV at the garage?"

"We can look," offered Moore. "But many petrol stations only have CCTV looking over the forecourt to catch petrol thieves. I don't think they'll show the gentleman stealing the lottery ticket off the counter and even if they do you would have to prove that he didn't put it back, as he claims." Both of the officers stood with a 'game over' sort of expression on their faces – the expression that they obviously practice a lot at Police College.

Rocco was incensed. He could quite easily have cut Milford's throat as he sat there looking like the victim. He looked over. Milford looked back, a slight smile briefly passing across his lips. The smile of the ferret. Rocco looked back at the police officers – their expression was still fixed. "This does not fucking end here." He spat, and stormed out of the pub. His feelings were frightening him. He felt out of control. He had to get home and regroup.

The following day, Rocco paid a visit to the police station to report the theft. After a couple of hours of trying he realised that he probably had more chance of kissing the Pope's arse than getting any sympathy or help from the police. No proof. Too much work involved. The CPS wouldn't go for it without a good strong case with plenty of evidence. Evidence that didn't exist! Rocco had to wipe his mouth and walk away. Every day for the rest of his and Pauline's lives they would be asking 'what if?' The ferret-like features of Paul Milford were indelibly etched on their minds. The temptation was almost overpowering. The word 'hate' was nowhere near strong enough for what he felt.

As a final insult, as he left the police station, he was warned to stay away from Paul Milford. He did.

You've got to be in it to win it

You've got to be in it to win it
So Rocco bought a ticket
But when the ferret stole it
He was on a sticky wicket

A £5 scratch card number three
He left it at the till
The medicine he had to take
Was such a bitter pill

The ferret man he swiped the lot
Such a load of money
Depriving Rocco and his wife
The land of milk and honey

How could Rocco put things right
And claim his rightful win?
To walk away and give it up
Would surely be a sin?

They went to see the policeman
Who didn't give a damn
You should have kept your ticket close
You silly little man

So there you see it's over
Goodbye to quarter mil
No-one seems to give a fuck
Not even the old bill

Chapter 5
The Plan

"What could I do to earn a lot of money very quickly?" It was a question that Ernest Gerrity had asked himself many, many times during his life but much more often recently. It was the first week of November 2009 and Gerrity was financially in the mire. He had probably six months before complete meltdown.

His girlfriend, Stella, had stuck by him. In her he had found someone who he fitted perfectly. They were both a little unpredictable and had many rows over anything at all, but ultimately would end up back together. The old 'soul mate' cliché was very apt. She was not, however, aware of the impending doom of Gerrity's financial situation. When she found out her resolve would be tested to destruction, and he knew it. The pressure was on to find a solution.

Crime was the obvious answer to short term riches – but did involve risk – so be it. But what crime? Drugs? Robbery? Extortion? Demanding money with menaces? Blackmail? Gerrity, not known by some of his friends as 'Snakesbelly' for nothing, was not opposed to anything, as long as the risk was minimal.

He needed a victim. A victim who had plenty of money, not much intelligence and preferably not much balls. He didn't fancy drugs or robbery as too many people would be involved and he didn't trust anybody. Extortion, blackmail or demanding money with menaces was probably the safest, if he could find the right victim.

He started racking his brains and talking to his colleagues down the pub. His local pub, The George and Dragon at Fenton.

Another of the locals there, a Paul Milford, had recently been bragging to the regulars there of a big win on the lottery, or a scratch card or something. Gerrity knew of Milford, the ferret man, indeed had spoken to him on a couple of occasions through mutual 'friends.'

He knew Milford as a wealthy man, business owner, a bit of a 'wet blanket' who seemed to crave attention and friends, of which he didn't have many that were genuine. One night in the past, Gerrity recalled, the locals placed a number of ferret soft cuddly toys strategically around the bar as a joke. Milford stormed out in tears like a mardy baby and was not seen for weeks. Big bullies.

Could this be a potential victim? Could Gerrity demand money from this guy without arousing suspicion in his own direction? Mmm… The profile fitted to a certain extent, but how would he react? Gerrity needed to research the man a bit, but time was of the essence.

He couldn't be sure. Milford was not an 'open book'. If the police were brought in things could get messy, and Gerrity would be on the front line. The police would check out the people closest to Milford first. Gerrity didn't have the confidence in his own ability not to get caught. He hadn't so blatantly broken the law before and not surprisingly was shit scared…but desperate.

One minute he was on, the next off. There was nothing else he could think of and time was running out. He then started to formulate a plan. An acorn of a plan that gave him a bit of a buffer against getting found out. He would simply get someone else to directly threaten Milford, someone who didn't necessarily have the money but was too shit scared to involve the police. A scapegoat. A Fall-guy as they say in the States.

The plan started to grow, as acorns do, into a mighty oak tree. He would find an intermediate victim. He would threaten to harm the intermediate in some way unless they did exactly as Gerrity told them to do. In that way, if the intermediary was caught, the police would not have a direct line to Gerrity. If the middle victim was terrorised enough they might even take the blame. If the police weren't involved, the drop off of cash could be arranged so that Gerrity picked it up himself. He was starting to get excited now and seeing the possibilities unfold.

Tuning, more tuning, then fine tuning was the name of the game. Who could he use as a middle victim?

Gerrity drew up a list of everybody he knew. He went through the alphabet listing everyone he could think of, however unlikely, from A to Z.

When he got to 'M', he was suddenly enlightened. Dean Muxlowe. Perfect in every way. Gerrity had known him since the early '90s when he briefly worked with him at a Citroen dealership. He was very respectable and solid. He'd been married for years to the same woman, Molly he thought, had three kids, his own business, own house. In other words loads of what Gerrity liked to call 'pressure points' – Aspects of his life that could be threatened. Muxlowe had never been in trouble with the police before, as far as Gerrity knew, had plenty of access to word processors and printers and, just as importantly, hadn't got a direct link to Gerrity himself. Nobody would think that Muxlowe would commit a crime at all. A perfect conduit to Milford's bank account.

So Gerrity had a plan and a couple of victims. If this worked well it could be a springboard to greater things. Maybe he'd set a few more going after the initial tester if it worked OK. If it didn't there was minimal personal risk.

Over the next few days Gerrity spent all of his time in preparation. He firstly went out and about doing research – research into both Milford and Muxlowe. He needed to know his victims. He was talking to mutual friends and contacts, casual questions, looking at their businesses, a bit of legwork in The George and Dragon. He even bumped into Milford in there one night and bought him a pint – asking him about his lottery card win – not too much interest as to arouse suspicion, but Milford did love to talk about himself and his money. To be fair he wasn't bright enough to realise that he was being pumped for information no matter how blatantly Gerrity's questioning was.

He 'bumped' into Muxlowe in one dealership and suggested a quick pint in the local pub. Muxlowe agreed and they sat for a couple of hours exchanging life stories and talking about the good old days.

Gerrity was certain that he had his two stooges. He had qualified them perfectly. The six 'P's – perfect planning prevents piss poor performance.

Gerrity also spent a lot of time on the internet studying past cases of blackmail and demanding money with menaces. This not only gave him ideas about avoiding certain pitfalls but helped him refine his plan and solve some of the problems that had been worrying him. He was now quite keen to get started.

Chapter 6

The First Letter

November 20th 2009, a Tuesday. Dean Muxlowe had just finished off at the office. It was six p.m. and he was feeling quite down.

Business had been excellent over the past few months but Muxlowe could not help feeling used and abused. The money had been earned by the company, or more accurately by him, but he was no better off. His business partner, James Hunter-Browne had been spending less and less time on the business and more and more time feathering his own nest, selling his own cars through Hunter-Browne Specialist Cars.

Dean had tried sitting down with Hunter-Browne and laying it on the line. He'd tried shouting and barking. He'd even had a general meeting including the wives in an attempt to tug at Michelle's guilt strings. Nothing had worked. All he got was, "don't worry, just a little longer until I've paid off this loan." There was always another loan though. At one point he'd promised faithfully to stop selling cars privately and shut down Hunter-Browne Specialist Cars and concentrate solely on MHB Finance Ltd. One hundred percent. It lasted one week and he was back to it. Dean was at the end of his tether.

Anyway, it was the 20th November and Dean was done for the evening. James had not even called in to see if any business had been done – obviously too busy himself. Frustration was eating into Dean's mind and bones, turning him a little bitter and twisted. It was causing arguments with Molly, who had come to really dislike, or more accurately resent, Hunter-Browne. She could see that Dean was being exploited and hated it. As a result Dean didn't relish walking into the house at night. He would get the same old questions every time: "Has James been in?"; "What's shithead been up to today?"; "Have you seen him?"

The one thing that could cushion this blow, indeed the only thing, was drink. The only problem was that Molly didn't like him drinking so it wound her up even more. Dean would drive back home past the large Tesco Extra store and call in for a half bottle of his favourite cheap white rum, or a full bottle if he was feeling particularly edgy, or felt that Molly might want to join him in a swallow. He could still get a full bottle of 'Superior' white rum and two litres of own brand cola for under a tenner, which would send both of them into oblivion – bargain!

Well, tonight was an edgy night so he got the full Monty. He called Molly on his mobile to tell her he was calling in and came upon the usual objections. The parting barrage from Molly being; "well if you're getting a fucking drink from Tesco you may as well get something to stick in the microwave 'cause I'm not cooking when you're pissed." The phone went down.

Twenty minutes later Dean walked through the front door with a bottle of white rum in one hand and Tesco cola in the other. He walked into the kitchen, greeted the dogs, who were always pleased to see him whether he had a bottle or not. He then poured a drink for himself and Molly before going into the living room, take a sip of rum and coke, gave Molly a kiss and sat down – all in that order.

The reception was its usual frosty one. The usual questions, the usual moans. Dean just sank into his chair as he faced the music. He took a long deep swallow of the sweet dark liquid. When he'd poured the drink he gave Molly half an inch in a three inch tumbler topped up with cola. Himself he poured a good two inches with a small dash of cola. The effect of the cold liquid was intense as he felt it travel all the way down his throat to his stomach and the warm tingly feel of ecstasy and relaxation radiate from deep within his body all the way out to his fingers and toes. Nothing mattered anymore. There was nothing to compare. He shut his eyes and gave out a long sigh.

"You've got a letter." Molly scowled just as Home and Away was starting on Channel 31. Her eyes didn't move from the television.

"OK," replied Dean. "Probably another bill or something, I'll open it later."

"No, it's not a bill."

"Oh. OK, then I'll open it now." Dean opened his eyes and took another swallow, virtually finishing the drink off. He got up to fetch the letter from the kitchen, using it as an excuse to get another drink. "You want another one yet?"

"Alright, then." She necked the weaker drink and handed her tumbler to Dean. It usually took her a couple of swallows to relax after a day bending and twisting out of shape.

Dean poured the drinks and picked up the letter. He didn't usually get mail at home apart from bills and bank statements. This was different. Dean was curious.

As Home and Away blared away in the background Dean sat down and opened his letter. It was anonymous, and at first he thought it was a joke. After reading it, he had another swallow, and read the letter again not knowing if it was for real or not.

"What is it?" Asked Molly, still entranced by Summer Bay.

"Oh, nothing." He replied. "Just something from the insurance. I'll sort it tomorrow." He put the letter in his pocket to deal with at work the following day. One thing was for sure was that he wouldn't be sleeping tonight, not unless he walloped the rest of that bottle… Which, of course, he did.

The following morning he went to work early. Having got pissed up the night before so that he could sleep, he had woken up at about three a.m. and been awake ever since. He now had things other than James Hunter-Browne on his mind.

Dean sat alone in his office, as usual, and took out the letter. He had seen nothing like it before. It began…

"Dear, Deano, you do not know me, so don't think you do. I know where you live. I know that you are married to Molly and that she works at Tesco Express, the supermarket over the road from your house. I know you have three children including Rose, who is nineteen and lives at home with you. She is very pretty. I also know that you have two dogs, Guinness and Gilbert, who play in your back garden regularly and jump up the fence at the bottom to bark at passers-by.

"I need you to do something for me and not to ask any questions. You may not involve the police, any friends, acquaintances or colleagues. You will do exactly as you are told to, immediately when you are told to do it. I'm assuming that you will obey my instructions. The consequences of you not doing EXACTLY as you are told or involving ANY other parties, are threefold:

*I will poison your dogs. (With pilchards and paracetamol.)
*I will damage your daughter, Rose.
*I will damage your wife, Molly."

The letter then went on to describe the 'damage' that was meant, in great detail. It involved breaking bones, cutting skin and worse. To be honest it was totally appalling. Dean felt both terrified and sick in the pit of his stomach. He couldn't believe the level of depravity that the letter's author had stooped to.

The letter ended, promising to be in touch with details of what Dean had to do to avoid the wrath of 'Myra' – the sender that was obviously not the Moor's murderer but someone not far off the same pathological mentality.

Dean read and re-read the letter, hoping that it was just a one-off. Some twat that had decided to let off a bit of steam and would get over it, or more likely sober up and forget they'd done it. He put the letter right at the back of the bottom drawer of his desk and decided not to tell anyone.

The following day – no follow-up letter. The day after – no letter. Great. He hadn't told anyone, even Molly. Particularly Molly in fact, as she would panic and start building mountains out of mole hills.

A week passed and still no follow-up. Dean felt that he was now safe.

The following Wednesday, however, the second of December, as he walked through the door at six-thirty p.m. with his two bottles, he was met by Molly. "You've got another letter." She said. "It looks like the one that came last week." Dean's stomach tightened and his head fizzed.

"Thanks." He replied. "I'll get us a drink." Molly frowned as she sensed that something was wrong. He shoved the letter in his pocket determined not to open it until the following morning. To make sure, after pouring the drinks, he walked out of the house and put the letter on the passenger seat of the car. Tonight he would have a drink with Molly and forget.

The letter was opened by Dean the following morning at his office. The tone of it was the same as the first one, but this one gave very specific instructions. When he'd read these instructions his first instinct was to go to the police. He was being told to commit a horrendous crime or else his wife and daughter would be mutilated and his dogs killed. The writer re-iterated that they knew a lot about Dean and was watching him continually. Dean picked up the phone, started dialling the police, and then hung up.

Again and again he went over the letter. What would he do? One minute he was calling the police, the next he was carrying out the instructions. His mind was a blur.

He went home that night with his bottles and Molly was waiting, this time with a hand stencilled note that had been pushed through the front door while she was at work. All that the note said was "DO THE RIGHT THING, DEANO".

Molly's face was annoyed and harassed. "What the fuck does that mean?"

"I haven't got a clue." Replied Dean. "It means absolutely nothing to me. I'll get us a drink and have a think about it."

Of course they had a couple of drinks and Dean skilfully switched subjects. After Home and Away came Emmerdale, EastEnders and Coronation Street. After they'd finished the bottle it was time for bed and sleep. Dean would deal with it the following morning. Tonight it was forgotten.

He opened and read the letter the following morning. His mind was tearing up.

The letter gave him a name and address – a guy called Paul Milford from Dagmar Road in Fenton, a small village just the other side of Nottingham. There was another letter enclosed written out in capitals using a kid's stencil set in green felt tip pen. The instruction was basically to type up and print off a letter using a word processor, and send it to Paul Milford, first class post, over the weekend. The letter was a threat demanding the sum of £20,000 from Milford, 'or else.' It didn't give a specific drop-off time or place for the cash but said that details would be sent 'soon.' If instructions weren't obeyed or the police or anyone else became involved, then the amount of money would be increased and the 'or else' bit would become more severe.

Dean looked at the letter in disgust but realised he was over a barrel. He had heard of Paul Milford, vaguely, and googled the name. His business came up and also a brief story from The Nottingham Echo about his lottery win. "Well." said Dean to himself. "At least he's got a few quid to spare. Probably won't miss it anyway. Would Dean risk pissing off this 'Myra' for the sake of this guy? If this 'Myra' was serious then he knew he may regret it, big time. And Milford would not thank him for not sending the letter.

"Fuck it." Dean said out loud. He fired up his laptop and logged on to the word processor. Hopefully it would be a one-off and this is the last he'd hear from it. He thought that last time. But he did type out the letter and he did send it off, taking care, as instructed, not to leave any fingerprints on the paper, or keep a copy of the letter on the computer.

As he had just posted the letter on his way home, he had the overwhelming wish that he could reach into the post box and get it back out and bin it. But of course, he couldn't. Still, he thought, forget it, that's the last of it, time for a bottle from Tesco.

Chapter 7

The Ferret's first letter

Monday morning Paul Milford liked to have a lie in. There were a couple of reasons for this. Firstly, even though he was sixty years of age, he still liked to live it up a little at the weekend that tended to wear him out. Secondly, at his place of work they were very busy and he would just get in the way. Yes, they would willingly pay money for him to stay at home.

At eleven a.m. on the 7th December 2009 the postman arrived with a letter for Paul. It was the letter that Muxlowe had posted on the Friday.

Paul was sitting at his wicker table in his large conservatory looking over his huge landscaped garden and water features, drinking his coffee, white, three sugars (but don't stir it because I don't like it too sweet). Heather came through from the kitchen with his mail. He discarded the bills and the junk as always and was left with just one letter.

Still a little bleary-eyed, he opened the letter and started reading. Heather had gone back in the kitchen.

The letter was supposedly from a woman called 'Myra', well that is what it said anyway, and was basically a malicious note demanding money from him.

"Who's the letter from, darling?" Shouted Heather.

"Just some fucking freeloader trying to beg some money off me. Obviously seen something somewhere about the lottery scratch card win. Well they can fuck right off," replied Paul.

"Quite right," agreed Heather. "Scrounging bastards."

Paul read the letter again, this time paying a little more attention to what it was actually saying.

"Dear, Paul. My name is Myra. I am a person that you know quite well. You have a very short memory when it comes to money, you still owe me £20,000 from way back and since you recently had a little good fortune I think that now is as good a time as any to pay me back."

Paul stopped and thought. He didn't remember anyone called Myra, or indeed anyone he owed £20,000 to. Yes, he'd ripped off a lot of people in the past and yes, he'd sent people and companies bust by refusing to pay bills due to a 'technicality', but nobody came to his mind straight away as the author of the letter. Still, he couldn't be expected to remember everyone he'd stuffed, he did that sort of thing for fun. Maybe his solicitor could recall. Anyway, he read on…

"I want £20,000 cash off you. I will tell you when and where and how. You will get the money out of the bank today and keep it handy, so when I get in touch you will be ready"

Paul stifled a little laugh at this point. "We've got a right arrogant prick here." He shouted through to Heather, and then read on.

"I will now tell you what will happen if you do not comply with my wishes. My plan comes in four stages. The sooner you pay me the money, the sooner I stop the contact with you and you live the rest of your life without me. Until then you do as I say."

"Twat," muttered Paul

"If you do as I say straight away, let's call it 'stage 1', I will take the £20,000 cash and say 'thank you very much, debt paid.' You will then never hear from me again. If you don't pay, or you contact the police, or any other third party we will have to move on to 'stage 2'.

"At 'stage 2' I will ruin your reputation and your life. I will send one hundred letters to households in your local area and fifty local businesses. I will also have one thousand posters printed and put up overnight on shop fronts, street lights, traffic lights, buses, cars, telephone boxes and anywhere else appropriate around Fenton. The theme of all this literature will be the accusation that you are a serial sex offender, paedophile, nonce, wrong 'un.

"Obviously this is all lies, Paul, but who will know that? Where there's smoke... The letters and posters will all have your name, address and phone number on. Who knows they may even have a photograph of you on, or at least a cartoon drawing of a ferret. Obviously 'stage 2' will incur costs and your bill will go up from £20,000 to £25,000.

Paul was now starting to panic a little as the gravity of the letter hit home. Who was this maniac? Was it a real psycho or just some crank trying to wind him up? Maybe one of the George and Dragon crew? There was more.

"If you still don't pay up, or insist on getting the authorities involved, we progress to 'stage 3' and the bill goes up to £35,000. This is where I pick on several of your friends and family getting them 'roughed up' a little and making sure that they know who is responsible for their pain. Each one will be told that they are to suffer because they are close to you."

Suddenly it wasn't some crank anymore it was some psychopath that was obviously very dangerous. Paul felt sick. The last paragraph read:

"Finally, ferret; at the end of it all I will put you in a wheelchair for life if we get that far. I will be in touch, lots of love and kisses, Myra. P. S.I know you will do the right thing."

"You've gone quiet," beamed Heather as she came back through the conservatory. She then noticed Paul was no longer smiling. "Paul whatever is wrong? Whatever does it say?"

Paul was stunned. He said nothing, just handed over the letter. Heather read it in silence, the colour draining from her face, her expression one of shock. "I'll call the police. She headed over to the phone.

"No," interjected Paul. "Not yet. Let's think a little about this. It might be one of them piss-taking twats down at The George and Dragon. They're always trying to wind me up. Let's just let it ride for a while. They say they will let me know what to do –that is when we'll get the police involved. It will probably blow over."

"I don't agree," countered Heather. "If it is one of them twats then they need to be punished for shit like this. It's sick."

"Yes it is, and yes they should," agreed Paul, but please, Heather, just leave it to me. I will deal with it as and when I think. OK?"

Heather looked to the ground. "OK." She said, solemnly. "But don't let the twats piss all over you as they always do. They're wankers down there; I don't know why you go."

That was the end of it for now. Paul filed the letter, making sure he put it, and the envelope, in a plastic wallet to preserve any fingerprint evidence that may exist, just in case he had to get the 'rozzers' involved.

It goes without saying that both Paul and Heather needed a few glasses of wine that night to get to sleep. That was after going over and over who the letter writer could be. Who would have a grudge? Well, maybe a few candidates to be fair, but to be that evil…

Anyway, all they could do was wait and see what happened.

The Blackmailer's pen

The letters from the blackmailer's pen
Cause heartache, fear and pain
The evil threats and hateful lies
Will leave a poisoned stain

He doesn't mind whose lives he wrecks
He cares just for himself
He digs in dirt and spreads it round
Just to increase his wealth

He must be caught, this evil beast
His freedom must be taken
For all that hate deep down inside
His life should be forsaken

So when the judge says "take him down"
Does the victim cheer?
Is his life his own again?
Or will he still have fear?

He hears the postman at the door
His heart goes all a flutter
He hopes its junk or direct mail
Please not another nutter

It never ends, it's always there
You try to sleep, you fail
It comes round quicker than you think
The bastards out of jail

Chapter 8

The Third Letter – Gerrity

December marched on and Christmas approached. Ernest Gerrity kept picking up his pen and stencil sheet fully intending to keep the demanding letters going. Deep down though he was a coward, shit scared of getting caught. He was hoping, really, that an alternative source of income would present itself so he didn't have to carry on with the rest of his scheme. He was still trying to trade cars and still made a crust, but his overheads were so high and his lifestyle so lush that his bank account was like a colander.

He'd go to the pub, have a few bevies, go home to Stella, some nights, and sit drinking scotch. At these times he would torture himself in a drink fuelled quandary. Should he continue his task, or not? Would any of them get the police involved? What would happen if they did? Would Milford pay up? What would happen to Muxlowe if Milford called in the police? Would Muxlowe then sing? Many, many questions all giving him different answers every time he asked himself them. He was driving himself mad and putting a great distance between himself and Stella. It surprised him that he seemed to have a conscience. Then he'd realise, "no I've not, it's only really me I've got to worry about and I have no other option. Fuck Milford and Muxlowe – I owe them fuck all."

Stella would try and talk to him. She knew something was seriously wrong. All Gerrity did was sit with his scotch in a kind of dream as if silently arguing with himself. As the drink flowed, the facial expressions became more pronounced and pained. Any attempt at conversation was futile and any enquiry as to what was wrong was met with hostility as if the problems were her fault, or at least she was reminding him, mocking him even, that the problems existed and were deep rooted. She stuck with it though, bless her. Most women wouldn't.

December 15th was a Tuesday. Gerrity had had a particularly shite day. Not only had he not bought or sold anything, one of his recent lucrative deals had gone pear-shaped. One of his few remaining dealer friends had bought a car off him the previous week, giving him £1,000 profit, which was very welcome at that time. Unfortunately the dealer had taken a customer on test drive that day and during the demonstration the engine blew up. Properly blew up. It was a Land Rover Freelander 1.8 petrol and the cylinder head cracked which was a lot of money. The dealer had gone to Gerrity insisting that he take the car back, and in his fury and embarrassment over the situation even implied that Gerrity knew the car was fucked when he sold it him. Gerrity not only lost his £1,000 profit but was now the proud owner of a £6,000 lump of scrap that needed recovering from the roadside where it had been dumped, and would probably cost him £2,500 to get back on the road.

After a couple of pints at The George and Dragon early doors, Gerrity headed back to Stella's with a fresh bottle of scotch – Glen Morangie – he needed a treat. Stella was going out that night leaving him alone with his thoughts, which he was pleased about.

One large scotch later and the stencil was out and the paper ready. He knew what he had to do – it was time for a 'Dear Paul' letter.

At this point, of course, he didn't know whether or not the first letter had been sent to Milford. A second letter would stir things up a lot more and maybe he would go and 'bump into' Milford at The George and Dragon one night next week to try and gauge his mood. Maybe it was time soon to befriend the ferret.

Chapter 9

The Third Letter – Muxlowe

"Dear, Paul." Muxlowe read. "Christmas is coming, the ferret's getting fat, please put a score into Myra's hat."

Dean had thought enough time had passed that 'Myra' had gone cold. But, no, he was wrong. Another letter had come demanding he do the same process as last time and forward the letter to Milford or the penalty clauses still stood. It was Thursday December 17th. The letter must be forwarded to Milford as before, over the weekend. It would arrive just before Christmas. Nice touch.

It was at this time that Dean considered contacting Milford himself to get his thoughts.

Who would be the loser then if Milford went to the police and this 'Myra' really was a psycho? Milford would have nothing to lose. The police would fuck Dean for sending the first letter and 'Myra' might kill his dogs and beat up his wife and daughter. No. Dean decided it was either 'him or me'. His thoughts, quite bizarrely, suddenly went to a James Bond film he had seen, he couldn't remember which one, where 007 was fastened to a table with his legs apart and a laser beam slowly burning its way towards his crotch. He wished he could remember how Bond escaped.

Dean read on:

"I bet you thought I'd forgotten about you, Paul.

"Of course I've not. I am just a very patient bunny, and also very busy. I now have everything in place to launch 'stage 2', should you wish to act the twat and not to proceed with paying your debt. In a way I wish you'd try to wriggle out of it but deep down I know that you are not a stupid man and that you will do the right thing." That phrase again.

"Remember, I cannot be caught and I am an extremely unstable person. The slightest inkling of outside interference and I will push the button to start 'stage 2'.

"I will be in touch again, Paul, early in the new year with further instructions. This is just a little reminder to you that I am still here, a little assurance that I am deadly serious, and a little hope from me that you have a lovely Christmas and a fantastic new year.

"All my love and kisses, Myra."

Dean re-read the letter. He needed someone to talk to. Someone to advise him. Another point of view. The trouble is that nobody would have the same point of view as him. Everyone would say that he should go to the police immediately, before he got too far in. That was the easy thing to say. It was not their wife, kid and dogs whose necks were on the line.

No, he would send the letter. He couldn't risk anything so valuable. The chances were still stacked very much in favour of the whole thing blowing itself out. A sick joke that he'd been dragged into? Someone with a grudge against this Milford man? But what had this got to do with him?

He sent the letter the following day. Happy Christmas, Paul.

Chapter 10

Second Letter – Milford

Milford got the letter the Monday morning. He recognised the envelope and his stomach dropped. He had raced to the post every day over the past few weeks, expecting the worst. Now it had happened.

He ripped the letter open with a roll of his eyes, directed at Heather who was equally as concerned, and who had just followed him through. "It's not?" She mouthed.

"I think so." Responded Paul.

"Let's have a look." She tried to grab a glance at the contents even before he got it out of the envelope.

"Just fucking wait, eh!" He snapped.

"Alright, alright. But I'm definitely calling the cops this time."

Paul was silently reading through the text. "Yes, it's Myra." He confirmed. "Just wishing us a merry Christmas and telling us, well me, to expect another letter next year."

Heather snatched the letter off him and read it for herself.

"Right." She stated in her authoritative voice. "No more fucking about, I'm calling the police."

And she did. She eventually got through to a Detective Inspector Shepherd of the serious crime unit at Nottingham Police Station. She explained what had happened and made an appointment, that afternoon, to meet at Nottingham's main station in Arnold, to show him the letters. Paul bagged up the new letter in a plastic A4 envelope.

Two p.m. at Nottingham cop shop Paul and Heather were shown into interview room 1, for their meeting with DI Shepherd.

He did not keep them waiting. He was a pleasant man, big smiles, seemed genuine although if anything, a little distracted in some way. He looked like a chap with a lot of problems. Maybe he got, as a lot of CID do get, a little too involved with his cases and huge work load. He was mid-fifties, five feet ten tall around twelve stone. He had obviously looked after himself physically quite well, hair fully grey, podgy round face with round nose and piggy eyes, his fat cheeks had the alcohol redness creeping in.

"Well, Mr and Mrs Milford, how can I help?" Heather did the talking, not correcting the 'Mrs Milford' bit at this point. She ran through the two letters and showed him the evidence.

"No we've not got any idea who it could be. No I don't think we've upset anybody recently. No Paul can't think of any money he owes people. Etc…etc…" All the usual questions.

After an hour and a weak cup of tea, DI Shepherd looked at his watch. His mind seemed elsewhere at this point. "Well, Mr and Mrs Milford, all I can do at this point is to take the letters for examination. We'll have a look at any possible fingerprints although I don't hold out much hope there. Meanwhile keep your eyes and ears open, rack your brains and make a list of any possible suspects that you know, as they more likely than not, know you. It may be someone jealous of your lottery win, or your business – maybe someone with a grudge, ex-employee, dissatisfied customer. Keep an open mind and let me know if you come up with anything. Any more letters let me know. Any more information you may come across, let me know. I have another appointment now but if this continues, I assure you, we'll get to the bottom of it. Is that OK?"

"Yes, thank you." Replied Heather, and they all stood up. At this point she informed him that she wasn't Mrs Milford but was Paul's long term partner so as good as. DI Shepherd shook their hands firmly and they left.

"Shit!" Said Paul as they sat in the car on the way back home. "It could be fucking anybody. Do you fancy a quick 'early doors' at The George and Dragon? I'm not going into work today, now."

"Why not?" Answered Heather. "I'm sure they can do without you for one day."

"I'm sure they could," smiled Paul.

After a quick bite to eat at KFC, Heather and Paul walked into the lounge bar of The George and Dragon at around four p.m. At the bar sat a chap that Milford had met before briefly, called Ernest Gerrity. He was reading *The Guardian* whilst cradling a pint. As they approached the bar Gerrity looked up with a huge, unexpected smile in Milford's direction. "Hello, there." He beamed." Paul isn't it? Of course it is. Can I get you and your good lady here a drink?" Milford was gobsmacked. Very rarely did anyone offer to buy him a drink. Very rarely did anyone smile at him or show him any affection.

"Thank you." He replied. "This is my partner, Heather. I know I've spoken to you a couple of times but I must admit I'm rubbish with names."

"Gerrity is my name, Ernest Gerrity. Call me Ernest. Yes I tend to frequent this place quite a lot, usually early on, on my way home from grafting." He turned to the bar maid. "Over here, love please." He turned to Heather with an enquiring look.

"Vodka and tonic, please, no ice."

"OK." He nodded to the now present bar maid to fulfil the order. "And Paul."

"I'll have a pint of lager please, if that's OK."

"Of course."

The bar maid poured the drinks and Gerrity got his wallet out making a point of exposing a thick wad of twenty pound notes to give Milford the impression of wealth. He didn't want any suspicions that he was hawking after some of that lottery card win. He wanted to be looked upon as a real genuine nice friendly guy.

"What do you do to get finished so early on a weekday," enquired Paul.

"Cars," replied Gerrity knowing that Milford had a passion for nice cars, in fact in the past he had indirectly supplied him with one of his VAT free disability specials. Thus the conversation was started.

"Will you join us, Ernest?" Asked Heather as they made to sit down at a table near the window.

"Certainly, I would love to." He grabbed his pint and followed them over.

Gerrity used all of his well-honed powers of befriendment – a salesman's best tool. He bought most of the beer and very shortly it was decided that the Milford car would be left overnight at the pub.

Time flew and before Paul realised it was nine p.m. and he had a gallon of moderately strong lager on board. The company was charming and he was so happy that he had found a new drinking buddy. The conversation went from cars to houses, to business, to mutual friends from The George and Dragon.

"Didn't I read somewhere that you had a lottery win recently?" Gerrity chipped in at one point.

"Yes, it's true," replied Milford. "But we don't like to broadcast it now – too many cranks around trying to skank money out of you."

"Really?" said Gerrity latching onto the theme. "What do you mean? Begging letters and stuff?"

"Yes." Heather stepped in, now red-faced and smiley with her vodka and tonics (Gerrity had got the bar maid to shove doubles in early on.) "And stuff." She looked over at Paul who had a glazed expression gazing into his beer.

"And stuff?" Pressed Gerrity, very casually. "Are you OK, Paul?"

"Yes." Paul slurred. Gerrity smiled and nodded at Heather, coaxing her to continue.

"Well, for instance…" She was also slurring now. "We've just had a letter from this absolute wanker. She stopped abruptly and went even redder. "Shit. I've only just met you and I'm saying 'wanker'. Do excuse me." She let out a girly giggle. Paul was still glazed over showing no interest in the conversation.

Gerrity laughed out loudly. "Quite alright." He quaffed. "What about this wanker?"

Another giggle from Heather at Gerrity's use of the word 'wanker'. "Well a letter came today demanding money off us or they'll tell people bad things about us."

"Bastards!" voiced Gerrity sternly and abruptly as if he couldn't believe the depths that some people could stoop to.

"Quite." Agreed Heather draining another glass. "The fucking police don't want to know."

"Really?" Gerrity sounded incredulous. "It makes you wonder what we pay our fucking council tax for."

"Indeed." Heather was drooping now; her eyes were starting to shut.

Gerrity went to the gents and on the way back got the bar maid to order a taxi of them. He then helped them outside. The cab arrived in minutes. They all said their 'goodbyes' and promised to meet up again soon for drinkies.

"You can bank on it," said Gerrity as he shoved them in the taxi, giving the driver their address. They drove off.

"Shit," said Gerrity to himself as they disappeared. He realised that he shouldn't have known their address. He'd only really met them properly that night and they'd not told him where they lived so how would he know to tell the taxi driver? Still, they were both as pissed as farts and so wouldn't realise.

Overall Gerrity felt chuffed at a good night's work: He'd established an information line that would be on-going; He'd found out that Muxlowe had done exactly as had been told to do; He had also learned that Milford had unfortunately gone to the police, however they had fucked him off. He'd just have to emphasise the penalty for police involvement a little stronger next time.

Gerrity used the festive period and the following few weeks industriously to build his relationship with Paul and Heather. Deep down he was worried about police involvement and had a suspicion that, although the pair didn't have much confidence in coppers, they would run to them as soon as another letter appeared.

Qualification was the name of the game, ask any good salesman. Get the qualification right and all the rest falls into place. What would frighten these people into paying up? Did they have all the funds available? Gerrity had to make sure that his plan was watertight and fool proof.

He would also have to do a bit of work on the other element-Dean Muxlowe. He had a part to play and Gerrity needed to know that he would play it well.

It may take a little time as too many bold, probing questions may cause suspicion. Slowly, slowly catchy monkey, as the saying goes.

The third Monday in the New Year, 2010, Gerrity sat at home with his phone. He had put in many hours of graft building his relationship with Heather and Paul. He had become more confident about his scheme. They had both, independently, discussed with him their lucrative business, money in the bank, cars that they both liked. In fact Gerrity, the first week after the New Year frivolities, had supplied them with a nearly new Mercedes-Benz CLK cabriolet ready for the spring. The car was at the time, quite out of season so the values were reasonably low. Gerrity convinced them to get in quick before they became expensive. They, of course, agreed wholeheartedly and gave him the go-ahead to get it for them. Heather's new toy. He took off them her old BMW 3 series and they were much chuffed, as Gerrity assured them he had done a 'mates rates' deal. In actual fact he had made a quick £2500 on the car he sold them and £1000 profit on their old BMW that he'd placed straight away. This gave him financially a little more time to cement his plan. Yes, this part was going well.

Gerrity dialled the number on his phone. It was eleven a.m. on the Monday morning. "Good morning, Dean Muxlowe speaking," came the reply.

"Hi, Dean, Ernest Gerrity calling. How are you?"

"Ayup, Ernest," Muxlowe replied cheerfully. "I'm fine, mate, how are you?"

"Brilliant," Gerrity Effervesced. "I may have a bit of business for you." Straight to the point.

"Oh, yes?" Muxlowe was always up for a bit of business. "Tell me more."

"Well," continued Gerrity. "I've got a chap looking at my Range Rover Sport – diesel HSE '07 57, black with black, 20,000 miles nice car, standard car but with extra Quentin Crisps. The guy's got some dough but wants to borrow £15,000 on the strap. Would you be able to sort it quick if he needs to?"

"I'm sure we can," answered Dean. "Has he got a budget in mind?"

"Don't know," snapped Gerrity. "At this stage the deal's not done but I just wanted to know that you were available to call him if I need you to."

"No problem," replied Muxlowe. "However if he's not quick I'll not be around so you'll have to talk to James Hunter-Browne."

"That's OK." Gerrity didn't have a customer anyway. "Are you going anywhere nice?"

"Yes," smiled Muxlowe. "Me and Molly are off cruising around the Caribbean for a month for our twenty-fifth wedding anniversary. We go at the end of January and come back at the end of February."

"No problem," continued Gerrity. "I'll talk to James if necessary. Business must be good."

"Yes, not too bad."

"Any problems with the 'credit crunch'?"

"We're doing OK."

"How are Molly and the kids?"

"Fine."

"Good." Gerrity thought that Muxlowe sounded very upbeat, not a care in the world. He'd have to put his plans back a month. Good job he'd called really. "Well, I'll get off now and if I don't get a result before you go away have a good one and I'll get hold of you when I get back. Meantime I'll talk to James."

"Spot on," confirmed Muxlowe. "Before you go…"

"Yes."

"What are 'Quentin Crisps'?"

"Rear entertainment," laughed Gerrity. "You know – Them TV screens in the front headrests so the kids can play on PlayStations or watch DVD's. See you, mate." And put the phone down.

Gerrity sat and pondered after the phone call. He thought he'd be talking to a troubled Dean Muxlowe. A Dean Muxlowe with a burden, a weight on his shoulders that he was struggling to bear. But no. An upbeat, happy guy that was about to embark on a four week trip around the Caribbean – strange. Still, fuck all he could do about it.

The following month, while Muxlowe was away, was spent schmoozing Paul and Heather. Not too much, just enough. Gerrity introduced Paul to some of his friends and even made up a foursome with Stella on a couple of occasions. There was logic behind it all.

Gerrity had realised that both Milford and Heather were quite insecure people. Paul more so than Heather. Years of buying the beer and having the piss ripped out of him had that effect. They were very suspicious and untrusting of others and were used to being let down and stabbed in the back.

The new found social circle had been very welcome. Paul was happy to have made, what he thought, were genuine friends, and Heather was pleased for him. She had been at The George and Dragon in the past when people were taking the piss behind Paul's back, and it hurt her. His so called 'mates' indulging openly in their 'ferret baiting' antics.

They were now both happy. They were wealthy, successful and had an active social life that revolved around the local pub. Paul thought of himself as a pillar of the community, respected and liked by all. He would do anything not to jeopardise his new found status.

By elevating his status, Gerrity had placed Paul Milford in the ideal position to be exploited. He thought that the risk of being slurred by an anonymous blackmailer would be too great for him to run squealing to the police when the money demand arrived in February when Muxlowe was back. The last thing Milford wanted was for his reputation to be tarnished and his friends to disappear. Even if the allegations and claims against him were untrue, would he be able to take the risk of people believing them? The old 'no smoke without fire' phrase would come into play.

Gerrity had done all he could with Milford. It was the end of February and the time was ripe. All depended now, he realised, on Muxlowe playing his part. He was back next week. Out came the paper, the pen, the stencil and the scotch. "Dear, Paul…"

Chapter 11

The Cruise

Dean Muxlowe had a crap Christmas. Nobody else realised the fact, but it was crap. He managed to smile and laugh, to drink and be merry, but he always had in the back of his mind the blackmailer.

Now was it the blackmailer that was the cause of his crap Christmas...Or was it that's what he felt comfortable in believing? Someone to blame? His excuse, in his own mind, to be unhappy. When really his reason for being so depressed was his life in general, from which he had no escape. His business partner's lack of effort, his continual arguments with Molly about the situation, the jibes from his friends and business colleagues about having the piss taken out of him. The ridicule. So he drank for the sake of clarity and illumination.

The true frustration in Dean's heart was, yes, his life situation, but also the fact that he could not do anything about it. No escape. He was frightened. He didn't like change. He didn't like admitting that he was wrong. He couldn't bring himself to move on and start again on his own. If he did it would drop Hunter-Browne in the shit – he couldn't do that. He was not ruthless, he was a doormat who people walked all over, and he was a packhorse that carried other people's baggage, a donkey.

Dean didn't know how to feel about the blackmailer and the letters. Was he appalled? Was he frightened? Did he feel guilty? Or was he excited? Did it give him a buzz? Was he looking forward to, or was he fearful of, another letter? Was he sorry for sending the first two? Really sorry? Or not? Did he regret not going to the police? He was all of these things and more. The blackmailer had certainly provided something in his life. Was that something a possible escape? An excuse? A cause?

Talking of escapes at the end of January 2010, the last Friday, Dean and Molly headed off to Heathrow Airport in their hire car to start their twenty-fifth wedding anniversary treat. They flew from London to Miami, stayed overnight at a hotel, then on to Puerto Rico to begin a four week cruise of the Caribbean. It was a trip that had been planned for months and they were greatly looking forward to it. They had been abroad very rarely in their lives, mainly restricted by money, children and work. They'd just had the odd trip to Spain, Portugal and France.

This was the 'trip of a lifetime.' The hot and sunny weather was virtually guaranteed. The ship was the 'Caribbean Princess'– the height of luxury. It was full of Americans that demanded nothing but the best.

Dean and Molly became friendly with many Americans and Canadians – yes, apparently there is a difference. The trip was full of sun, booze, food and relaxation. They visited many islands: Granada; St Lucia; St John; Aruba; Barbados.

When at sea they had everything at their fingertips. The ship was seventeen decks high with a theatre, three swimming pools one of which had a cinema, a gym, a shopping centre, eight bars, four restaurants, ice cream parlours, burger bars, plus much, much more.

After a day on shore sunbathing, shopping, scuba diving or sight-seeing, they usually spent early evening sat on their private balcony with a bottle of cheap white rum that they'd managed to smuggle on the ship from the local shops ($8 for a litre as opposed to $15 for a half bottle off the ship – worth the risk.)

They would sit and have a few rum and cokes, watching the sun set on the horizon, as the ship left harbour to set sail to the next island destination. Fantastic. If they got hungry they would call room service or wobble along to the nearest buffet restaurant for something to eat – lobster, prawns, all sorts of seafood, all sorts of meat, and indeed all sorts of everything.

Both Dean and Molly got very sunburnt and put on a hell of a lot of weight, but thoroughly enjoyed it. Molly had to be held back from booking for the following year. Just as well as it turned out.

They arrived back in the UK on the last Friday in February. The journey had been horrendous. From Puerto Rico to Miami, a five hour wait at the airport, followed by a nine hour flight back to Heathrow. Molly had picked up a bug and felt like a blob of jelly with a pounding head and sickly stomach. So much for 'the holiday of a lifetime' – never again.

From Heathrow they got a hire car back to Nottingham. Dean had lost his counterpart drivers licence which delayed things even more. They eventually walked through their own front door at two p.m., exhausted but still buzzing about the memories that they had.

They had obviously brought back a couple of bottles of white rum, one of which was opened on arrival in a vain attempt to continue the holiday spirit.

As they sat down to relax with a drink and tell Dean's mother all about it, Dean went through the mail from the last month. Dean's mother, Madge, had been over every day to make sure Rose had been behaving on her own and that Guinness and Gilbert were fed and let out in the back yard.

The letters were just bills, all paid on direct debit, and junk...apart from one. It had arrived that morning and Dean immediately recognised it as being from the blackmailer. Whilst Molly, despite her headache, was rattling nineteen to the dozen about the holiday to Madge, Dean opened the letter.

He'd almost expected one to have arrived whilst they were away. Shit, surely, he thought, that he wasn't feeling that he'd been hoping for one. The feeling worried him. It was a strange co-incidence that it had arrived just that morning.

"Dear, Deano." The usual opening. "I hope you and Molly had a fantastic cruise around the Caribbean and that you got plenty of rest. I know you've been busy at work lately and you were ready for a break. I hope the journey back wasn't too brutal."

Shit. How did they know that he'd been on holiday, and to where. They were obviously being watched. Maybe it wasn't a co-incidence that it arrived that day. Dean read on.

"I enclose the latest letter I need you to send to Milford. As you will see it identifies the drop-off procedure for the £20,000 cash. You will not have to send him any more letters after this one but you will have to send him a couple of texts from a mobile phone. I will provide you with the phone and all the necessary instructions on the day that I collect. Do not worry, Deano, you will not have to collect or handle any money yourself – that risk will be mine.

"Well thanks for that kind consideration," thought Dean. Molly was still rattling on. The white rum had kicked in a little and the vocal speed and volume had both increased somewhat. Madge just listened. Dean read on.

"I would like to take this opportunity, Deano, to thank you for all of your help and co-operation thus far. Believe me this is money that I have been owed by Paul Milford for a long time. He is a robbing, slimy, deceitful little ferret bastard who has caused a lot of people a lot of misery."

This was an obvious attempt by the blackmailer to lower Dean's feelings of guilt. It did have a little effect – Dean appreciated the excuse to send the letter on, although he would have probably done it anyway.

"May I remind you though, on a very serious note that if you fail in any of my instructions the consequences will be very severe; your wife will suffer greatly, your daughter will never forgive you, and you dogs will die. As I inflict all sorts of pain on Molly and Rose I will tell them that their suffering is your entire fault. Let's call it a revenge attack from the jealous husband of some old slag that you've been having it off with.

"Anyway, Deano, I do hope that the holiday went well. I'm so glad that you are home, I know that you will do the right thing, lots of love, Myra."

The fact that the blackmailer had said 'as I inflict all sorts of pain' was the first clue to Dean that 'Myra' was a man rather than a woman as the name would suggest. Was this a genuine error or did they want him to know or think that? It didn't really matter, he supposed.

Dean had been given a couple of days to send the letter on to Milford. He put it in his pocket and put all the other mail on the kitchen worktop as he went through to refill their drinks. He then sat down with Molly and Madge to join in talking about the Caribbean. "Anything interesting in the post?" Molly enquired.

"Nothing," Dean answered. "Bills and junk – I'll go through it all tomorrow."

"Good."

Would Dean send on the third and, supposedly final letter? Of course he would.

Chapter 12
Milford's last letter

The first Monday in March 2010. The day Paul Milford received his final letter. He was expecting it, and dreading it. It was the letter that would tell him how to hand over his £20,000 in cash to 'Myra'.

"Dear, Paul. Hello, it's Myra. The time is upon us; time to pay the piper. I hope you had a good Christmas. I hope Heather likes her new car; it looks nice although I would have gone for black with black leather." The car was dark metallic red with cream leather.

"The £20,000 has to be paid in used notes. I will not tolerate any notes being marked, any transmitters or other devices hidden within, any magic water or invisible ink. Any attempt to catch me will result in stage 2 coming into play immediately. Don't be a twat. I will have the money checked before I get hold of it.

Contact will be made by text. You will have the money ready, packed tightly in a black waterproof bin liner.

"When you receive the text you will follow the instructions to the letter. The instructions will take you to several locations. At each of these locations you will have to answer questions, by text, both before and after you drop off the money.

"At one of the locations you will drop off the money. You will be watched at every stage. Any suspicion of the police or any other company and the drop is off. Stage 2 will start and the bill will go up considerably. Paul, do the right thing. Do not get silly.

"Once the money has been dropped off you will continue to obey instructions and answer the text questions at each location. This will give me time to get the money picked up and checked. I have a team of kids hired for the day to run around for me. They don't know me – they work for a third party who they will not, dare not, betray if caught.

"The money will be checked by a forensic student from Nottingham University for any adultery. His services have cost me a lot of money.

"Once the money is declared as clean and my team confirm to me that there has been no third party interference, then I will thank you very much and send you home. You will never hear from me again.

"It may be this week, it may be next, and it may be in a few weeks. Just get the cash out of the bank and be ready to act immediately that you get the first text.

"I wish you luck and once again urge you to do the right thing. You will regret it if you try and fuck me around.

"Lots of love and kisses, Myra"

"Mmm…" voiced Paul as he read the letter for the umpteenth time. Heather had also read it. They'd decided to go to the police. They knew that there was a possibility that texts could be traced if it went to that – they regularly watched 'Spooks' on the TV – The MI5 drama. They also did not believe that it would not all be over if they paid up. How many times would they end up having to 'pay the piper?'

DI Shepherd at Nottingham read the letter. They had, as he expected, had no joy with fingerprints, but the introduction of the mobile phone gave him hope.

"We can trace mobile phone signals," said Shepherd, excitedly. "We can also trace where pay-as-you-go credit has been bought."

"Sorry?" Heather was puzzled.

"Well," explained Shepherd. "The phone that they use will probably be a pay-as-you-go. The number will show up on your phone, Paul. It has to because you have to respond to instructions and answer questions by text – if the number was blocked then you would not be able to. The blackmailer thinks we cannot trace the phone. We can trace where the phone credit has been bought and allocated to that number from the phone network supplier. We might be lucky with CCTV coverage. When the phone starts being used to text you we will be ready to trace the signal."

"So there's a good chance?" Asked Heather.

"I would say 'yes'," smiled Shepherd. "Once we know who it is we need to move fast to confiscate any paper, envelopes, computers, printers etc. that we can. This is where we will get all our evidence to build a watertight case and charge the culprit. There is nothing worse than getting the right man, or woman, and they get off on a technicality because we've fucked up and left a door open."

"Great," she says.

"So," continued Shepherd, "as soon as you get a text on Paul's phone, call me, day or night, on Heather's. We will use delaying tactics as much as possible. Time will be of the essence."

"Certainly," said Paul. "Let's hope we get her then, or him, or whatever."

They left the police station feeling confident of a result. They had been warned not to tell a living soul of the plans as it could be anyone writing these letters, and it was, more than likely, someone that they knew.

Chapter 13

Preparation for the sting

It was the first Monday in May. The last eight weeks for Dean had been a bit of a blur. He was well and truly in a rut – the old work, drink, food, bed, work cycle was eating up his life. He was having a traditional African breakfast in the mornings (fuck all) and drinking himself into a stupor at night. It was, he realised later, like sitting on the outside looking into his life, watching it pass him by out of control. He was neglecting Molly and the kids, but just could not help himself. He was on a carousel and couldn't jump off. "HELP, HELP, HELP!" He heard himself screaming into his bottle. But nobody ever did. Why would they? Everyone apart from Molly thought he had the perfect life. He put on such a good show that nobody was ever the wiser.

There were no brakes. He knew he would lose Molly but couldn't do anything about it. Most of his time was spent trying to convince himself that life was OK. He was arguing with himself. When he had a drink in front of him he was very convincing. He sometimes believed himself; he felt a joy, a sort of elation. The 'life is good' part of his mind took over and he wouldn't listen to Molly saying that 'life wasn't good'. Too much drink, too much work, putting everyone else in front of her and the kids. Dean wasn't fucking interested.

In the mornings when the drink had worn off the 'life isn't good' part of his mind would take control back. A hollow feeling of deep depression. No light at the end of the tunnel, no escape. He was frustrated that he seemed unable to control his life. Why could he not jack everything in and start again on his own? Why couldn't he face facts and change his life? – Weakness – that was the answer – weakness. And it was this that frustrated and depressed him even more.

Almost every day Dean would contemplate suicide. When he stopped and thought about what he was thinking about, he became scared. It seemed such an easy way out. Surely he wasn't serious about that? Fuck! It didn't sound in his own head that he was joking.

He couldn't face evenings without a drink. It became his only temporary relief and his only pleasure. He sometimes sat at work thinking about the taste, and the relaxing effect as it took over his mind and body. He couldn't handle his life so he would hand it over to the bottle. It was just such a pity that the bottle always gave the bastard thing back. He didn't want it.

On the Monday morning the doorbell rang; it was the postman. Dean got up and took the package off him. "Sorry, pal, can't quite get it through the letter box."

"No, problem," replied Dean. He took the package, it didn't need signing for. It was a brown paper wrapped oblong package about eight inches by three inches by three inches, addressed to himself. He wasn't expecting anything apart from maybe another letter from the phantom blackmailer.

Dean sat down in his favourite chair and opened the package. He couldn't think what it could be. As he progressed, realisation kicked him like a punch in the chest. It was a mobile phone along with a stencil written letter. It was an old flip-top type Nokia, a little bit worse for wear but probably worked. In silence he put the phone on the arm of the chair and read the letter.

"Hello, Deano. The time has come. It is nearly all over. Just one final task for you. I hope Molly, Rose and the dogs are all well, please give them my regards.

"I have enclosed a present for you as you can see. It is an old Nokia that was on a T-Mobile tariff at one point. All it needs to work is a T-Mobile pay-as-you-go simcard and a credit voucher. These can be purchased from Tesco. The simcard is 99p, the credit voucher will cost you a tenner. A small price to pay to get rid of me for good I'm sure you will agree.

Well, once you've got them I want you to send a text on this Thursday, ten a.m. to arrange the pick-up of my £20,000 do not worry, Deano, you will not have to pick-up or handle the money."

Dean wondered why this prick insisted on calling him 'Deano'. Nobody called him 'Deano.' Myra then laid out a script of texts he had to send at specific times.

"1. Initial contact – send out the text dead on ten a.m. – 'are you ready ferret man? You had better be. You were warned.' I'm assuming he has got the money. If he says 'no' then send him another text telling him he has one hour to get it and get to the car park at Brimshill School, NG7 6LP. Tell him if he is not there by eleven a.m. then stage 2 will kick in.

2. At eleven a.m. send him another text; 'are you there yet ferret man?' I'm assuming that he says 'yes'. If so ask him what colour the school's front door is. He should text back to say that it is blue to prove that he is there.

3. Once that he has confirmed the colour we know that we have him. Text him immediately saying 'good boy, now wait.'

4.Next text is at eleven-thirty a.m. Send: 'Drive to Miller Vauxhall at NG7 4LF, you have fifteen minutes, text me when you are there, OK?' Miller is two miles away and so he should be there well before eleven-forty-five a.m.

5. Next text is at eleven-forty-five a.m. Confirm that he is at Miller by sending: 'WF57PUL is a Vauxhall Astra on the front forecourt, what colour is it?' The car is white. It is on their front and should still be there. Await confirmation. If the car is not there ask him the colour of the sporty Sigma in the showroom (it is red.)

That should be enough to establish that Milford is playing ball. Send him a text then telling him to go to the car park at Brimshill Nature Reserve at Fulford Lane, NG7 6LT, it will take him ten minutes. Tell him to text once he is there.

When he texts it should be about twelve-fifteen p.m. Tell him to get out of the car, follow the path over the wooden bridge for approximately half a mile. There is a seat with a red bin next to it. Tell him to make sure nobody is looking and put the money inside the empty Tesco bag on the top and then push it to the bottom of the bin. Tell him to then go back to the car and text you to say it has all been done.

Once you have this text tell him to drive to Anthill Mercedes-Benz at NG12 6LF. This is about thirty miles away and will take him about an hour. Tell him to text you when he is there.

When he texts ask him the colour of the SL350 registration number PT59SWA – it is red – not silver like most of them

When he confirms this send him a final text saying: 'thank you, you will never hear from me again.' Then ditch the phone – the best bet is remove the sim card then smash it up and post it down a water drain in the road. Either that or launch it into the River Trent.

After that, Deano, you are free. You will never hear from me again. I will get the money picked up and you will know that you played a big part in righting a great wrong.

Love and kisses, Myra XX"

Myra then gave Milford's mobile phone number for Dean to send the messages to.

This was real; Dean's heart was thumping fast and hard. The letters weren't real to him, it was distant, something that disappeared once he put it in the letter box. This texting business was real. If Milford had involved the cops there was a real chance of getting caught. The unthinkable. This was the sort of stuff you read about; something that Ian Rankin or Jeffrey Archer would come up with. This was blackmail or demanding money with menaces; heavy shit. Could he do it? Did he have the balls?

If Muxlowe had been in a normal state of mind things wouldn't have got this far. He was subconsciously looking for an exit point to his life. Some excitement and risk. He'd never had this. It was almost, he thought, like a drug. It was if he'd found something that had been missing in his life. Had it been the lack of contact from the blackmailer that had caused him to get so depressed? When all this ended what would he do? Where would he get his next fix? What would happen if he got caught? Maybe, deep down inside, he wanted to.

Yes, he'd do it. Of course he would: what was the worst thing that could happen? Blackmail isn't that serious is it?

That night Dean called at Tesco to pick up his usual bottle of white rum and a two litre bottle of cola, but also grabbed a T-Mobile sim card and a ten pound credit voucher.

When he got home he tested it out and everything worked. He had two days to build up his courage. Uncle white rum and aunty coke would help convince him. Better not let Molly suspect anything

"Drink, Molly?" He shouted through.

"Just a wee one." Came the usual reply.

Chapter 14

Text and arrest

Two days later Dean was up with the larks. Molly was working the early shift and so was up at four a.m. for a six-thirty a.m. start. She was a cashier at the local supermarket convenience store and was a bit 'OCD', so she needed plenty of time to get ready, clean the toilets, have a coffee and watch, for the third time, the re-runs of 'Heartbeat' on ITV 3. Routine was king. She could tell you exactly the plot of each episode from the opening credits. Her favourite character was Claude Jeremiah Greengrass.

Dean had had the mobile phone on charge all night, tucked away in the garage so nobody would see it and ask awkward questions.

He was up at four a.m. with Molly – he couldn't sleep anyway when the booze had worn off. Despite Molly's attempts at conversation Dean seemed distant. She put it down to the early start – he didn't usually get up with her.

"What's up with you?" She thought she'd have one more go.

"Nothing."

"Yes there is." She persisted.

"For fuck's sake, Molly," he snapped. "It's fucking ridiculous 'o' clock, I've got a fucking headache and I'm sitting watching poxy re-runs of a programme we first watched together fifteen or so years ago, that you are constantly reminding me, as if I need to be reminded, what is going to happen next and how it all ends up. So just get ready and leave me to get to myself, eh?" Molly received the comment in silence and continued to apply her make-up. She still had to have the last word.

"Fuck you then." She muttered – hardly audible. Dean ignored her.

The time dragged until ten a.m. Molly had left at six-twenty-five a.m. After Breakfast TV, at nine a.m. Dean went to work. Coincidently he was on his own the whole day. The others has excuses – kids, vets, doctors, whatever. Dean had stopped listening to excuses for time off. He knew he was on his own in this business with his partner just hanging on for the benefits without any constructive input or effort – that, thought Dean, was not far off the definition of a parasite. It certainly was not, sticking to biological terms, a symbiotic relationship that they had.

He'd made a conscious effort over the past few weeks to try and think about something else whenever these thoughts came into his head. He felt his whole body tensing up and his mind twisting and bending. Surely this couldn't be healthy. He was heading for meltdown.

By sticking his head in the sand like an ostrich, and trying to avoid the real issues, he was becoming more and more distracted. His thoughts were festering. It was becoming more and more difficult to present the persona of a dedicated, focused professional who people would want to do business with. It became increasingly hard to supress those acidic little comments that would jump from his lips when asked how his business, or his business partner, were doing. He felt like a victim of The Bloody Red Baron, spiralling downwards to destruction, no way out, no parachute.

Yes, he would send the texts. He had no feelings at all for Paul Milford. He had heard rumours that he was a back-stabbing little ferret look-alike that thought he was a Lord, but that was irrelevant

– it could have been anyone. Dean's mind was a blur; it no longer belonged completely to him. He just wanted something to take away the pain; free him, if only temporarily, from his cage. Yes, of course he'd send the texts. And if he got caught? He didn't even think about the possibility or consequences at this point. He just felt the buzz.

Ten a.m. came and he sent the first text. 'Are you ready, ferret man? You better be, you were warned.'

As he pushed the 'send' button on the phone, he walked out of the office. He got in his car and drove to the car park down the road looking over the river. He needed a change of scenery – he didn't know why, but he definitely needed a change of scenery.

'Beep beep' went Paul Milford's mobile phone; He had a message. It was ten a.m. on the Thursday morning and it was from a number that his phone didn't recognise. His heart leapt, as it had done several times over the last few weeks when he'd had a few false alarms; this was no false alarm. "Are you ready ferret man…?" He read on.

He was sat with Heather in the conservatory having a coffee before going to work. "Shit!" He exclaimed as he read the text. "It looks like this is it; it's actually fucking happening."

"Let's have a butcher's." She grabbed the mobile off him and read it. "I'll call the police – you try and stall him like they told you to." She picked up her mobile and called Shepherd.

Milford replied to the text; "I have your money but I've got a slight problem – I am very busy over the next couple of hours." He sent it. The reply took less than two minutes to arrive.

"Well, wanker, you'd better fucking well get yourself un-busy. You will be at NG7 6LP, Brimshill School car park, with the money at eleven a.m. or stage 2 will start immediately and you wouldn't want that, twat." As Dean sent the message he couldn't help asking himself the question as to why he'd used the extra 'wanker' and 'twat.' Was he enjoying himself? No, no, no… That couldn't be normal. No, maybe he just wanted to force the message home.

"OK, I'll be there – I don't want any trouble," came back the reply.

At eleven a.m. Milford sat in the school car park. He didn't have any money – he had absolutely no intention to pay.

Heather had spoken to DI Shepherd who had immediately sprang into action, smelling a result. He was very happy and excited – he had half expected a call at midnight on a cold rainy night, or even worse, whilst sitting down to his Sunday dinner. This morning was easy for him. He had all the resources at his disposal. He'd got his technical team mobilised to trace the text messages – it was just a case now of waiting and hoping that the messages continued and they could get a fix.

'Beep, beep.' The eagle had landed. "Are you there yet?"

"Yes."

"What colour is the school door?"

"Blue."

"Good boy, now wait."

Milford had Heather's mobile to keep in touch with Shepherd. His own mobile was actually at the police station being monitored – the questions to be relayed through Heather's. The only risk was that the blackmailer would want to talk to Milford, but Shepherd thought this was very unlikely.

"We should have a result soon," fizzed Shepherd with the excitement of a hunter bearing down on a fox. Heather was sitting with him. "Keep on the phone and just keep doing as I say and we'll be OK."

Dean Muxlowe sat in his car at the side of the river. The time was 11.20 a.m. He had Radio 2 on hardly loud enough to hear, and his seat ratcheted slightly back, head on the restraint and his eyes closed. He was wondering what the fuck he was doing. It would have been better not to have had thirty minutes between texts – maybe Myra realised this and was getting a perverted sense of enjoyment at cruelly torturing both of them.

Far off, Dean heard the sound of wailing sirens. You didn't usually hear that at that time of the morning. They seemed to be getting closer. His eyes were still shut.

Louder and louder, closer and closer, came the sirens. Dean's eyes remained shut." I wonder…" He thought. The possibility of capture started to dawn on him. He didn't open his eyes, his heartbeat remained constant. "Surely this can't be right? Why aren't I scared?" He asked himself. They were almost on top of him. They were on top of him.

He opened his eyes as the sirens stopped. All he could see were the blue flashing lights all around. Two police cars and a bike. Two officers, one male, one female, were marching towards him. Dean closed his eyes again. The male officer opened the driver's door. "Dean Muxlowe?" He barked. He was probably early forties, dark hair, rugged good looks, no smile. He was wearing blue latex gloves.

"Yes." Replied Dean – very calm, his eyes slowly opened to look at the officer.

"Dean Muxlowe I am arresting you for the blackmail of Paul Milford. Anything you say can be used in evidence against you. Anything you don't say but later rely on in court may count against you. Do you understand?"

"Yes I do," confirmed Dean.

"Step out of the car please."

Dean climbed out of the car. He'd left the pay-as-you-go mobile on the passenger seat. The copper quickly searched him, and then led him over to one of the cars, depositing him in the back. Several other officers had appeared and, all wearing the latex gloves proceeded to crawl all over his car. Dean remained silent; his heartbeat had still not changed. He was consciously waiting for the fear to hit him. It didn't.

"Are you OK, Sir?" The female police officer had climbed into the back of the car next to him. She seemed very young, early twenties maybe, quite pretty, the sort you'd have expected to see on 'The Bill.' She also seemed quite genuinely concerned.

"Yes," sighed Dean.

"Do you understand what is happening?"

"Yes," sighed Dean.

PC Templer, the newly arrived lady, had expected protests, arguments, denials, but no. Maybe this guy was in shock? "Are you sure you are OK, Sir?"

"Yes," sighed Dean again. Templer decided to try and lighten the mood a little with small talk.

"Nice car. I bet it can shift. How much have you had out of it?" She chirped nodding towards the Subaru.

"Seventy miles per hour," sighed Dean again, in a totally disinterested manner.

"Oh, really?" She laughed. "No, off the record of course," Dean remained silent. Templer stopped the nervous, forced laugh and several silent minutes passed.

The male officer came over to the car, his radio crackling away. He'd reported the successful arrest. "OK, Mr Muxlowe." He sat in the front of the car and turned to speak to Dean. "You've been arrested for the blackmail of Paul Milford. We are now going to take you to Mansfield police station as it is the only local with room at the moment. You will be interviewed by detectives up there. Any questions?"

Dean thought a little. "Can I let my wife know where I am?" His tone was flat and he almost sounded bored with the situation.

"No," replied the copper. "In the case of blackmail you cannot talk to her before we have finished our investigations. We will be searching your car, your business premises and your home. We may take away anything that we feel may aid our investigations."

"Whatever," Dean sighed and looked away out of the car window. He then closed his eyes and put his head back on the headrest as if trying to shut out a bad headache. His mind was still a blank; his pulse still had not changed. Not another word was said during the forty-minute journey to Mansfield.

"We've got him!" DI Shepherd was ecstatic. Paul Milford was confused.

"Him?"

"Yes, 'him.' Myra is a bloke. Do you know Dean Muxlowe?" Paul could hear Heather 'whooping' in the background. He could picture her walking round 'high-fiving' with the team of police.

"The name rings a bell."

"Well, that's who it is. We've arrested him and are now gathering more evidence from his home and work place. It is definitely him though; we've got the phone he was texting with. We will now try and find the computer that he wrote the letters on and the printer, plus paper and envelope matches, CCTV pictures of him buying the sim card, which is Tesco so that should be no problem. We've got the bastard."

"Good, thank God." Milford gave a huge sigh of relief. He could still hear Heather's excited squeals in the background. "Is it over then?"

"Nearly," replied Shepherd. "I'll get the boys up at Mansfield to hammer a confession out of him. I just need a statement from you tying up the texting today. Once we've got all we need we'll put a case together for the CPS and get him charged."

"Brilliant!" Said Milford. "I'm on my way over to pick Heather up – I'll see you shortly."

Milford takes a bow

We've got the bastard bang to rights
He's made our last few months' pure hell
Why did he write those poison notes?
Let's hope the police can make him tell

No longer will I fear the sound
Of postman strolling down the drive
Of what he has inside his sack
At last, again, I feel alive

He thought that he could rob me
Demand my hard earned money
But I am so much sharper
I find it rather funny

I'll claim it caused a heart problem
I'll say for weeks I was not sleeping
The constant fear, the mental stress
My girlfriend Heather, always weeping

Please Mr Judge, do your worst
No longer can this man stay free
I want him jailed with all the scum
Lock him up and sling the key

Molly was back at home. She had done her four-hour shift and had just made a cup of coffee at twelve midday. Rose had not long got out of bed. As she sat down in her usual chair by the window Molly saw two police cars and a dark blue Volvo estate pull up outside the house. Several uniforms got out along with a couple of suits. They came to the front door. Molly's heart was in her mouth.

Chapter 15

The Search

There was a loud knock on the door. The police didn't use the doorbell. Molly opened the door to a rather large detective in a blue, ill-fitting suit. He was well over six foot, quite slim, probably fourteen stone. He had a pleasant fleshy, round featured face but a very stern, serious expression. His voice was very deep. "Mrs Muxlowe?"

"Yes," Molly squeaked.

"I am sorry to bother you but I have a warrant here to search your home. My name is Detective Inspector Fox of the Notts police." He flashed up his credentials. Molly stood there unable to speak. She couldn't think of anything to say. She stepped aside as the uniformed officers marched past and spread throughout the house. Eventually she found her voice.

"What the hell is going on here? What are you looking for?"

"Mrs Muxlowe," said Fox, "your husband has been arrested on suspicion of blackmail. We have officers currently searching his work place and I am here to conduct a search of your house. I may have to take away any items that I feel may be relevant to our investigation."

"My Dean wouldn't blackmail anyone." Molly was recovering from the shock and starting to get angry. In fact she was starting to get very angry and irate. Her vocal volume was steadily on the increase. "How dare you accuse him of blackmail? How can you possibly think he'd do anything like that?"

"Please, Mrs Muxlowe. We wouldn't go to these lengths without good reason. We do have evidence to confirm his involvement now please have a seat and let us do our job. We will try not to disturb too much."

Molly went back to her chair and picked up her coffee. She didn't want it; she felt sick. Everything was running through her head.

The police moved through the house like a raging fire. They were in the cupboards, under the beds, in the loft, out in the back garden. They even dismantled some of the toilet cistern and pipes, apparently looking for bundles of cash that Dean may have extorted off possible past victims. They carried out a couple of computers, bank statements, credit card statements, blank paper found in one of the cupboards and other bits and pieces that Molly didn't even notice.

They were very thorough but also very considerate in that they left the place virtually as they had found it. Molly sat in silence, not able to believe what was happening.

"Where is Dean now?" She enquired of Fox.

"Don't worry, he's safe and well. We have him in custody up in Mansfield."

"How long will he be there?"

"I can't tell you, I'm afraid. Not because I won't but because I don't know. He's being interviewed now but I don't know how long it will take."

"Can I call my mother?"

"No, I'm afraid not. Not yet."

They were there in total for just over two hours. DI Fox thanked Molly for her co-operation and told her he'd have anything that they didn't need back to her as soon as he could. Throughout the search,

Rose had sat in stunned silence on the settee gazing onto space. She spoke up after the last copper had left. "What the hell has he done, mum?"

"Fuck knows, darling. I can't imagine he's done anything. They said he's been blackmailing somebody."

"How can they think dad has done that? Blackmail's not that bad anyway."

"Apparently it is, and they seem pretty sure he has done it."

"When's he coming back?"

"Fuck knows. Probably when they've done with him."

"I bet all that lot got a good eyeful." Rose nodded out of the window as the nosey old git, Mrs Stenson from three doors down walked past staring in; trying to see what was going on.

"Fuck them. I don't give a shit. All I'm worried about is Dean. I'm going to give your gran a ring; you go and get us a drink – and I don't mean coffee – I know it's only two o'clock in the afternoon but there's a bottle of Bailys in the fridge – go and get us both one." Rose went through to the kitchen while Molly picked the phone up to her mother. This should be fun.

Meanwhile at Dean's office a similar scene was being acted out. The police had to break the door to get in because they couldn't get hold of anyone with a key. They didn't take long to search the place because the office was very small and sparse. They took away a computer, a printer, a mobile phone, samples of paper and envelopes, a few bank statements and Dean's diary. It would be found that the paper and envelopes matched that of the blackmailer's and the computer would contain traces of the letters that Dean had created on behalf of Myra.

James Hunter-Browne was sitting on his ride-on lawnmower surveying his huge garden that he couldn't afford. He was torn between finishing off his lawn, and driving into work to show his face. He decided to just do a little bit more. He thought he'd got an appointment that evening to show someone a Jeep Cherokee that he'd bought very cheap. His true motivation was that he'd not had to pay for it yet. Hopefully he would turn it round for a cheeky little two grand profit before he had to. Well, he'd have to because he didn't have two ha'pennies to rub together.

Yes, he'd like his lawn to look nice and trim to give a good impression to the punter. Two grand would be more than welcome, with that and the MHB money he would be able to live for another month.

His thoughts were interrupted as he saw Michelle running towards him, pained expression on her face, waving her mobile, yellow wellies on her feet, and marigolds on her hands. She started calling James' name.

"What's up?" he called, switching off the engine of the lawnmower.

"You're not going to believe this," she shouted. It was two-twenty p.m. "Dean Muxlowe has been arrested for blackmail!"

"What?" James indeed couldn't believe it, not one little bit. He thought someone was having a joke. "Who's this?"

"It's your accountant. Molly has called him; the police have just finished searching his house."

James took the phone and was given the brief details that Andrew Deptford, the accountant, had been told. As he hung up he was picturing his big expensive house falling into the ground as his wife and kids climbed into a taxi and fucked off. "Shit!" He said.

"What is it? What's happened? Is it true?" Michelle was hysterical. James didn't answer. He was too stunned. His mind had immediately switched to 'what does this mean to me' rather than 'I wonder what's happened to Dean and it's time for me to step up and take over the reins until this is sorted' mode.

"Well? Well?" Michelle was screaming now.

"I'm not sure." James Replied. "But I think we need to make some plans. MHB Finance may well be over, we may have to distance ourselves from it."

"What about Dean? What's he done?"

"Not sure, exactly. But whatever it is we can't be associated with him. I'll start telling people we've split up. I'll deal as Hunter-Browne Specialist Cars on my own." James was now babbling, thinking out loud. He sounded a bit crazy. As it began to sink in, so the panic grew. Fuck the lawn; he had other things to do. He needed to get to people before his ex-partners misdemeanours were general knowledge. He couldn't be anywhere near this. His wife, house, kids, business all depended on it. Fuck Muxlowe.

He hit the phones. His thinking was that if he told people what had happened he could make his excuses and put his side first, in effect 'ring-fencing' himself and maintaining his own reputation.

Most of the people he rang couldn't believe what had happened. That wasn't important. What was important was that it was fuck all to do with James Hunter-Browne. "And, oh, by the way, MHB Finance no longer exists. Don't phone Dean, phone me, I'll sort your finance out for you, just a change of name." He actually started thinking that it may actually help him – people might give him a bit of sympathy business as a victim himself.

Most people were stunned into silence. What had made such an honest and trustworthy man do something to get arrested, banged up and lose his business? They all had so many questions. Hunter-Browne couldn't answer these questions, he didn't really have time to, and he just wanted to get to as many people as quickly as possible. The pressure was on.

Paul Milford walked into Nottingham Police Station just before eleven-forty-five a.m. Heather was waiting for him, along with DI Shepherd. Smiles were everywhere. As he walked through the door she rushed over and threw her arms around him. "At last, at last." The joy in her voice gave it a little quiver of anticipation. "It's over."

"Yes, it is." He replied as if he were some sort of victorious soldier returning from a hard fought war. DI Shepherd approached and stuck out his hand. Paul pulled away from Heather to shake it firmly.

"Well done, Paul," smiled the policeman. "We'll just take a brief statement from you regarding the texts then I suggest that you take this little lady here for a celebratory glass of wine."

"Not half," agreed Paul. "Let's get it done."

By two p.m. Paul and Heather were sitting in The George and Dragon. Paul ordered a mixed grill, extra onion rings, and a pint of lager. Heather went for the vegetarian three bean chilli and a glass of medium white wine. She wasn't a vegetarian by any stretch, but she liked the way that the beans made her fart at night. Some people find pleasure in the strangest things.

After they'd eaten they sat drinking; babbling away to each other like they were teenagers again. Normally when they were on their own they had very little to say to each other; today they were conquering heroes.

By four p.m. Paul had three pints on board, heading for the half gallon. Heather had gone onto the vodka and tonics. As he approached the bar who should walk in? Yes, Ernest Gerrity.

"Ernest, my dear boy! What can I get you?"

"Hi, Paul." Ernest appeared a little sheepish, as if he was expecting something. "I'll have a pint of usual lager. Have you been in long?" With the excitement of the day and the three pints of lager Paul's face was slightly rouged, giving him the appearance of being half pissed.

"Yes, mate. We've had a bit of good fortune today. Have a seat with Heather and I'll bring your drink over." Gerrity went over to Heather who stood to give him a welcoming hug.

"What's happened?" Asked Gerrity.

"Have a seat," replied Heather. To build the drama she added; "We'll tell you when Paul gets here."

So the story was told. Heather and Paul competing for floor space, interrupting, contradicting, correcting and exaggerating like two school kids who'd just witnessed a car accident. Gerrity listened with interest to the blow by blow account nodding, smiling and laughing at all the right places.

Of course he knew something had gone wrong. He had felt a little sick at eleven-twenty a.m. that morning as he approached Brimshill Nature Reserve. There had been an almighty cacophony of police sirens somewhere locally that had lasted for about ten minutes. He'd parked up anyway hoping that it was nothing to do with the reason that he was there. At twelve-forty-five p.m. though, when he was still sitting in his car parked at the side of the road and Paul Milford hadn't turned up to go into the car park he knew there had been trouble. He then felt really sick. He had driven home to see Stella. She had still been at work when he got home which was lucky, because when she got back at two p.m., he'd claimed that he didn't feel too well and had only just got up. Just in case he needed an alibi.

After a couple more pints, and a couple more repeats of the overdramatized details, Gerrity decided that he could face no more. His main emotion was relief – relief that he had put someone else in the frame to blame and the hope that he swallowed it and took the punishment, or at least that if he did spill the beans that the police would be more interested in getting their result than expanding the investigation to implicate anyone else. He did find comfort from the thought that he knew the police generally didn't like complications. They didn't usually like to cloud the issue with the truth.

He did admit to Milford that he knew Dean Muxlowe and even expressed a little surprise by his actions. But then he made the excuse of feeling a little off colour, as if to confirm his alibi for earlier, and left them to their celebrations.

Paul and Heather stayed until nine p.m. by which time they were totally bladdered, they deserved it, they thought. On the way home Paul phoned the local Indian takeaway delivery service.

"What do you want, lover girl?" He asked Heather.

"Well, big boy." She smiled. "What have they got with beans in?"

Gerrity's Conscience

Whoops, it's all gone pear-shaped
I've fucked up Muxlowe's life
He'll lose his house, his job, his car
His, dogs, his kids, his wife

I'm trying to ignore what's done
Try and remove it from my mind
And hope that it will go away
I'll keep my head down to the grind

I know he'll go to prison
Can't see him staying free
It could of course be so much worse
It could of course be me

But can I really do it?
Leave him hanging out to dry
Abandon him, it's all my fault
But if I speak, it's me who'll fry

Out of sight, out of mind
He's over twenty-one
I shut my eyes, it disappears
What is done is done

Chapter 16

The custody suite

Dean, Dean, Dean... What have you done?

Have you ever been taken into police custody? Spent time in a depressing cell or 'custody suit' as they call them these days?

Well, let me tell you it's not that much fun.

The cell was probably sixteen feet long and ten feet wide. It had a burgundy painted concrete floor, the concrete walls being a pleasing shade of battleship grey, intermittently marked with black scuffs from previous occupant's shoes. The 'bed' was a solid concrete block seven feet by about two and a half to three feet – also grey with a lovely red, one inch thick foam filled mattress. Earlier a pleasant little copper had brought Dean in a bed sheet – nicely folded – made a lovely pillow. Next to the 'bed' were the stainless steel toilet and an odd hand washing device. Filthy, covered in piss. (The toilet not the hand washing device).

The lighting was constant; yellow and constant – no daylight so it was impossible to tell whether it was day or night. The 'window' was a series of thick glass blocks arranged in a rectangular grid at the top of the wall facing the door – it was about three feet square but impossible to see through.

The door was big and steel and blue. There was a small 'window' in the door that didn't look outside but into a black space – presumably a peep hole to check that the inmate was still alive.

From outside the big 'window' somewhere there was a monotone whining/rattling mechanical noise – maybe a generator or air con unit of some kind. This was complimented by some faint music – not very clear, maybe opera? Never changing tone or volume.

Dean estimated that he had been in the cell for about thirty-six hours. He'd already been interviewed by the C.I.D. twice and told them a complete pack of lies. He had been arrested earlier for blackmail – quite a serious crime apparently – certainly a fuck's sight more serious than he'd thought. Oops! Caused quite a stir – he even got a visit from the Chief Superintendent or somebody to tell him he'd been in custody for twenty-four hours and he was authorising a further period of twenty-four hours as they needed more time to investigate. Wankers – seemed a little over the top to him.

Wait…footsteps…are they coming to get him again? He fucking hoped so – He's going to admit everything now – he'd done with all of this. He knew he did it and they knew he did it. He even thought that they knew that he knew that they knew he did it. He thought he should come clean. He needed to get out of there, he needed to go home, he needed to check on the wife, poor bitch; he bet she was spinning on the roof, he needed a fucking drink.

Silence…shit.

Dean had not had any sleep or food now for nearly two days. Every time he shut his eyes it was as if there were springs behind them pushing them open. He lay staring at the ceiling thinking, not so much of what he'd done, but more of how he would explain himself to friends and family; going through different speeches to different people. The more he thought the more people popped into his head to deal with. With every new face came a new problem and he felt a surge of adrenaline – his heart was already in his throat and he felt sickie sick sick.

He looked over to the opposite side wall – WOW! The whole wall was alive – like a massive aquarium full of fish, lobsters, shrimps and seaweed, all swimming and swaying in the slow steady current. His heart flipped again – what the fuck? He stood up to get a closer look but as he got nearer the 'sea creatures' stopped moving and turned back into scuffs and graffiti. He was then aware of a face at the little black window – an Asian woman in a blue turban waving at him! As he moved closed she disappeared into the blackness. Shit – this must be what sleep deprivation does to you.

He lay back on the 'bed'. Down in the far corner of the burgundy floor was a small, saucer size pile of glowing ash. Around it in circles flew a number of tiny dragons with bright red wings – the brightest red he'd ever seen – almost glowing. There were four or five, maybe six – he tried to get a bit closer to count them properly – no good, away they go. The Asian woman at the door is back – smiling now.

The friendly little copper, who brought him the blanket earlier, also brought a magazine for him to read – some old edition of Chat or something. He'd tried to read bits of it – tried but failed. Funny how your mind works. He looked at the mag thinking not of its content but more of its staples. He remembered an old police drama programme he was watching once – The Wire in the Blood I think – something along those lines. Anyway the mentally ill prisoner had managed to get hold of a staple, or was it a paper clip? Whatever, Anyway, the whateveritwas was used to sever the prisoners own carotid artery, thus spraying blood for many metres all up the walls and ceiling. Very impressive. The prisoner of course died and the police were in a major stress. Dean could do that. Wouldn't that just fuck off Mr Superintendent and mess up his lovely 'custody suite'. Problem is he didn't know the difference between his carotid and his jugular – the jugular wouldn't have the same effect – it seeps rather than spurts, apparently.

Come on, come on for fuck's sake – let's get this over with.

More faces, more excuses, more sickness.

Clip clop, clip clop. Either that was one of the three billy goats gruff or he was out of there – He hoped.

The bolt in the door slid open and there stood the Desk sergeant. "Interview time," he chirped, almost sung with a cheeky little smile across his face.

"Thank fuck for that," Dean replied, not quite loud enough for him to hear and gain any satisfaction from his situation.

Dean was escorted to the interview room by the desk sergeant where he was re-introduced to the two detectives who were processing him. DC Burdett, who was a typical copper from Ashes to Ashes – the TV series about the woman DI that got mysteriously transported back to the eighties (Dean never did quite figure it out). Burdett even had the same dress leather jacket that Bodie wore in The Professionals. The other one looked more like a mature student – a little bit too skinny with an ill-fitting suit and cheap glasses. He spoke very slowly emphasising particular words, lingering on others – watching all the time for reactions to his questions. DC Elliott was his name – obviously been on the 'interview techniques' training course.

It was silent as '80s cop loaded up the recording device – 3 discs: one to analyse later; one as back-up in case the first one failed; and the final one to seal in sticky back plastic so that the police couldn't get into it to 'edit' it.

Studious then reminded Dean of his rights and offered him a solicitor again. He declined the offer.

The interview then began:

STUDIOUS: "Well, Mr Muxlowe, as you know we have been carrying out extensive enquiries regarding the blackmail of Paul Milford."

80s COP: "Yes, mate there's not just us two coppers on this one you know. We've searched your home, workplace and car. We are actually the homicide squad normally, so we don't cut corners and we will get to the bottom of this."

STUDIOUS: "Is there anything that you wish to tell us?"

DEAN: "No." He could feel some bile acid coming up his throat at this point so had to keep swallowing. Keep the talking to a minimum. He felt as if he was in another room looking in on himself – head very light and dizzy'

The two coppers looked at each other rather too smugly. That look told Dean more than any words – it told him that they had found something.

STUDIOUS: "We have removed a computer and printer from your workplace and our very clever technical people have spent many hours interrogating them,"

The use of the word 'interrogating' seemed a little odd at the time.

DEAN: "OK, so what have you found?" Again an exchange of glances between the two.

STUDIOUS: "Very interesting really. You say that you didn't produce and send these blackmail letters." Dean nodded. "Please answer for the benefit of the tape."

DEAN: "Yes." Dean's lips were dry, he'd refused the glass of water offered earlier by the 80s cop.

STUDIOUS: "Well from your computer we have managed to extract remnants of one of the letters that was sent to Mr Milford… What have you to say about that?"

Dean stayed silent still swallowing back the bile.

80s COP: "Does anyone else have access to your computer?"

DEAN: "No."

80s COP: "How do you explain what we have found then?" A creepy smile spreading across his face. Studious was glaring at Dean, analysing his every movement. He would probably know he was nearly choking on stomach acid.

A long silence passed. At this point Dean knew that they had what they needed and he was done. Any resistance now was pointless and potentially damaging. It was time for damage limitation.

DEAN: "OK. OK. Let's not waste any more time. I produced the letters, I sent the letters and I was responsible for all of the malicious texts that were sent to Mr Milford." Shit, he'd not asked them if he could go home if he confessed. They'd have probably lied anyway.

STUDIOUS: "So you did do it?"

DEAN: "You sound surprised."

80s COP: "We're not surprised, Mr Muxlowe, just a little disappointed that you lied to us earlier." Dean wasn't aware that it was a crime to lie to the police.

DEAN: "I bet you get disappointed a lot in your job." Shit, he probably should not have said that – he needed a bit of sympathy at the moment. 80s Cop just smirked.

Studious then went into great detail re-affirming Dean's confession for the benefit of the tape. He then confirmed it was all his own work and that he didn't have an accomplice somewhere out there.

STUDIOUS: "You are going to prison, Mr Muxlowe." Dean couldn't really take this comment in.

DEAN: "How long for?" Stupid question – he wished he hadn't asked.

80s COP: "Years."

The recording equipment was turned off, the discs removed and one of them sealed and labelled. This is when 80s Cop's attitude changed remarkably.

As Dean stood up he reached out to shake his hand, a warm smile across his face. At first he thought he was taking the piss. Dean took his hand and he shook it. He could smell the whisky on the policeman's breath.

"Look," he said. "No hard feelings, eh? Thanks for coming clean it will help your sentence. You may even get a suspended if you plead guilty straight away and be a good lad." He winked and Dean smiled. Why did he smile?

Dean had never ever contemplated the possibility of prison or a criminal record. What had he done that was so very, very bad? Nobody had died or even been injured. He'd not stolen anything or kidnapped anyone. All he did was get into a ridiculous situation well over his head. Stupid, stupid schoolboy error.

Still, he thought, he couldn't 'un-ring the bell.'

Dean's emotions were all over the place. Sudden panic attacks followed by rushes of euphoria, then deep, deep depression. There must have been all sorts of chemicals and hormones sloshing around his brain.

80s Cop removed his hand. "Well, then. What do you think that you will do with your life now?"

"Probably suicide," Dean replied flatly. The smile was no longer on his face. 80s Cop stared. Silence. "No job. No house. Reputation in tatters. Wife will probably fuck off back to Scotland in disgrace. Ruined life. Ruined business and the lives of those people who work for me. Forty-eight years old up to my neck in debt and will not get a job in finance anywhere with a criminal record. Three grown up kids that will now have no respect for me. Sorry to go on but on a scale of 1 – 10 of stupid fucking questions, that has to come somewhere close to the top." 80s Cop blushed and looked embarrassed.

"Still," Dean carried on, "at least this bit is over and you pair can go and get a pint. Call it a celebration. What happens to me now?"

"Well," pipes up Studious. "You go back to your custody suite for a couple of hours whilst we contact the CPS. You will then be bailed, go home, and return here in approximately six weeks to be formally charged."

"Six weeks?"

"Yes that will give us time to conclude our investigations."

"But I've confessed. You've got evidence. Why waste time and money pissing about. Let's just get it sorted. I can't sit around for six weeks waiting for the axe to fall."

80s Cop: "Sorry, mate that is the process."

With that they left the interview room and Dean was led back to the custody suite with the fish tank and red dragons.

He wasn't there long. He had a visit from a couple of prisoner welfare people making sure that he had been treated properly. It lasted about fifteen minutes. Shortly after that the desk sergeant came back with his belt, shoelaces and wallet, and then took him to explain bail conditions and when he had to go back. Six weeks it was. Shit!

Molly was on the way with Bernie to pick him up.

Chapter 16

Sentencing

It was Tuesday the 28th September 2010; the day Dean Muxlowe was to be sentenced for his crime of blackmail, although on the official charge sheet it stated 'demanding money with menaces.' He walked into Nottingham Crown Court and took a seat outside of court number 6.

The past four months of summer had been one long nightmare. He'd not been to work often and had spent all his time reading, drinking or explaining his actions to his friends and family. He'd had to report to the local police station every week as part of his bail conditions. He couldn't wait to get this over with and move on with the rest of his life.

After being charged he had to await a magistrate's court date. From there he was referred to crown court, where he pleaded guilty. He then had to go back for sentencing.

Dean found himself surprisingly calm now. The prospect of a custodial sentence was very real but, though he thought he should be, he could not even force himself to be frightened, or even too concerned. As he sat and analysed his situation, thinking as he thought a forty odd year old first time offender, married, kids and up to now, totally respectable, should think, his lack of concern is what worried him most. He daren't admit it openly but he was quite enjoying the cleansing of his life and the excitement, almost, that he was experiencing. He was the centre of everyone's attention and felt as if he'd been transported to a movie set. He could not grasp the seriousness of the trouble he was in. Surely the British justice system would show common sense and let him walk free.

He sat and took a look around at all the barristers, solicitors, clerks and 'hangers-on' dressed in their ridiculous outfits and gowns. They swanned around as if part of some solemn, ancient ritual, each one with their part to play. No smiles, just neutral expressions. So much belief in their own self-importance. The word 'aloof' came into Dean's mind. It took all his effort not to just stand up and scream at the top of his voice, 'you're all just a bunch of fucking wankers.' He smiled at the thought and wondered if anyone had actually ever done it.

If he had been on his own he pictured himself as one of these gangsters on News at Ten; the ones who stand in the dock and laugh at the judge, or stick a finger up at the victim's relatives. Contempt of court – fuck the court and all of its outdated little fucking pompous, childish rituals that should have been binned years ago in the annals of time.

But he wasn't on his own – he had Molly, and family, and friends. Molly was the one that worried him if he was sent down. She would lose it, he knew. She would need help from everywhere. She would feel so alone. Dean had sorted the finances for a year or so away by borrowing money and consolidating current outstanding loans, but Molly would panic. The future was uncertain, out of his control. Would the house be sold? What about the business? What would the neighbours say? Will they have to move to another area? Back to Scotland? What happens when the money runs out? All these were questions that Molly had asked Dean a hundred times over the last few months but he could still not answer. He tried to answer, and sometimes was quite convincing, but deep down he didn't really know himself.

Molly was with him, along with Mike from MHB Finance for support. She kept trying to smile; the smile that was used to try and cover up the fear in her heart. She kept talking of her 'butterflies' in her chest, like when she was a kid and she got separated from her mother in a busy street for a few minutes, but thought that she was lost forever. 'Are you OK?' was all that kept coming from her lips, more out of nervousness than need for an answer. It was starting to irritate Dean but there was nothing more to say. It had all been said. Mike was in the background with the odd funny comment in an attempt to lighten the situation, but Dean was not really listening. He was in his own world. So many different personalities in his head, all jabbering away, fighting for attention. Then a voice from the outside.

"Mr, Muxlowe, good morning." It was Dean's barrister smiling down from way above. Dean peered through the haze.

"Good morning," he said trying to reciprocate the smile.

The smile, obviously false disappeared from the barrister's face. The neutral expression took over. Dean thought he almost sensed a flicker of concern. "Shall we pop into a consulting room where we can have a chat in private?" It was not a question, he strode over to the open door just opposite the waiting area chairs, and Dean was dragged along in his wake.

"Shall I come?" asked Molly.

"No, no – I'll not be long." Dean, for some unexplained reason was expecting bad news in some way. He shut the door of the consulting room behind him and they both sat down. The barrister, Paul Reynolds, was in his black gown and curly wig. If someone from another planet could see him what would they think?

"How are you?" The barristers first expected, but unnecessary question.

"Fine," replied Dean. "What's happening?" Dean had been sat in the court waiting area for two hours and wanted things over. He was fed up to the back teeth of this weird micro-universe that he'd entered that seemed so distant from reality as he knew it.

"Well, I'm afraid that I'm not the bringer of good tidings." This time Reynolds did not try to hide his concerned look.

"What's up?" Dean sighed. "Tell me everything."

"Well, firstly the psychiatrist's report is good for us, or it should be," frowned Reynolds.

"How do you mean 'or it should be'?"

"Well, the report states quite clearly and categorically that you have been suffering from severe clinical depression for at least two years, and that this condition has caused you to act quite out of character in doing what you have done i.e. sending these vile letters to Paul Milford." The barrister paused, the frown still across his face.

"That's good, isn't it?" Paul jumped in.

"Hopefully." There was a short pause before Reynolds continued, rather embarrassed. "The problem is that the report was late getting to the probation officer, so your pre-sentencing report that she provided for the judge doesn't take into account any of the medical evidence."

"OK, so whose fault is that?" Dean was incredulous. "I went to see the shrink over a week ago."

"Well, it's nobody's fault," Reynolds was now on the defensive. He didn't want to implicate anybody, especially the solicitor, effectively his employer. He continued, smiling, trying to diffuse the situation. "These things take time to produce and get to the relevant people; a week is a very short time in legal terms."

"Yes," Dean spat, "of course it is. At two hundred odd quid an hour you wouldn't want to be rushing would you?" Dean's frustration was quite apparent.

"What I intend to do is ask the judge for an adjournment. This will allow us to re-submit the medical evidence to the probation people and ask them to produce a new report reflecting the evidence."

"So that's more time? More waiting? How many more weeks?" Dean sighed.

"I don't know," Reynolds' voice had dropped. He paused. "We do have another problem."

"What's that?" Dean shot back

"The judge…" The barrister paused for thought, trying to choose his words carefully. "The judge is notoriously awkward. He is renowned for not allowing such adjournments, unfairly in my view, but it is his decision whether to allow the new evidence."

"New evidence!" Dean was again incredulous. "It's not new evidence, its past evidence that hasn't been delivered to the right people on time. It's not my fault that a report can't be prepared, typed up and taken around the corner to the probation office in over a week. I went to that assessment with the shrink probably 800 yards away from their building. Half a fucking mile away and it was late! What's going on here?"

"I understand your feelings, Dean, but…"

"No you fucking don't," Dean jumped in. "You're not the one stood in court about to be sent down, leaving your wife and family to fend for themselves, just because some frigging solicitor spends too much time guffawing over long lunches and not enough time building a decent case for his client. They fucking charge enough." Dean was shaking his head.

"Look, let's not get too excited yet." Reynolds was pacing the room now. "Let's see what the judge says, we can always appeal the decision if it goes against us."

"Fuck that!" Dean paused for a few moments to collect his thoughts. The past few minutes of conversation had hit him like a train. "Do you think it will work, or will I get sent down?"

The barrister thought for a while, aware of Dean's heightened agitation. "At another time with a different judge I would be ninety percent sure that you would come away with a suspended sentence or at the very least an adjournment. The police said the same and so did your solicitor. But now...I don't know."

"So what you are saying is that it doesn't really matter what the crime is or the circumstances behind it, the most important factor is what fucking judge you get? So it's more a game of chance than a fair, consistent judicial process that treats everyone the same? What a load of shit! I can't believe what I'm hearing."

"I didn't say that," protested Reynolds.

"Yes you did! It's bollocks." Dean was shouting now. "Look, just do what you can, I can't be bothered anymore. I'll expect the worst."

Reynolds opened the door for Dean and he left to re-join Molly. "Well?" she was concerned by the red face and angry expression.

"Fuck knows," spat Dean. "Apparently the solicitor didn't get my psycho report to the probation twats in time and so their pre-sentence report doesn't reflect the fact that I'm a nut job, so it slates me. Along with that, the judge is apparently a right wanker and will probably not adjourn the hearing to allow the depression to be taken into account. In a nutshell, I'm fucked. I'll be going down as sure as I've got a hole in my arse."

Molly's eyes filled with tears. At that point DI Shepherd waltzed into the waiting area with Paul Milford and Heather. Dean stared over at the couple, he was ripe for a brawl, but they had obviously been well briefed and didn't acknowledge Dean's presence.

It wasn't until after lunch that Dean was called into court. It had been a long, hard wait. Dean was glad things had now progressed. Molly's 'butterflies' felt like they were on speed.

Molly, Mike, Milford, Heather, Shepherd and a few other interested parties took up their seats in the public gallery. Dean was led to the dock.

The dock was a little glass-fronted room about three metres square with a couple of benches. The resident security officer emptied Dean's pockets into a polythene bag that he put on a table just through a door leading out of the back of the dock. The door led to the cells underneath the court.

Dean was instructed to sit on the bench, facing the court. It was very quiet, silent even. All the officials were sat in position with their neutral expressions and self-importance in abundance. Not one smile. Minutes passed; Dean wondered what the fuck the delay was. He'd pleaded guilty, just get on with it!

Eventually a door at the back opened and the judge walked in. Everyone stood up. When the judge sat down, everyone else sat down. Dean wondered why he hadn't got a gavel. Surely all judges had a gavel to bang when they shouted 'order, order!' Such a strange thing to come to his mind at that particular point. He later found out that no judges use a gavel in UK courts. Dean was asked to stand.

The hearing was announced and the judge made various noises, and then asked the prosecution to present the Crown's case. At this point Paul Reynolds stood up to ask for an adjournment due to the medical evidence being missing from the probation's pre-sentencing report. Dean could not help but be completely unimpressed and underwhelmed by the barristers performance. It was like Oliver Twist asking for more gruel at the workhouse. The judge swatted him away as if he was nothing more than an annoying little wasp on a hot summer day. He turned to the prosecutor and asked him to continue.

The prosecutor outlined the facts of the case and the contents of the letters. The sexual perversion, the hatred and obvious malice they contained. He painted beautifully the picture of mental torture that Milford and his loving partner had been mercilessly subjected to. How Milford had suffered severe chest pains as a direct result and how Heather could not sleep and was afraid to leave the house on her own. They had been frightened beyond belief and anyone that had done this to them must, must, must be removed from society. The public would be in danger if this man was allowed to remain on the streets.

Dean looked on impassively; face forward, in his own world, like he was watching this from outer space. The prosecutor sat down and Reynolds stood up to plead for the defence.

It wasn't too bad a performance to try and mitigate the result as much as possible. Clinical depression was blamed, no past history of offending, married for twenty-six years, three kids, two of which had graduated at university, own house, own business, uncharacteristic behaviour – all the usual, but Dean wasn't convinced.

The judge looked directly at Dean once Reynolds had sat down. "Well, Mr Muxlowe, I have taken note of all the defence arguments for mitigation. I also give you credit for admitting your guilt and in doing so saving a great deal of time and public money in performing a trial by jury. I must admit we get very few blackmail cases and this is a particularly unusual one

"Having also taken into account the evidence and the effect of your actions on your innocent victims, I find it impossible to impose anything other than an immediate custodial sentence." Molly burst into tears suddenly and the judge paused for a few seconds to give her a chance to compose herself.

"This is a very serious case and the effects are extreme. You must face up to your responsibilities despite your claim that your illness has affected your behaviour.

"Taking everything into account, I am imposing a reduced sentence from forty months to thirty-two months, of which you will serve sixteen months in prison starting immediately. Take him down."

Dean was immediately led out of the dock through the back door, along a corridor and down some stairs to a room deep down in the bowels of the Court. A dungeon would have been a better word.

Molly was inconsolable. She'd always held the belief that Dean would be walking away. When she realised that he was being taken away for nearly one and a half years she completely broke down. She could see no future. Paul Reynolds went over to try and help, give a bit of hope by talking about an appeal and early release on HDC (Home Detention Curfew) or 'tag' as it was known. Nothing helped, nothing at all.

What also didn't help was Paul Milford and Heather jumping up and down in the waiting area whooping and laughing. High fives with the coppers like little kids. Briefly Molly felt something that she had never experienced before; she thought that this is what true deep hatred felt like. She could quite easily have soaked the pair of them in unleaded petrol and set fire to them.

Mike took her home where her mum was waiting. She'd recently made the journey from Scotland at Dean's request. That helped a little but she couldn't stay too long – Molly had to cope – sink or swim. It might even do her some good in a way. It could be worse; Dean could have died, or even worse fucked off with another woman. Eighteen months wasn't that long really – try telling Molly that.

The Wrong Judge

It's all a fucking game to them
They play with people's lives
The barristers, the briefs, the judge
All wielding deadly knives

They laugh and joke, guffaw, do lunch
Like gods they flounce and swagger
It's not about who's right or wrong
It's whose got the sharpest dagger

Our justice system is not fair
It laughs at common sense
It's all about the dough you spend
To buy the best defence

People needlessly rotting in jail
Building up a bitter grudge
Their lives thrown in the wheelie bin
Because they got the wrong judge

Chapter 17
Prison Life

Down in 'the dungeon', Dean was being processed by the officers or 'screws' as he would have to start calling them. After a strip search and a few forms, he was 'banged up' in a cell to await transport in a 'meat wagon' to Nottingham Prison. One of the screws gave him a paperback to read – an old Dick Francis novel called 'Silk' or something – he quite enjoyed it, and they let him take it to finish off when he was escorted to the 'meat wagon' for transfer.

From the cell to the 'meat wagon' policy dictated that the prisoner had to be hand-cuffed – right up to the point of being locked in the single compartment in the van. This brought home to Dean that he was now a criminal.

The van was a Luton box shape housing seven single compartments, each probably thirty inches square with a hard plastic seat looking out onto the street through a small tinted one-way window. The compartments were all full of mainly young twenty-one to-twenty-five year olds full of nervous energy trying to show their fellow prisoners that they weren't scared and that this was just another day to them. They were overly loud, overly cheerful, overly friendly and full of bull shit. Dean just smiled, nodded and kept himself to himself. He didn't want to be associated with these criminals.

Jeffrey Archer described Belmarsh Prison as 'Hell'. Dean thought the same about Nottingham. After being unloaded and escorted through processing, he was put into a holding cell with all the latest batch of newcomers. In that two hour period he first came to realise something that surprised him, and he would later find quite worrying from society's point of view.

There were a dozen other guys in the holding cell whilst they waited to be taken through to collect their clothes, see the healthcare people, and get put into their cells. There were four Arabs, none of which could speak a word of English, or so they said. They were in for ringing cars that they had illegally imported. There was a gypsy traveller who was in for hugely overcharging for paving a pensioner's drive and then demanding the money with menace. There was a drug dealer from Mansfield who was covered from head to toe with tattoos. A couple of black kids on drug charges, three others in for burglary, and Dean. Apart from the four Arabs and Dean they all either knew each other or had common acquaintances. The conversation was all about what prisons that they'd been in, who they knew, what they'd done and how long they'd got. Even the young kids were on their 4th, 5th, 6th sentences. This was their way of life. An occupational hazard. Dean listened with great interest how the gypsies dealt with the blacks, the whites and the Asians. He learnt about a Chinese cannabis farming gang that operated growing in houses and distribution centres stretching the full length of the M1. Car ringing gangs, crack cocaine processing labs, drug importers and smugglers. They were all clambering for their floor time. Whether a lot of it was bollocks or not Dean didn't know, but it sounded credible.

This was a whole new side of life to Dean. He'd been brought up to believe that prisoners were sent to prison to be punished and as such should be terrified of going back. Was that not the whole point of prison? – A deterrent? – To punish? To concentrate the mind on what they'd done and probably most importantly, to discourage them from offending again? Well these guys were certainly not discouraged; they seemed, if anything, happy to be back inside. They couldn't wait to renew old acquaintances, meet new people and make new friends and contacts. They wouldn't have to worry about where their next meal was coming from or where they were going to sleep. They could complain if it was too hot or cold in their cell, or they didn't like the food. It was a break from the pressures of their normal lives, a holiday almost.

Nottingham is a category 'B' prison. The 'B' relates to the risk level and thus the level of security employed. Most men sentenced at Nottingham Magistrates or Crown Courts were taken to Nottingham Jail to be held. Many are then, after a few weeks, transferred to another category 'B' or a lower risk 'C' prison. As a result Nottingham's prison population is very fluid. Dean realised very early that the best policy was to smile and nod and try to get on with everyone; prisoners, screws and governors alike. You were watched very closely while you were inside and any 'nickings' by the screws or 'negative comments', were added to your file and would always bite you on the arse later.

Part of the prison staff's job was to assess the inmates and try to spot any potential hot heads. As time went on, Dean thought of it as a huge reality TV show, everyone jostling for points. Applying to do a 'victim awareness' course, 'thinking skills', or gaining a certificate from CARATS (the drug and alcohol awareness people) would get you points. The important thing was that you were seen to be making the effort to address any potential issues. Volunteering to sweep the exercise yard got you points. Being friendly to screws got you points.

You could lose points quite easily; fighting; drugs; brewing and/or drinking 'hooch'; not being in your cell on time for 'bang-up'; cooking food in your kettle; throwing litter out of your cell window; being abusive to prison officers; not taking the rehabilitation courses seriously e.g. making silly comments, even if as a joke, would attract a negative comment and would probably be analysed by the experts to try and identify any underlying psychological issues that may lead to re-offending tendencies. These psychological issues must then be addressed at all costs before this person was allowed to be released back into society. What bollocks.

Anyway, two hours later Dean was called for further processing, a full strip search and allocation of his new prison uniform. This consisted of a horrible 'corned beef' pink sweatshirt and matching jogging bottoms, six pairs of boxer shorts, six pairs of socks, three 'corned beef' tee-shirts and a pair of prison trainers. He then had an interview with the prison doctor to talk about his depression and anti-depressant medication. To be honest, Dean thought, after spending two hours in the holding cell with such a bunch of arseholes he felt a hell of a lot better than any 'happy pills' could make him. There is nothing like an insight into the lives of some of these career criminals to make you realise that your own life isn't really that bad. Doctors should realise this and use it more often rather than keep shoving anti-depressants down people's throats. 'Appreciation therapy,' Dean thought, a new concept. Maybe some of these celebrities or sports stars that hit the booze or drugs because their life has bombed now that they are down to their last few million quid, should do a stretch and see what it is really like to be on your arse.

After the doctor, Dean was taken up to his cell on 'B' wing, the third floor, or the 'threes' as it is known. On the way the officer allowed him a thirty second phone call to Molly. "Hi, Molly."

"Oh, my God! Are you OK? Where are you? What is happening?" Too many questions.

"Listen, Molly. I'm at Nottingham and I'm fine. I'll call you tomorrow. I've got to go to my cell now so I can't talk."

"OK, OK, I love you and I'll speak to you tomorrow." Dean's heart was in his mouth as Molly burst into tears.

"Fine, I love you too." Dean hung up, also quite tearful.

Dean was then taken up to his cell. Nearly all cells in Nottingham are 'double-bangers', i.e. two sharing. Dean however was, for some reason given a cell on his own. He thought later that it may have been because he was a non-smoker. It seemed everyone else smoked. It was probably some European human rights thing that a smoker and a non-smoker could not share a cell. Whatever the reason, Dean was not complaining.

The cell was about three metres by two metres. There was a bunk bed, toilet, wash basin, wardrobe, drawers, TV and kettle. Very clean and tidy. The view wasn't much good, just lots of high fences and razor wire, but all in all much better than expected. The officer left him to settle down and get some sleep. It was now nine p.m.

Dean thought that he would struggle to get some kip but to his surprise, after getting his bed set up and a cup of coffee, he watched a bit of TV and dropped off into a deep sleep.

The routine in a cat 'B' prison is fairly strict. You were locked in the cell at all times apart from half an hour for meals at lunch and teatime. There was one hour exercise every day, weather permitting, and one hour 'association' every other day, which allowed you to mix with other inmates, have a shower or make a phone call. The only other time you were allowed out of your cell was if you had a job within the prison (usually cleaner or kitchen worker), a gym session, or education class, usually literacy or numeracy. Dean found that a high proportion of the prison population that he met, he would have classed as effectively illiterate and/or innumerate.

Still, Dean kept his head down and his mouth shut. He did find it difficult sometimes, not so much with the inmates who he could accept as being arseholes to a certain extent, but the prison officers, who he would have expected to be professional, effective and command a bit of respect. Generally this was true but on many occasions, and he was only in Nottingham for four days, he had to bite his tongue. There were some screws that were not in the job for the money. They were there for the pure love of the job. The love of the power – the ability to be arrogant and ignorant without any reprisals. They could talk to people like shit, act the bully, and their language was worse than the inmates. Dean thought they modelled their selves on the Cool Hand Luke guards (some even had the 'Aviator' style sun-glasses). As a result the inmates, especially the youngsters, gave them some attitude back, leading to tense situations. It was like parents arguing with their kids, but the kids not showing any respect for the parent.

Dean found it quite funny to smile warmly at the screws. They'd look puzzled, try and understand, attempt to smile back, but the smile would be fleeting and soon curdle with the thought that he was up to something, because they all were. Dean would laugh and walk away.

Dean was only in Nottingham for four days. On the Tuesday, out of the blue, which is how most things happen in prison, Dean was transferred to Onley category 'C' prison near Rugby in Warwickshire. A much better prospect.

Chapter 18
The Ring-fence of JHB

The news of Dean Muxlowe's sentence sent shockwaves around the motor industry. How could such a straight arrow fly so far off course?

The local paper, The Nottingham Echo, splashed the story over the front page. They really could turn a crisis into a drama. Muxlowe was painted as a serial monster, stalking his prey over several months with the final kill planned to a fine, calculated, almost surgical degree.

Mike and Bernie kept MHB Finance running, looking towards James Hunter-Browne for help, but to no avail. He effectively walked away from the whole thing – total disassociation – which was a shame as the model of the business was sound and could be profitable, but by walking away he was throwing Mike and Bernie to the wolves. Would they cope?

The answer was yes. Over the next few months they rallied and kept the business afloat. Muxlowe kept in touch intermittently from home whilst awaiting sentencing, but there was only so much he could do. Once sent down they visited him weekly to keep him updated, and wrote regularly. Fortunately, many customers stayed loyal.

Hunter-Browne carried on with his specialist car business. He became quite successful over time and managed to at least pay his bills at the end of each month. Although he no longer had anything to do with MHB Finance Ltd., he did hang on to his fifty percent share, just in case they started making money and he could step back in and claim some dividends, or maybe even take the company and change its name if Mike and Bernie got into trouble. That was for the future though, at the moment Hunter-Browne lived his life day to day.

In the September that Muxlowe was sentenced, Hunter-Browne did sign all of his shares over to Molly as an attempt at total disassociation. He also emptied the MHB Finance Ltd bank account, paying over £40,000 to Hunter-Browne Specialist Cars as a 'consultancy fee'. He thought that this would sentence the company to certain liquidation. It didn't.

Chapter 19

Big Fish little pond

Onley was a much different environment than Nottingham. It was not a holding prison so the inmates were more settled for longer periods. As a result it was more relaxed and friendships amongst prisoners were formed – well, short term prison friendships anyway. There were a lot of reunions.

Dean settled in very quickly. The prison officers were much more relaxed and professional, friendly almost, calling Dean by his first name.

All cells were 'single-banger' apart from 'I' wing where mainly the younger ones were stashed for a while. All other wings you were given your own cell with the usual bed, TV, kettle, drawers, wash basin and toilet. Dean was put on 'B' wing, again on the 'threes'. Some of the cells on Onley's 'J' wing had their own in-cell showers.

Three meals per day – breakfast, lunch, tea. You were also given a job, but being an educational jail, most of the jobs at Onley involved learning a skill such as plumbing, carpentry, bricklaying, painting and decorating, plastering or others.

Dean had been inside now for two months. The novelty was beginning to wear off – a routine was definitely in place. The good thing about routine is that it does make time appear to pass quicker. Somebody once said that 'procrastination is the theft of time' – Dean started to feel that this was also true of routine.

Monday morning Dean was woken up at eight-fifteen a.m. to get ready for 'work'. 'Work' was a carpentry class he'd been enrolled in to earn some City and Guilds qualification. Although he'd be let out of his cell at eight-forty a.m. to get to the workshop at eight-forty-five a.m., they didn't start until nine-fifteen a.m. as the instructor, Will, had to count everyone (usually ten to fifteen depending on who could be bothered to turn up) and report numbers to prison administration. The ones missing then had to be tracked down, usually to the healthcare, some rehabilitation course or the barbers. If you didn't turn up you didn't get paid (£10.50 per week – which was the best paid job in the place, other jobs could pay as little as £7.00 per week.)

Morning classes finished at eleven-fifteen a.m. and the inmates would sit around for another thirty minutes until they were let go back to their wing. They had to be searched before they left to make sure they weren't concealing any tools that might be used as a weapon. Dean was never sure what the thirty minute blank period was for, but Will had to wait to be given clearance to let them walk back.

Once back on the wing they could get their lunch, which was collected from the servery and taken to the cell to eat. At twelve-fifteen p.m. the doors were locked up and Dean would either read his book or watch some old film matinee on the TV until one-forty-five p.m. when they were let out for the afternoon shift.

Again there was the delay in starting until two-fifteen p.m. and the session lasted until four-fifteen p.m. Dinner was at four-forty-five p.m.

After the dinner, again collected and eaten in the cell, the doors remained unlocked so that the inmates could socialise and interact, have a shower or use the phone. 'Association' it was called, and lasted until seven-fifteen p.m. when the cell doors were locked up for the night.

Dean didn't like to interact too much with the other inmates. He usually sat in his cell watching 'The Chase' until six p.m. – this was a current game show that he and Molly used to watch together. After 'The Chase' he would wander down the three flights of stairs to give Molly a call then maybe have a shower ready for 'Emmerdale' at seven p.m., followed by the rest of the soaps, then maybe a film at nine p.m., or settle down with his book. Dean read a great number of books whilst in prison, usually Jeffrey Archer, Ian Rankin, James Patterson or John Grisham, although he did drift into Wilbur Smith territory for a bit of historical drama and Terry Goodkind if he was in an escapist fantasy mood.

Dean usually dropped off to sleep around eleven p.m., depending on TV. To be fair, and to his own surprise he slept very well all night every night. He almost looked forward to the door being locked at seven-fifteen p.m., so he could relax in his own company. When he slept he did tend to have the most vivid, weird dreams – dreams that he couldn't remember much about, apart from the fact that they were weird. He put the dreams down to the lack of alcohol in his body.

Tuesdays were pretty much the same for Dean apart from the TV programmes and the fact that at lunchtime it was the 'canteen' day. The 'canteen' was the delivery of goods, ordered on the previous Thursday, from a list of groceries, toiletries, stationary and the like. Each prisoner was given a 'spends' account that their wages were paid into and they could use to buy these things. Friends and family could also add to the 'spends' account by sending cheques or postal orders, although a prisoner was only allowed to spend £15.50 per week. The 'canteen' included phone credit, stamps, soap and shampoo, shaving foam and razors, biscuits, sweets, tins of vegetables, meat and fish etc. Dean spent most of his on phone credit and stamps, although he did treat himself regularly to a packet of 'Happy Shopper' fruit shortcake biscuits to dip into his coffee.

Tuesday night was shite on the TV so Dean usually picked up his book again.

Wednesday was a day off. The instructor, Will, was in college all day so Dean and the others had to spend it 'banged-up'. Dean would write letters or watch daytime TV – real mind numbing stuff – Bargain Hunt, Cash in the Attic, Jeremy Kyle – if he was lucky there would be an old western film on in the afternoon, James Stewart, John Wayne or the like. Oh, dear Dean!

Wednesday night was worse than Tuesday on the TV.

Thursday was the same as Monday and Tuesday but there was the added excitement of ordering the 'canteen' and even better, a trip down the corridor to the library to get some fresh books to read.

Friday was only half a day out and Dean had to spend the first few months at the education department to assess and examine his literary and numeracy skills. It was prison policy that all prisoners were educated up to a level 1 standard. Dean was educated at Grammar school and then progressed to university, attaining a BSc (Hons) Degree. Because he had not sat a new style 'key skills' examination, he had to sit in a classroom whilst Kim, the teacher, waffled on about fractions, decimals, apostrophes and spelling. Stuff he'd done when he was about thirteen years old. Dean sat most of the time twiddling his thumbs but some of the inmates could only just read and write, if at all. Dean thought this a great shame – he was astounded of how bad the general level of education was and how in this day and age, in the United Kingdom, literacy and numeracy levels could be so low. What sort of future did these guys have in store? How could they be employed? Was it any wonder that they were in prison? These people had been let down early on in life

147

whether it had been by their parents, their teachers, the social services or whoever. It was a crying shame.

Friday afternoon all through to Monday morning was spent in the cell 'banged-up' – apart from a few hours 'association'. Dean hated the weekends unless Molly was coming over to visit. Initially he had three visits per month at one hour each but after a while he became an 'enhanced prisoner' which meant that he could have four visits at two hours each per month. He was also then allowed to wear his own clothes, spend £25.00 per week in the 'canteen', and if he wanted, was allowed a DVD and PlayStation in his cell. Dean did a lot of thinking whilst in his cell at night; his past, his current state and, of course what would happen when he was released.

Leap of Faith

I'm bursting in here
I'm waiting to fly
Like a scared little fledgling
Perched way, way up high

That first leap of faith
Will I live, will I die?
God please give me strength
Help me not to be shy

I've had quite too much
As Her Majesty's guest
Don't want to come back
To this spikey old nest

From my very first steps
Through that big prison gate
I'm back on my own
To make my life great

To re-learn to smile
To dance and to play
Be strong and love life
And enjoy every day

It was true that time was passing much quicker now for Dean. If he was a good boy and didn't get any 'nickings' he would end up serving less than a year. A thirty-two month sentence would be spent half in prison and half on licence – if he was granted a HDC (Home Detention Curfew or 'tag') that would reduce the time inside by four and a half months. The HDC system allowed an inmate of very little risk to the public, to be sent home as long as they didn't go out between the hours of seven p.m. and seven a.m. This would mean a release date around early September 2011.

Although Dean kept himself very much to himself whilst inside, he could not help but amuse himself by categorising other inmates around him. There were several distinct types, all trying to get on together, whilst trying to set up a hierarchy within their own little prison world. Dean refused to be a part of it.

It certainly wasn't like *The Shawshank Redemption, Escape from Alcatraz*, or *Cool Hand Luke*, with gangs, usually ethnically based, challenging each other for superiority through violence and fear. No, this was Onley 'C' cat prison in Warwickshire – a cross between 'McVicar' and 'Porridge'. Not that many of the inmates with Dean would have remembered any of those.

The 'big fish' in Dean's wing, 'B' wing, were the black kids and the 'wannabe' black kids – the early 20s white kids that walked and talked like the black kids, slapping each other's skin and listening to 'tumpin' bass' until late at night, sometimes rapping the lyrics at the top of their voices until after midnight. Now that was annoying. The 'screws' didn't seem to give a shit, or they were too frightened to say anything.

When these 'big fish' communicated with each other they didn't talk – they shouted. Communication was loud and aggressive, even when standing next to each other. It reminded Dean of wildlife programmes he had watched where the males of the species competed for status and superiority. Dean usually had his cell door shut on association as he couldn't stand the constant roar of these kids barking about how much 'burn' they were owed, how many 'reps' they could do in the gym, and how they were the 'big man' of the wing. God help them in the real world.

Dean laughed at the way they walked around with their elasticated waistband trousers pulled down below their arse. This was the 'big fish' fashion statement. It originated when kids in the streets in the USA started to copy the inmates over there jailed in the penitentiaries. Prisoners were given poorly fitting clothes to wear including trousers, but weren't allowed belts to hold the trousers up in case they used them to top themselves, or other inmates, or 'screws'. This, coupled with the weight loss due to eating shite food, led to the trousers hanging round the arse. The street kids copied this look to emulate their heroes. Dean wondered if some of these 'B' wing bad boys knew this as they sat around looking angry whilst squawking about the X-Factor and Big Brother evictions.

The big statement at meal times was to walk to the front of the queue as if they were special, the ruling class. Dean was sure that a couple of them thought that they were Mr Bridger, from the original film, *The Italian Job*; the guy played by Noel Coward that virtually ran the prison and set up the heist.

These guys were no Mr Bridger. A lot of the other inmates got upset by their behaviour and squealed at the prison officers; who did fuck all. So what do you do? – Go over and give them a good kicking and risk having time added on to your sentence, or ignore it and treat them like cheeky little kids? You still got your food, and just as quick.

Dean just laughed, inwardly – in fact sometimes openly. He just wondered how these arseholes coped outside, where if someone slapped them into place they would get away with it. All of a sudden

151

they weren't such 'big fish' – all of a sudden they were in the real world where if you shouted your mouth off you got told to shut the fuck up, if you pushed in a queue you got sent to the back and if you picked on the wrong guy, or took the piss, or sometimes even looked at someone the wrong way, there was half a chance you could end up in A & E.

Dean could see why they were inside – because they were only 'little fish' on the outside. Inside they were somebody, or at least they thought so – 'legends in their own minds'. All the fifteen and sixteen-year-old kids would look up to them in awe as they told stories of how they ruled the prisons and terrorised the 'screws'. "Gee, Mister, I want to be just like you when I grow up!"

One little incident that did make Dean smile, happened at Christmas. The gangsta boys were having a 'Christmas party' in one of the cells – about seven of them in all. They were smoking weed and downing large amounts of 'hooch', the home brew fermented from orange juice, raisins, bread and sugar – quite potent by all accounts. As the volume increased everyone started to focus in on the gathering; everyone it seemed except for the prison officers.

Now in a prison, strategically placed around the wings, are a number of alarm buttons. They are bright green and if pressed set off a loud bell. The bell is a sign to all other officers that someone is in urgent trouble and so everyone available races to the scene. One of the Christmas party goers decided that it would be a hoot to set one off, particularly as they were on the 'threes' and so the screws had to sprint up three flights of stairs. Another of the party decided it would be even better fun to empty the contents of his shower gel bottle all over the landing at the entrance of the 'spur' corridor where the bell had been set off.

After a few seconds of deafening ringing the first red-faced screws raced up the stairs and across the landing to where the supposed attack was taking place. Of course they hit the shower gel at full pelt and their legs went from under them. Three screws hit the deck at once in a writhing pile, several others slamming on the brakes so as not to come to the same fate. An almighty cheer went up, followed by raucous laughter and chanting from the gathered expectant crowd of prisoners.

The red-faced guards were livid, looking around trying to suss out who the culprit was. Of course every one of the prisoners retreated to their cells knowing that shortly the wing would be 'locked-down'. There would be no 'grassing-up' of the culprit and the screws would probably not even bother investigating. It added a little excitement to the festive period.

The Gangstas

I am da big man
Strong and lean
I run dis prison
Hard and mean

Do as you told
We get by fine
While you in here
You mine all mine

You join ma crew
You live well, innit
You want respect
You know you get it

Hey there big bloke
What you on
You keep up that shit
You be gone

Relax your arse
And don't you shout
It won't seem long
Before you out

Big fish in here
This tiny pool
Out there you just
A tiny fool

A lot of the kids inside were young. Young but very experienced in the ways of prison life. Dean's neighbour in the next cell was twenty-five years old and been convicted of 152 crimes so far in his life. He had been in and out of young offenders' institutions and prisons since he was sixteen. His father was in Leicester Jail and his brother, or rather half-brother, was in Lincoln. He was due to be released in one month. Dean remembers the first conversation he had with the guy;

"Well, Greeny, are you looking forward to getting out? – Stupid question really, I bet you are buzzing aren't you?"

"Yeah, mate, buzzin'" Although Dean didn't detect much 'buzz'.

"What have you got lined up work-wise?" Dean did try sometimes to make conversation, then regretted it immediately afterwards.

"No, mate, fuck all," replied Greeny. "I still don't know where I'll be living yet."

"Oh?" whispered Dean, not really knowing where the conversation was going and looking for a way to end it. Greeny then opened up and Dean got the idea that he wasn't really looking forward to getting out. He could move in with his sister or his mum. His sister had a room spare but also a six year old daughter, no partner – he'd fucked off when the child was born. The prison authorities were not keen on Greeny going there to live because of the kid. His mother lived in a small, one-bedroomed flat and was looking after Greeny's two year old daughter. Greeny was still supposedly with his girlfriend but she couldn't cope with the unwanted kid and so dumped it on his mum. She was living with her mother and was definitely being faithful to him. (Dean later found out from one of the other inmates that she'd actually had more cock-ends than weekends whilst he'd been inside.) The other option was a place in a hostel in Leicester. The problem with that was that he

155

couldn't trust himself not to get smashed on super strength lager and white cider all day. No job, no home, no future, no hope. This kid was the norm rather than the exception.

It seemed that it was a combination of poor upbringing, failures in society and the prison system that had created a whole section of a generation dependent on prison as a way of life.

A lot of these kids couldn't read or write, had never done a day's proper work, or ever been bothered with school or any education. They had drifted into crime, got caught and been introduced to an escape from their shit life. Three meals a day, their own room, a job, social activities – gym, badminton, pool, table tennis, darts (darts in a fucking prison!), own in –cell colour TV, kettle, telephones – What would Papilon have had to say?

Dean had to laugh at one newspaper article that he read in The Sun. The headline read 'Jail Fail', and was outlining the scandal that around a quarter of all prisoners re-offended within a year of being released. He could believe it. What he couldn't believe was that some Right Honourable arsehole in Parliament had stood up to preach about how prison sentences should be made longer to provide a bigger deterrent to people to re-offend. What a totally out of touch individual. How could this man be allowed to have any influence over prison policy with such little idea of reality? Dean thought what a good idea it would be if the people that governed the prisons and dictated policy were planted inside the system for a few weeks to see what really went on. They would see the processes and see how effective, or not, that they were. They would experience the problems, talk the talk and eat the food. They'd live the life twenty-four hours a day. Don't lengthen the sentences, you twat, shorten them. Take the TV, DVD, and PlayStations out of the cells. Stop the gym, the library. No pool, no table tennis, no darts, no cards. It's a fucking prison. It's fucking punishment. We don't want people to go back. We don't want people to recommend it to their friends. Spend more of the government money on making things better for these people on the outside and less money on keeping them in longer and making life easier for them on the inside. Apparently it costs around £35,000 per year to keep a prisoner behind bars. You never know, if it was a little more uncomfortable inside, people might want to stay out. What would these penal reform politicians come up with next...? Frequent flyer bonuses...? Loyalty cards?

Why I Need Prison

On the outside, I despair
No job, no life, no hope
Day to day I just exist
My only aim, to cope

Every day I hate to wake
Another day of fear
Fear of reality, what do I do?
Weed and burn and beer

Oblivion helps waste my life
Whilst numb I feel no pain
It's sad, it's sure and I know well
That soon I'll have no brain

How do I escape this downward slide?
My life destined to fail
There's only one way I know for sure
That way, my friend, is jail

The greatest institution that there is
Inside I'm scared no longer
Three meals a day, friends and a gym
I'm somebody, I feel much stronger

I get my own room, kettle TV
Why would I want to leave?
My life has meaning whilst I'm here
All I have to do is thieve

Getting caught, some say is bad
Those dum dums need correction
Prison has saved my life
It is my one direction

When I get out I'll tell the rest
That's the last of me you'll hear
As I walk away from jail
All that I feel is...fear

I'll be back, I know deep down
It's only a matter of time
When no more can I cope with life
I'll start again with crime.

There were a few of the older generation on Dean's wing at Onley. These were guys that had been doing petty crime all of their lives. They'd not had the cushy early years inside – indeed most of the 40+ year olds could remember the days of 'slopping out' – sharing a cell with another inmate, each having a bucket to piss and shit in, that they had fixed times to empty and clean. No toilets, no kettle and certainly no TV. Some of them still came back though. It made Dean worry that the younger lads, according to the old boys, were almost encouraged to come back.

Most of these old boys were in for burglary, drugs or fraud, and most of them seemed to have had a fairly successful career so far. A lot of them accepted a stretch in jail as an occupational hazard. They had salted away a damn sight more money from crime than they would have done working as a factory worker or dustbin man.

Time in prison was more of a frustration to some of these old boys. It wasn't a hardship, just an interruption to their earnings. Some looked upon it as a vacation.

Dean was told by one of his fellow inmates about how he broke into his local chip shop. Chester, his name, went out on the piss one Sunday night and decided at the end of the evening to get a bag of chips. Unfortunately the chippy was closed so Chester decided to break in instead, filled as he was with a few Stella's.

The chip shop owner had been away for a fortnight and was due back the following morning; the Monday. Chester hadn't realised this and also that none of the staff had been to the bank with the takings for the past two weeks. The bigger and more important fact was that the guy in charge hadn't locked the safe properly the previous night.

As you can imagine Chester was most surprised and delighted when he broke in, opened the safe, and saw £21,000 sitting there waiting for him. "Take me!" It said to him. Chester just could not say no, it would have almost been rude to walk away without it.

Chester was never caught and not even questioned, not even after walking into the local motorcycle dealership the following week and paying cash for a brand new Ducati – £14,000 in used notes stinking of chip fat. Yes the boys certainly had a few stories to tell, Dean sat for ages. He gathered enough stuff to write a book if he wanted.

The Career Criminal

I live my life beyond the law
I like to ride my luck
Do I squeal when I get caught?
Of course not, do I fuck

I get sent down, I do my debt
Of that you have no fear
I've never killed, I've never raped
My conscience is quite clear

Crime has been so good to me
It's let me live so well
To be a teacher or bank clerk
Now that's a living hell

Someday I know, I'll have to stop
And hang up my old tools
Stay at home and mind my own
With all the other old fools

There was the odd enigma. The con that didn't seem to fit into any category. Dean considered himself as one of these. He didn't even think he should be in there. He never intended to go back to prison. It was OK for a break, something to tell the grand kids, but any more than that was a complete and utter waste of time.

Solomon – Dean wasn't sure if that was his real name or not – was a first time offender. He was seventy-three years old, but seemed pretty healthy. He was in for sending death threats to somebody. He had lived in a caravan for years and years, as his home. The guy who owned the land, his land lord, had sold it. The new owner wanted Solomon off, so sent him an eviction notice. Solomon flipped and refused to move. He then sent death threats, drawing pictures of gravestones and wheelchairs amongst other things.

The police marched him off, sent him to court and he was sent down for twelve months. Seventy-three years old! First time offence! Is that really in the public interest to send this man to jail your honour? It seemed to Dean like the old 'luck of the draw with the judge' syndrome. A sensible judge would have slapped his wrist and let him live the rest of his life in peace. What a travesty.

All in all though everybody got on relatively well. They were all in there for a reason. Some looked on it as a way of life, some as an occupational hazard, some as a miscarriage of justice, some as a mid-life crisis – a sub-conscious way to escape a dead end life that they have sleepwalked into and needed a jolt to get them out of – sound familiar, Dean?

Mid Life Crisis

Sometimes in life we reach the point
When all we've been is giving
We do our best, and then some more
So others enjoy living

Things go wrong, the cracks appear
The arguments they start
The ones you love; your wife, your kids
Your lives they drift apart

The years go by, the fights get worse
But no-one else can know
You're wasting life, you're losing grip
And time is running low

You're so afraid, you can't go on
Depression gets so deep
The best thing you can hope for now
Is dying in your sleep

Death sounds good, the great escape
Such warm relief that would be true
Your wife, your kids, you thoughtless fool
You can't deny their love for you

You've done a crime, you've been sent down
Twelve months you'll be inside
Deep down you know, that nasty judge,
Saved you from suicide

Dean was determined to keep his head down. Not get noticed. He saw all the others smoking weed, drinking hooch, grinding painkillers and watching pornographic movies on their DVD players. Dean had none of it. He read his books and wrote his letters, watched his TV and phoned his wife.

The only time he didn't conform was when one of his neighbours, a big black drug dealer called 'Mush' asked him to piss in a small pill bottle for him. 'Mush' was a regular cannabis smoker but was on a rehabilitation program where he had to give regular voluntary urine samples to prove he wasn't using the drug. The crazy thing was that the screws that collected the samples didn't watch him fill the bottle. Dean, as a non-user regularly pissed in Mush's bottle so he could show them how he was behaving. In return 'Mush' told the guys on the food servery to give Dean exactly what he wanted for his meals, the best bits of chicken, leanest pork chops and freshest fruit. Dean found the arrangement very advantageous.

So, for prisoner A6840CG, cell number B45, time trapped on as he slipped into the routine. He phoned Molly every night at six p.m., when possible. (Three p.m. on Friday, Saturday and Sunday as it was 'early bang-up' straight after tea.)

He started to feel better than he'd ever felt. He couldn't drink, so he lost quite a bit of weight. A by-product was that he instantly ceased to have headaches and physically he had no, what he had thought of as age related, joint pains and unexplained aches and pains around his stomach, chest and kidneys.

He had time to look back at his life. His mistakes. How he'd ended up where he was. He began to question whether it was a bad thing that he was in jail or whether it was all part of a universal plan; a second chance. A wake up call. Everything that had happened to him seemed to have happened for a reason. The business; Mike and

Bernie holding the fort; Hunter-Browne turning his back; Molly learning to cope with life without him; his friends and family showing so much fantastic support. Yes, he felt great, he was making plans, and he felt like a young kid again, excited about starting a new life again on his release. New challenges – a world to take on again. He realised that he regained something that he'd lost over the years but hadn't been aware of losing – a purpose, drive, ambition.

It was enlightening to have the ability to look back on your life and be able to plan a new one without making the mistakes of the old one. To be able to appreciate and embrace the good things, and appreciate and learn from the bad things.

Chapter 20
Brother Derek

The second Monday in January 2011, Molly was home alone and feeling down. It was the miserable time of the year just after Christmas and the New Year when everyone else was trying to cheer themselves up by booking a holiday. Not Molly. Her misery was compounded by news from Fife that her brother, Derek Rafferty, wasn't very well.

Derek was Molly's younger brother, slightly. He was thirty-eight years old and had joined the police force in 1995. He'd done very well and was recruited to CID, spending most of his past time specializing in fraud cases. He'd reached the rank of Detective Inspector. Most of his time, these days, was spent with the Edinburgh Serious Crime Unit.

At thirty-eight years old he was five feet ten tall, solidly built at sixteen stone, with the beginnings of a beer belly, but not overly obvious. He'd long ago shaved his head to cover up the hair loss in places, and Molly had always said that he looked like Grant Mitchell off EastEnders, the actor Ross Kemp in real life, although in his 'teens when he had big spikey hair, she swore he was the spitting image of Gary Glitter.

Derek was very committed to the force. It was his life. He'd been married briefly and had a couple of kids he never saw; every relationship he'd ever had since had failed – the job tended to frighten off most women; the long, irregular hours, the nights out cancelled at short notice with a less than adequate excuse (I've got to work again, hen), nights away – he felt like John Rebus, the imaginary Edinburgh detective of the Ian Rankin novels.

Over the last six months, despite his legendary commitment, he had lost his appetite for the job. He had put it down to a combination of things; Obviously Dean's circumstances didn't help and had a knock-on effect upsetting his big sister who he always considered his 'wee sister,' in that he had always looked after her at school even though he was slightly younger.

He'd had a few difficult cases recently, also. After putting in even more hours than usual, putting in a massive effort and getting, what he thought, were some great results, he and his colleagues had watched as the clever solicitors and barristers for the defence had chipped and chipped away finding technicalities, loop holes and procedural discrepancies – anything to destroy all of their hard work. The criminals, who it was obvious were guilty, seemed to be walking away smiling, more and more regularly. They were showing complete contempt for the system that he once believed in. It was getting Derek down. He was feeling sick, depressed and disillusioned. He no longer wanted to go to work. His head was gone.

He was sent to see a psychiatrist by his superiors, who had seen this sort of thing before and recognised the warning signs. The shrink told him to take time off. It sounded like the same problem that Dean had been suffering from – depression, lack of appetite, lack of energy, lack of interest. "Go away somewhere," Dr Stevenson had said, "take four weeks off at least, get a change of scenery and we'll see how you go." The way Derek was feeling he had no intention of ever going back. He was on the verge of a breakdown and needed a new direction in his life.

He decided that the real solution was to take time off and go to Nottingham to see his 'wee sister.' He would stay with her to keep her company and she would be there for him in return.

So, in early January Derek Rafferty headed down the A1, across the M18 to the M1 South and off at junction 25. It took him seven hours in a little Citroen van he'd picked up on a three month hire quite cheap from a local company. He stopped off at a Little Chef for his favourite, the Olympic breakfast.

Molly was over the moon to have some company. Someone to moan at and commentate on 'Heartbeat' to.

He would have time to plan his future. Maybe he would change his mind and continue to be a cop – but would he regret it if he did and find himself in the same situation in a few years' time?

His dream was to set up a seafood bar. It was an idea that he'd talked to Molly and Dean about on several occasions in the past – usually when they were all pissed up at Christmas or Hogmanay.

When he was much younger and had just started drinking in the pubs, he could remember that later on in the evenings a little chap would wander around the bars selling seafood – cockles, mussels, crabsticks, and prawns. All of a sudden it had stopped and he'd often wondered why. Was it lack of demand? Competition from other things? Was it some sort of European law or guideline – the sort of thing that stopped peanuts being put out on bars in open bowls? Who knows? His plans were to investigate the licences required to set up a seafood bar in a city centre at night. Pissed-up people, especially the older generation, he could see quite fancying a quick prawn or cockle, or even a smoked trout and salad roll with a touch of horseradish sauce.

It was just a dream, but without dreams what do we have? – We have a routine, a dull rhythm to our life to drag us along to the end of it.

Still, that was for the future. The immediate plan was to take some time out and try to recover a little, to put him in the right frame of mind to make his decisions.

One day late February, whilst Molly was at work, Derek was given the job of clearing out the attic. Molly had been meaning to do it for months, but without Dean she couldn't manage it. She got dizzy at any height and didn't want to fall from the ladder and do herself some damage.

It was a big job as the attic was full of everything from old record collections to boxes and boxes of old children's VHS videos – Thomas the Tank, Trumpton, Camberwick Green, Poddington Peas, – hundreds of them. So one Tuesday morning he got started.

Time flew by as he discovered all sorts of interesting rubbish, when all of a sudden he came across something he certainly didn't expect and, as he read through them, horrified him.

He had found a number of letters, written using a stencil in a green pen, that were basically threatening Dean, or 'Deano' as they called him, or rather Molly, Rose and the dogs, if he did not go along with a blackmail plot to extort money from some guy called Paul Milford. The letters had been hidden under a box of old 45 rpm records, obviously to keep them away from detection by Molly or Rose.

As Derek read the letters through his blood began to boil. It became obvious what had happened and Dean had been the fall-guy for this 'Myra' person who had been pulling his strings. Why hadn't Dean said something? He'd obviously been so frightened by the threats to Molly and Rose that he'd been carried along on a tidal wave until it was too late to jump off. In the end he'd probably been so confused and bewildered that he'd taken the consequences knowing that by doing so at least Molly, Rose and the dogs would come to no physical harm.

What would Derek do? His first reaction was to go to the police – but would they get justice? Dean still did what he did and had been sentenced. The police would probably just look at the letters and sweep them under the carpet. They didn't want any old wounds opening up. For all they knew Derek had produced the letters himself in a plan to get his brother-in-law freed. No, Derek would have to sort this problem himself in some way. Should he tell Molly? Should he go to this Paul Milford character? He didn't know what to do. He didn't trust the police.

After a few minutes pondering, he put the letters away under the heat insulation felt and continued his task of clearing out the attic. All the time he was running through the different options, often stopping to go back and re-read some of the letters.

When Molly got in later, Derek finished off and went to join her for a coffee. He couldn't help looking at her and feeling such pity and sorrow. This was his 'wee sister' that had been the victim of some malicious twat that had used Dean as a shield in order to try and extort money. When it all went smelly, Dean went to prison and Myra walked away free.

One thing that was for sure in Derek's head was that things couldn't remain unchanged. People couldn't remain unpunished. All the instincts and feelings that made him such a good copper were sloshing around in his head. He would not sleep for days, he knew that he had to make plans. He had to right the wrong. Justice must be done and that certainly didn't involve the fucking police.

"Are you OK?" asked Molly. "You seem a bit vacant."

"Yes, I'm OK." He smiled. "A little bit of time and relaxation and I'll be fine. I guarantee it." Molly thought she detected his jaw stiffen as he finished the sentence.

Chapter 21

The Funeral

March 1st 2011, Molly received some bad news. She got a phone call from a lady called Valerie Forsyth, who she only very vaguely remembered as having worked with Dean in the early '90s at Citroen. Val was the assistant to the accountant at the dealership, a guy called Andrew Foster. Andrew had helped Dean get the job and had become quite close whilst they were together, sharing a mutual interest in squash, which they played together weekly. When Dean had left they still kept in touch, the squash games however, becoming less frequent.

Andrew had died very suddenly from a heart attack and Val was doing the 'ring round' making everyone aware of the funeral arrangements.

"Oh, I'm very sorry to hear that," replied Molly to the news. It was two p.m.

"Yes," Val had obviously gone over the same ground many times that day. She sounded, although obviously not intentionally, rather bored and robotic. "It was very sudden. We all thought a lot of him and I know… Dean." There was a slight pause as if she'd forgotten who she was talking to and had to refer back to her tick list. "Dean was close to Andrew. I know that they used to play squash quite regularly."

"Yes, years ago," said Molly. She did remember Andrew and had liked him. She and Dean had been out several times with him and his wife, Penelope, in a foursome.

"Well," Val continued, "just to let you know that the funeral is Thursday at Bramcote crematorium, two-thirty p.m., with a bit of a drinkies after at The Peacock. Do you know The Peacock?"

"Yes," replied Molly. "The big pub come hotel on the roundabout."

"That's the one." Val seemed quite pleased that she didn't have to troll through the directions again.

"One problem, Val," said Molly after a slight pause.

"Yes."

"Well, Dean won't be able to come."

"Oh?" questioned Val.

"Yes. I'll explain more on the day, but Dean's in prison." Silence for a few seconds that felt like minutes.

"Prison?" Val eventually came out with.

"Yes. He got into a bit of trouble, and the long and the short of it is that he was arrested in May and is now banged up at Her Majesty's pleasure."

"Oh, right." Val was caught off-guard and didn't really know what to say.

"I'll be there though," continued Molly. "I'll come with my brother if that's OK."

"Yes, of course," stuttered Val. "I'll see you Thursday and you can tell me all about it then. Bye, bye." The phone went down.

"Cheerio." Molly smiled to herself. Something told her that the rest of Val's conversations that afternoon would probably be a little less boring and robotic.

Dean called that evening at six p.m. as normal, and was quite upset to hear the news about Andrew Foster. "He was a good bloke," he commented. He was pleased that Molly was going and that Derek was going with her. He knew she would be getting some interrogation and would appreciate Derek's support.

Derek was fine with the idea of the funeral. He was getting a little bored now. Often he would take Guinness and Gilbert for a walk, but apart from that there wasn't much to do. A funeral would kill an afternoon, excuse the pun.

He'd even talked to Molly about getting a job, even part-time. "You've got a job," she told him. "You're off ill!"

"No, I've got another few weeks off yet," he replied dismissively. "I still can't face that shower of shite." In reality, at that moment in time he had no intention of ever going back to that 'shower of shite.' He'd even borrowed Rose's computer to find out the ins and outs of setting up a seafood bar – licences, regulations, permits etc. Still a dream.

Thursday came and at two-thirty p.m., dentist time, Derek and Molly turned up at Bramcote Crematorium in Derek's white van. Derek had extended its hire period, even though it had not expired yet, to an open-ended agreement.

The service was 'nice', 'lovely', 'heartfelt', all the usual stuff. Plenty of tears and solemn faces. Certain people were trying to laugh and joke; an attempt to 'lighten the mood'. In general a typical, standard funeral that happened every day in every town. The only difference was the darting glances and secret whispers aimed in Molly's direction as the contingent plucked up courage to approach her and ask about Dean; Get the real story, not some overdramatized version from Val, that seemed to get more and more elaborate as time moved on. Nobody was brave enough to offer more than the odd concerned 'nod' at the crematorium. The Peacock would be another matter, Molly knew. A few bevvies would loosen the tongues.

They walked into The Peacock at just past a quarter to four. Most had already arrived and were tucking into the cold buffet and their first drink. The atmosphere was more relaxed. Many were crowded around a large board that Penelope had put up with with photographs attached of Andrew throughout his life. From his old school photos through adolescence into marriage. There were a lot of foreign holidays and fishing trips. At sixty years old he was very young to have suffered a heart attack. He wasn't a heavy drinker and Molly wondered if it was the pressure of work that had caused it, although Dean had often mentioned that he wasn't the sort to get stressed. Maybe his wife had other ideas. Maybe he was one of those that appeared dead laid back to everyone else but showed his true side after hours. Molly knew the type well.

Molly walked straight over to Penelope to offer her condolences. Penelope's eyes were puffy and red, but she'd stopped crying for a bit, cradling a short drink of some description. Molly thought that after a few more of them that the tears would be back.

"Hello, I'm Molly – Dean Muxlowe's wife." Just in case Penelope didn't recognise her. With all that was going on, with all those people floating around, she didn't want the woman to be embarrassed because she couldn't remember her name.

"Hello, Molly. Of course I recognise you." Nevertheless grateful for the thought, she took Molly's hand. "I've heard about Dean; I couldn't believe it. How is he?"

"Well," she responded, quite used to the enquiry now, "sometimes things happen that don't have much of a rational explanation. Dean is fine, well, as fine as can be expected in the

175

circumstances. I'll just get myself a drink and I'll fill you in properly a bit later. This is my brother, Derek." Derek smiled and shook her hand. They both made their way to the bar before Penelope could probe further.

As they stood at the bar waiting, a little wispy woman came hurtling up. "Hello, Molly, nice to see you again after so long, how are you? How is Dean?"

"Hi, I'm fine. Val, isn't it?"

"Yes, yes, yes, I'm sorry. Yes, I'm Val." The force of nature known as Val. Molly had recognised her voice and had a vague recollection of her from the Citroen days. She was fussing around like a mother hen. "And Dean? I know you said he's inside. What happened? Nobody can believe it." She'd obviously asked many opinions on the subject.

Well nobody really knows – even Dean if truth be known. We put it down to one of life's mistakes. Derek had got the drinks in by now and Molly tried to move away. She'd decided to be as elusive as she could. Just a show of face, a brave front to show Dean's friends she was with him and not ashamed of him. Val stuck with her, bombarding with questions for the next hour. Many other people came across to ask about Dean as the booze loosened them up a bit. Molly coped admirably and with dignity. Derek thought that she fought the corner very well.

Val finally gave up and retired to the bar for another large one, and to report her findings to anyone that would listen.

Molly and Derek at last got a bite to eat and a seat. "Fucking hell," Derek muttered as he plopped into a red leather armchair at one of the tables. "You wouldn't want to be married to that."

Molly sat down opposite. "You wouldn't want to be married to anyone," she chuckled.

"I've just not met the right one yet." Derek defended. "I thought I did but the police force saw her off."

"You'll never meet the right one in that fucking job. There's no woman stupid enough to put up with that." Over the last few weeks Derek had poured out to Molly about his job and how much it was getting him down. The hours, the stress and all the shit that went with it.

They sat back and relaxed in their own company, viewing the crowd in the lounge. It had been hired for the exclusive use of the funeral party. The mood was lightening by the minute; more jokes and laughter, celebrations of the good times. There was a spare chair at their table. It didn't stay spare for long.

"Molly, how are you?" Ernest Gerrity sat himself down. He was smiling and jovial.

"I'm fine." Molly had a puzzled smile on her face. She didn't remember the name but the face was familiar, like most of them here.

"I'm sorry," he realised. "Ernest – Ernest Gerrity." He reached out and shook her hand. "And you are…?" He turned to Derek.

"I'm Derek Rafferty. I'm Molly's brother."

"Oh, brother!" False laugh from Gerrity. "I thought that Molly had found herself a temp whilst Deano was inside. How is the old lag?" Gerrity was obviously well pissed.

"He's fine," smiled Molly. If Gerrity wasn't so drunk he probably would have realised that it was not a smile of true warmth.

"And what about you, Molly? And your daughter…Rose, isn't it? And of course the dogs – I'll bet that they're missing him?"

"All fine." Molly was quite surprised that Gerrity obviously knew Dean better than she thought. He'd never talked about Gerrity to her. Still, if he knew they'd got a daughter and two dogs they were obviously better acquainted than she realised. He certainly seemed very familiar.

177

Derek took an instant dislike to Gerrity. He got the impression that if he had not been there that Gerrity would be trying to get into Molly's knickers. Why was he the only person so far, and he'd met a few, that referred to Dean as 'Deano'? Something was not right. Suspicion was eating at Derek. This guy was a snake – or was it just that much practiced copper's nose of his?

Gerrity got more and more pissed, much louder, and more arrogant. Molly toddled off to the bar for a bit of relief and was surprised when she looked back over that Derek and Ernest were deep in conversation like old buddies. She had realised that Derek was a bit 'prickly' and had half expected an argument, but they seemed fine. At that point Val, who was by now quite blotto, stepped up for round two.

At six p.m. Gerrity and Derek were still laughing and joking together. Molly was still fencing with Val and had just about lost the will to live. "I'm going to have to go, Val." She had to almost shout into her ear. "The dogs will be sitting with their legs crossed."

"Oh, you've got dogs? What have you got?" She would not be dumped easily.

"Cocker spaniels." Molly started to move off smiling and nodding at Val as she tried to arrange a night out. One of those drunken arrangements that never happen. "Derek," she shouted, "are you ready?"

"Have another drink," Gerrity called back trying to lift himself out of the chair.

"No, thanks," intervened Derek, "we're off – dogs to sort out." He reached out and shook Gerrity by the hand.

"Yes, of course," he slurred, "lovely to see you both, we'll have to do it again sometime. Don't forget, Derek, if ever you're passing The George and Dragon at Fenton do pop in – I'll usually be in early doors. Give my regards to Guinness and Gilbert."

"Will do," Derek frowned.

Molly and Derek said their goodbyes to Penelope, who was now snivelling again, and left.

"You were getting on like a house on fire with Ernest." Molly turned to Derek as they walked out of the door.

"Wanker!" Derek snarled.

"Well, you were talking to him for long enough. You even told him the dogs' names"

"Not me," Derek replied curtly.

They went home.

Six p.m. had passed so Molly had missed Dean's 'phone call. "Shit," she thought, time had flown. Still, he'd call again tomorrow. When they got back they had no milk, so whilst Derek got changed Molly had a walk to the shop.

The 'phone rang.

"Hello." Derek picked it up.

"Hi, Derek – it's Dean."

"Hi, mate." Derek was pleased to hear his voice. It was six-thirty p.m.

"Yes, I'm late tonight; I didn't know whether you'd be in or not. I know you've been to the funeral today."

"Yes, it was fine. Molly's gone to the shop – she'll be angry that she missed you."

"Well, don't worry. Tell her I'll call her tomorrow, it'll save me some credit and there's a massive queue here anyway."

"No problem," replied Derek. "While you're on though, mate…Ernest Gerrity?"

"Oh, yes?"

"How well do you know the twat?" Dean laughed. Five minutes later Derek hung up just as Molly walked through the door.

"You've just missed Dean," he called.

"Shit!"

"Don't worry, he'll call you tomorrow. He's just filled me in on our friend, Ernest Gerrity."

"Didn't you have anything better to talk about? I hope you've not wasted his credit."

"No, no." Derek took on the defensive palms up by his shoulders facing forward stance. "We were just on for a minute – very interesting though." With that he walked out and went upstairs to finish getting changed.

Early April Derek told Molly he had got himself a part time job and he was far from going back to being a copper.

"All that time in the force and you're going to throw it away," she protested.

"Well," Derek was adamant, "the way I feel at the moment I just can't face it."

"Fair enough, then." Molly was quite happy that Derek was staying so didn't protest any more. She didn't want people to think she was guilt tripping him into staying so she had to show a tiny bit of resistance. "What are you doing, anyway?"

"Delivering and collecting stuff for a catalogue company. If anyone buys anything and then wants to send it back, I will pick it up from their house. I then take it to the delivery company and back it goes. I also pick items up from the delivery company and take it around the houses."

"Is it good pay?" She enquired.

"No, it's shite," replied Derek. "But it'll give me something to do at evenings and weekends. My police sick pay is still in play anyway."

"And they don't mind you working, even though you're meant to be off sick?" There was a pause – a little too long.

"No, of course not." Derek didn't sound too convincing.

"Well, you know what you're doing." Molly frowned.

"Yes, I do."

Chapter 22

D Cat Status

After six months in Onley, which was a 'C' category prison, Dean had a category status review. This essentially meant that he was downgraded to a 'D' cat prisoner and could be moved to a 'D' cat prison – basically an open prison where you could roam around free for most of the day and, after a qualifying period of eight weeks, were allowed all day town visits and three day home visits. Deans only motivation to move prisons was to be allowed to go home to Molly and his family for three days. He was overjoyed to be re-classified as a 'D' cat prisoner.

April 27th 2011, Dean was transferred to North Sea Camp – an old 'D' cat prison on the East coast of England near Boston, around fifty miles from his home in Nottingham. The place was an old naval camp that was well overdue to be closed down and flattened. The only endearing features of going there were the prospect of getting out for a few days to visit Molly.

The site was split into a North block, a South block and two other blocks set away from the main buildings that housed around seventy-five inmates each – Harrison and Llewellyn. There was an old communal dining hall, and education block consisting of three classrooms and an office, a portacabin converted into a library and a few other little temporary buildings that looked like they'd been there for twenty years, that were used for other things such as drug testing suites, auxiliary classrooms or storage areas. The whole site took around twenty minutes to walk around including the football pitch.

As the 'meat wagon' pulled in to the reception area, Dean started to wonder if even this was worth the move. At Onley he had his own cell, TV and kettle – here he would have to share a cell with at least one person, probably a paedo or rapist, or maybe even more – some of the inmates were staying in three, five or seven man dormitories. It didn't describe the place very accurately in the brochure.

After getting unloaded, searched and processed, Dean was sent over with four more newbies to the initiation block, where they would spend a week learning about the place – the education facilities, day and home release, stores, employment, what entertainment was laid on, religious facilities, etc.

The first thing they did was get allocated accommodation. This was the part that Dean was least looking forward to. Most of the new boys were put in the seven man dorms, as to a certain extent, once you'd settled in and made 'friends' you could move out and find your own cell mate. Dean was not in a dorm, however. The orderly announced to him, with a look of surprise on his face, "You're in 'Harrison', mate. You've had a right result there." Dean wondered what a 'right result' could possibly mean.

Dean grabbed all his belongings that had been all slung into a clear polythene bag, and made his way over to 'Harrison' block under the directions of the orderly, who still had a somewhat puzzled look on his face.

'Harrison' block was one of two separate buildings each containing around forty cells, most double but a few singles. Dean was to share a double. He walked into the reception struggling with his gear. The screw on reception was quite friendly, which put Dean at ease a little. She was around her early fifties, quite attractive, blonde and a bit dumpy, chubby face with a huge smile. "Hello, who have we here then?"

"Muxlowe," gasped Dean, by now out of breath.

"Splendid," she grinned. "Your room isn't quite ready; the bloke that's moving out hasn't gone yet so you can either wait over there," she pointed to an area on the other side of reception, "or you can fuck off and come back in a bit."

"I'll wait over there," replied Dean. He was taken aback a little by the woman's use of the word 'fuck'.

Several minutes passed as Dean began to get his breath back. Then a rather large, aggressive looking Scottish guy walked in to the reception. He scanned the room and his eyes came to rest on Dean. "Are you my new fucking pad mate?" he barked.

"I don't know," replied Dean hoping desperately that he wasn't. The Scotsman scowled.

"Sixty-six," he shouted, turned and walked back through the door from which he came that led to the cells. Dean approached reception again. The female screw had an even bigger smile on her face.

"Yes, you are number 66, sharing with Mr Scott. He is ready for you now."

"Can't I share with someone else?" asked Dean.

"No you can't. We've not got the room. He's not that bad when you get to know him."

"Great," replied Dean.

Dean dragged his baggage through the door, down the corridor and opened the door to cell 66. "It looks like I am your new cell mate," said Dean. The mad Scotsman was sitting on his bed, face like thunder, steam coming from his ears.

"That's your fucking bed," he grunted and nodded towards the other bed in the room.

"Thanks." Dean took a seat on the bed and decided to grab the bull by the proverbial horns. "So what's your problem?" He asked Scott, in as an aggressive way as he could in an attempt to show him he wasn't scared.

"What are you in for?" asked the Scot.

"Blackmail," replied Dean.

"Really? But what are you really in for?"

"Blackmail," repeated Dean. "Why, don't you believe me?"

"I'm just fucking sick of fucking nonces," came the reply. "The twat that was in here before you was a raving faggot that was in for shagging kids. I used to wake up at night and catch him wanking whilst staring at me. The other night I woke up and the bastard was standing next to me stark bollock naked pulling his todger! You sure you're not like that?"

"Definitely not!" exclaimed Dean. "I'm married with three kids. In fact I married a Scottish girl twenty odd years ago and am still married to her." This last statement had a very cooling effect on the jock.

"Really?" his expression softening a little. "Where's she from?"

"Fife," replied Dean. "Just outside of Kirkcaldy; a little place called Buckhaven."

"Well, fuck me," smiled the Scotsman. "I'm from Dundee just up the coast."

"I know it well," smiled Dean. "I've been there a few times." He now knew that he should be OK. He knew the Scots could be aggressive but deep down most of them were OK, particularly if you'd got a connection to their home land.

Dean and Steve Scott spent the next few hours getting to know each other, talking about Scotland, what they were in for, their backgrounds, and mutual hatred of nonces (Sex offenders).

Steve was about five feet ten, and built like a brick shithouse. He looked the typical convict; short cropped hair, scars around the chin where he'd probably been glassed at some point in his life, plenty of tattoos – particularly the self-done prison type – the type you do when feeling very low, using a sharp object and biro ink. His skin was very red and blotchy – he explained this by the fact that he had had some illegal steroids smuggled into the prison that had allowed him to train harder in the gym, but had given him horrible spots.

His crime, the reason he was inside, was for battering a bloke close to death outside a UDA pub. He claimed he was an 'enforcer' for the mafia and was often employed by them to collect debts and threaten people. He told Dean how easy it was to get hold of guns and explosives. As he went on Dean couldn't help but sense the faint aroma of bull shit. He was in a long term relationship with a girl from Manchester who had a fourteen-year-old son, not Steve's. He rang his Sonia every night and was truly in love with her. She was very loyal and would stand by him. He was in for another year.

Apparently the 'faggot' who was sharing with Steve previously had to be moved to a single cell for his own safety. Steve was close to doing him some serious harm if they remained together much longer.

At meal times Steve Scott took Dean with him to the dining hall and introduced him to his friends. Dean, as a friend of Steve's, became accepted very quickly and soon settled in.

Dean, although being pleased that his initial feelings about his new cell mate were wrong, could not help thinking that something wasn't quite right. Steve was overly friendly at times; not in a gay way, on the contrary more of a macho, pub friend type way. He would comment on every woman on the TV and how he'd like to 'ruin them'. He had a collection of well-hidden pornographic magazines and went out of his way to show Dean that he was off to the toilets down the corridor for a 'read'. At any and every opportunity the mad Scotsman would bring up the subject of guns and violence and how he'd like to massacre all gays, paedos and rapists – something though just did not ring true.

The following Monday, the 2nd May, Dean was lying in their cell on the bed, reading a book. He'd not started work yet and was still officially on induction. Steve Scott was out at work – he was the painting and decorating orderly – in other words he cleaned and tidied up in the workshop where they taught City & Guilds decorating to the prisoners. He'd done his qualification and got on well with the tutor and decided to stay on as orderly. He actually got Dean a place on the course to start the following week.

As Dean lay on the bed, his eyes starting to shut as he drifted off to sleep, there was a sharp knock on the door and it opened. Dean looked up to see a pair of rather aggressive looking prison officers, one of whom had a black cocker spaniel that reminded Dean of Guinness, his own dog back home. "Where's your pad mate?" One of the screws asked.

"Painting and decorating workshop," replied Dean. "He works there." The two officers left without a word and shut the door. Dean carried on with his book.

Ten minutes later the door came in again, this time no knocking. The same guard as spoke before spoke again. "Can you give us a minute, mate. This has fuck all to do with you; we just need to spin your cell. What stuff is yours?"

"This half," Dean pointed to where his belongings were. He then left them to it. As he walked out there stood Steve Scott, very worried expression on his face, eyes watering, looking at the ground. "What's up?" Dean asked.

"Nothing to concern you," interrupted the screw. "Just go out and leave it to us."

Dean walked out of Harrison block and sat on a bench outside, continuing to read his book.

The search lasted twenty minutes and at last the two screws walked out with Steve Scott in hand cuffs. "You can go back in now mate but we'll be back in a short while to get the rest of his stuff." The officer with the dog was carrying a black polythene bag with stuff in – Dean couldn't see what it was but assumed it was drugs. He went back in to continue with his book.

True enough the prison officers came back and removed the rest of Scott's property, but wouldn't give any clue as to what was removed. They just told him that Steve Scott would be 'shipped out' to Lincoln Prison immediately. Lincoln was a cat 'B' nick that people who misbehaved at 'D' cats got sent to.

So Dean was allocated a new cell mate. The guy that moved in was a thirty-eight-year-old chap, quite pleasant and quiet, claiming to be in for aggravated burglary. He was only a little bloke – he reminded Dean in features and personality, of a mouse – one of those off 'Bagpuss'.

One talent this boy had was art. He could draw brilliantly and showed Dean some of his portfolio. As the time passed and days turned into weeks the two of them got to know each other quite well, as two cell mates were bound to do. As with Steve Scott though, Dean didn't believe all was as it appeared with Stuart Worth.

One Friday late in June, Dean was looking at some of Worth's drawings. "These are really very good," he commented. "Are you going to be doing something in this line professionally when you get out?"

"No," replied Stuart. "I used to do a bit, but I'm not that bothered now."

"Why not," enquired Dean.

"I don't think I'm that good." Worth then started collecting the drawings up to put away.

"I disagree," countered Dean, picking up one of the drawings. "In fact I've got a photo of my wife, Molly with her niece, Kayleigh that you could draw for me. I'd pay you for it."

"No, I couldn't." Worth then went very red.

"Why not?" probed Dean.

"How old is your niece?"

"Thirteen, why?" There was a long silence as Dean waited for an answer.

"Look," Worth was stuttering and now very red faced. "I'm not in for aggravated burglary at all. It's time I levelled with you."

"Go on," Dean said, knowing what was coming.

"I was arrested and convicted for downloading pictures of young girls." Silence.

"You must have done more than that to be in here," accused Dean.

"Well, I took some photos of some of my nieces and their friends also, but I never touched any of them." Stuart Worth spent the next couple of hours telling Dean what he had done and how he had been caught with images on his computer. How his friends and family had beaten him up on several occasions and his family was still suffering abuse and shame. He could never go back to Southampton, which was where all his family came from and most of them still lived and how he was on a ten year licence when he was eventually released which he didn't know because he was in the hands of the psychologists and probation service, all of whom hated paedophiles and were very reluctant to allow them back on the streets in case they re-offended and they got the blame.

Dean listened with interest and disgust. Worth did continually stress that he never touched any of his victims and that he had been very hard done by. Dean now had a decision to make; did he request to be moved or did he put up with the paedo? If he moved he couldn't guarantee what other sort of weirdo he'd be shacked up with. If he stayed he might be tempted to bash the nonce. He decided to stay until he possibly found someone relatively normal to share with. As it would turn out he was more tolerant than he thought and lasted there until he was eventually let out on tag.

Over the next few weeks he found out that he'd not been far off the mark with Steve Scott, the mad Scotsman. It appears that he had been 'shipped out' because things had been found in his cell. Drugs, yes, but not just drugs. They'd also found homosexual pornography, cash and a dildo. Allegedly the 'faggot' that had shared his cell before Dean, was not a sex pest but his lover. The guy had moved from his own single cell to share number 66 with Scott. He had been paying Scott for sex and moved in with him to make things more convenient. When he moved in he got the wrong idea and assumed that he and Scott were now a couple and didn't need to pay him. When the payments stopped, Scott became angry and started to beat his lover up. This is when Dean walked in, effectively on a lovers tiff. Hence the anger and aggression. Dean wondered if he had subsequently been 'groomed.'

Dean heard many strange stories whilst at North Sea Camp. He often heard the noises of cellmates shagging each other. One morning as he walked along the corridor to the toilet, all he could smell was a vile mixture of rubber and shit. It made his stomach turn. On induction he had been told that if anyone wanted condoms they would be given them free of charge but he, naively, didn't think that sort of thing happened on a large scale.

Drugs were openly available to all inmates. Cannabis was the usual smoke but some inmates used 'Black Mamba' – which was a 'legal high' drug sold at some of the shops in Boston. Inmates picked up some whilst on town visits. Many other prisoners used pills; painkillers and the like that they ground up to hit the spot quicker. These were tamazapan, diazepam, subbies, pregabbies, all sorts. Many of the inmates walked around in a daze most of the time. If they were caught in possession they were 'shipped out' but most got away with it.

One of the guys he regularly walked around the camp with was called Adam. He was a big bloke from a town close to Dean's home, built like a brick shithouse. He was quite a good looking chap but was a user of methadone, a heroine substitute administered by the prison in an attempt to wean him off the real stuff. It was taken in the form of a liquid and was given by the medical centre quite liberally. Every morning you could see them all lined up in the 'juice queue'. The methadone had got into Adams bones and rotted his teeth. He only had three left in his head.

The prison authorities had sent him to a local dentist to have a new set of dentures made to give him back his good looks. It had taken many weeks but eventually Adam turned up at Deans cell with a big toothy smile, very chuffed as he was to be released in a couple of weeks and wanted to be out there with his new teeth.

A few days later Dean returned from a town visit to find Adam distraught. That morning he had crushed up a few painkillers and got himself 'shitfaced' as he wandered around the site. He couldn't remember much of the day apart from coming round in a drug-fuelled haze without his teeth. Some nasty fucker had decided that it would be a laugh to nick them while he was spaced out. Dean went with him to look for them around the usual haunts but with no success. They even went to reception to put a call out offering a reward for the lost dentures. This only had the effect of causing great hilarity amongst the other inmates and the screws. They never did turn up

The drugs were all concealed in oval plastic containers, the sort you got in Kinder Eggs to house the little toy. The containers were then shoved up the rectum so they couldn't be found by the screws. Recently the specification of the Kinder Eggs had changed and the containers came with a hinge rather than the two halves just pushing together. The hinge stuck out a couple of millimetres and so could cause some discomfort. It didn't stop the practice though and some inmates could get two or three up quite easily.

Once into a routine at North Sea Camp the time started to fly. He'd get up at five-thirty a.m. to have a shower before anyone else got in and shat on the floor. He'd then have to 'roll-on' at seven a.m. The wing officer took a roll-call at certain times during the day to make sure nobody had fucked off, or absconded as they called it. Many people did abscond, usually because they got into debt to other prisoners and couldn't pay it back.

Dean went for a cooked breakfast at eight a.m. before going to 'work' doing his painting and decorating course. At twelve-fifteen p.m. he'd leave work to go for roll-call and lunch. He'd return to work at two p.m. until four-fifteen p.m., when it would be roll-call and dinner. He'd then either watch TV or walk around the grounds of the prison, taking a break at six p.m. to call Molly. The penultimate roll-call was eight p.m. when everyone had to be back on their wing. Final roll-call was ten p.m. – Dean was usually asleep not long after this. It was either sleep or playing PlayStation games with a pedantic little paedophile that got very angry if he lost.

The weekends were quite boring but the Chapel put on the odd film and quiz night to keep the inmates happy. The Sunday dinner was quite good, something to look forward to, but generally the week ends did drag.

Once Dean had finished his painting and decorating course he was employed as the education orderly. His role was to make sure that all the training courses provided by the prison were full. North Sea Camp was basically a rehabilitation establishment which essentially meant that after these murderers, rapists, paedophiles and the like had spent twenty or thirty years behind bars, they were sent there to be integrated back into society. Impossible. Too late. Already institutionalized beyond repair.

Along with the town and home visits, the inmates were enrolled onto training courses, which very few wanted to do but were considered advantageous, if not essential to some prisoners. The courses included Community Living, Volunteering, Employability, Business Start-up, Peer Mentoring, Customer Services and a few others including Art and Sculpture. The prison employed two teachers that taught all the courses in turn. The courses were supposedly to help prisoners coming up for parole to be granted release.

It was a steady job for Dean and helped pass the time. Oh, and of course there was a wage – £7.50 per week to spend on phone calls and 'canteen'.

Molly visited three times a month, even though it was a pain in the arse to get there. She wouldn't have missed a visit for anything and Dean would not have wanted her to.

Days turned into weeks, turned into months. Dean had his first town day release to Boston – the first time he'd visited the town. It was quite an interesting place although not the sort of place he'd want to visit twice. He preferred Nottingham. After that came his home visits which he was allowed once per month and lasted three days. The three days flew by. He'd get a shuttle bus from the prison to Boston Train Station, a train to Nottingham where Molly would meet him, something to eat in Nottingham, a bus back home, a shag followed by a bottle of white rum and oblivion. The second day was spent entertaining friends and family and the third day travelling back to prison. Still, it broke the month up a bit.

As September approached Dean dared to look forward to release on tag. It was never guaranteed but he spent a lot of time filling out all the correct forms and lobbying the relevant Offender Supervisor. Things were looking good but he didn't want to tell Molly unless thing went 'tits-up' – as they often did when the prison service were involved in anything.

Chapter 23

Another Letter?

Friday 1st July 2011, a very pleasant sunny summer morning. Paul Milford and Heather were having breakfast, as usual, in the conservatory. The postman commeth.

Heather picked up the post with one hand, a half-eaten slice of toast in the other. It was ten-thirty a.m. and both were dressed.

"Anything interesting?" Paul called through although concentrating on the newspaper.

"No," came the reply as she walked through. "Just one letter that's not junk or a bill. It looks like one of those blackmail letters we had last year," she joked. Paul laughed, knowing that that was impossible. The blackmailer, 'Myra', was still behind bars. His jaw dropped.

"Hello, ferret man…"

"Oh, my God!" Paul was gobsmacked. "It's from Myra." He read on ignoring Heather as she tried to snatch it from him and look herself. She thought he was trying to carry on the joke.

"Hello, ferret man, long time no speaks, eh? You were a very silly boy getting the police involved after I specifically told you what would happen if you did. Paul, Paul, Paul, what have you done?

"Firstly, may I tell you that stage 2 of my plan WILL come into force. You cannot change that now. I have 1,000 letters addressed to residents of Fenton plus fifty to local businesses. I have 2,000 posters printed also. These letters will all be sent out to arrive at the end of

July. The posters will be put up the night before. You may think that this is a hoax. It is not. I don't really give a flying fuck through a rolling doughnut if you do think it is. You can't change a thing anyway. Did you really think that Dean Muxlowe was Myra?

"The posters will be pasted to shops, lamp posts, cars, buses, mailboxes, indeed anywhere that people can see. Others will be posted through people's doors.

"The letters and posters will have your name and address, telephone number, car reg number and business details. They will give details of your links with gay and paedophile organisations and various sexual acts that you have carried out in your past. The campaign will ruin your reputation within Nottingham. You will be a social leper. These posters and letters are very graphic. I have a team of kids ready and waiting to distribute the posters. I need from you £35,000.

A lot of money, eh? Costs, Paul, costs!

"Towards the end of July, 2 days after the letters and posters have hit, let's call it D-Day shall we? I will send you some bank details. It is a numbered account in the Caribbean. You will transfer the £35,000 to that account within forty-eight hours. If the money isn't there within that time stage 3 of my plan kicks in. If at any point the police or anyone else is informed stage 3 kicks in. If I get any bad feelings about your lack of absolute confidentiality stage 3 kicks in. If I suspect any delaying tactics stage 3 kicks in. Believe me, ferret man, this is your last chance. If stage 3 kicks in it will not end there and your bill will rise to £50,000

"Let me remind you about stage 3 – that is where a selection of your friends, family and business associates have the shit kicked out of them whilst being informed that it is your fault that it is happening because you don't pay your bills.

"Do the right thing, ferret man."

Paul handed the letter over to Heather. She read it whilst he remained silent.

"I'll call D I Shepherd," said Heather as she finished the letter.

"No." Paul put his hand over hers, stopping her from dialling the number. "Let's think about this."

"What exactly is there to think about here?" She protested.

Well," Paul continued. "It may be some crank. It probably is some crank, who just read about the case and sent this to scare us. It may even be some twat from The George and Dragon."

"Yes but what if…"

"Just listen." Paul stopped her in her tracks. "If we get the police involved it would throw everything into confusion. They would probably not want to cast any doubt over Muxlowe's guilt so would tell us to ignore it. They won't want the wounds opening and the possibility that they got it wrong."

"But what if these letters and posters are sent?"

"Well, we'll have to cross that bridge at the time. This paper and envelopes are not exactly the same as the others so it seems as it is probably a different person. The police are also adamant that Muxlowe produced the letters, and if it wasn't him, why did he plead guilty?

"What if he had an accomplice?" Heather frowned.

"The police said that he was acting on his own – they are one hundred percent certain of that."

"I still think that we should let Shepherd know." Heather was not easily dissuaded.

"Not yet. Let's talk it through some more." Paul was not comfortable; he sensed malice on a different level to before. He had the £35,000, it was a small part of the money he'd stolen from Rocco. He was starting to wonder if he should have paid the £20,000 when he had the chance.

The argument was continued through the morning. The wine came out about mid-day and continued throughout the afternoon and evening. One minute they would tell the police, the next they would ignore the letter. So many 'what ifs?' Not enough answers.

They had nearly three weeks to get the police involved. As every day passed, and time ran out, anxiety levels increased. They were both like ticking bombs, liable to go up at any time. The arguments became more frequent and more intense.

What would happen if the letters and posters went out? Would Paul then involve the police? He would probably have no choice at that point but would he pay the £35,000? If not he would be risking physical harm to his friends and family. Could he do that? If he did involve the police at that point, what reason would he give for not letting them know earlier? Every time he asked himself the questions, he gave himself different answers.

As each night came he put the decision off until the next day. Days passed in the blink of an eye. The point of no return had arrived and gone before they realised it. They would just have to wait and hope to God that it was just a hoax – an evil, malicious wind-up from some monster that had a grudge, or was playing a sick joke.

Many people had a grudge against Paul; business associates that Milford Park had ripped off; businesses that they'd sent bankrupt; even a lottery ticket player that claimed he'd had his scratch card stolen by Paul and lost £250,000.

They stayed away from The George and Dragon. If it was someone from there, Paul and Heather didn't want to give them the pleasure of gloating and watching their misery.

July 21st, Thursday. Tomorrow was the day. Paul and Heather had one last sudden rush of inspiration and called DI Shepherd's number. Before he answered Paul hung up. They both looked at each other and opened a bottle. That night they got very, very drunk and passed out on the bed. It was the only way that they would get any sleep that night.

Chapter 24
Stage 2

At eight a.m., they were up, hoping that the phone would not ring. Neither of them could face any breakfast – a combination of hangover and nerves. Paul could now understand the term 'hung-over'. His whole body literally felt 'hung-over' his bones. At eight-thirty a.m. his mobile phone rang – it was an unknown number. Paul's heart rose to his throat as he answered. "Hello."

"Paul Milford?" It was a voice that he did not recognise.

"Yes, speaking."

"Paul, I don't know what is going on, or how I'm involved, but I've just had a letter through the post with your name and number on it."

"Really?" Paul was horrified but not too surprised. He hoped that he was wrong about what was coming. He was close to being physically sick.

"Yes," continued the caller. "I'm John Flax from the village. This letter claims that you are a vile sex offender. It's extremely graphic actually, and I'm glad that my wife didn't open it." He had an accusing tone to his voice and made it sound like it was Paul's fault. As Paul was listening the 'call waiting' sign came up on his phone. "Well?" Flax pressed.

"Sorry, Mr Flax," replied Paul. "This is obviously a ridiculous hoax – a plot against me. The police have been involved previously. Can I give them your name if they need to speak to you?"

"Yes, certainly," confirmed Flax. Paul hung up to get the next call. There was another call waiting. The phone didn't stop ringing all morning.

The 'stage 2' had been implemented by Myra, or whoever it was that had picked up the baton. Yes, there had been many letters sent out and yes, there were shed loads of posters all over the town, just as the blackmailer had promised.

Heather was in bits. She had never felt more damaged and ashamed. Surely people wouldn't believe this shit. She stopped answering her phone for a while, but then thought that people might take this as an admission of guilt. She avidly rang everyone back to put over their side of the story.

Paul was constantly taking calls. Most were from confused recipients of the letter saying that they knew it was probably a hate campaign and that any help they could be, they would. There were some though that had read the posters. Many choice phrases were shouted down the phone from 'unknown numbers' – "Fucking Paedo!" "Vagina decliner!" "Nonce!" If Paul Milford needed any convincing that Myra meant business then this was it. The only big question now was regarding the £35,000. Should he pay it or risk the safety, even the lives, of some friends and relatives.

At three p.m. there was a knock on the door. It was DI Shepherd and a colleague. Paul opened the door – he certainly looked older than sixty. His phone was ringing in the background. Shepherd came straight to the point. "Paul, what the fuck is happening here?"

"You've heard then." Paul shook his hand and invited him and his colleague in. They had a seat in the living room. Heather put the kettle on, remaining in the kitchen until it boiled.

"Well, this is a twist," said Shepherd.

"Mmm…" agreed Paul. "Any ideas?"

"That's what we're here for – to see if you have any ideas."

"Nothing," Paul lied. He was broken. He had decided to lie to the police and pay the £35,000. It was a 'no brainer' – Myra meant business – damage limitation was now his only concern. Heather brought in the tea and biscuits.

"What about you, Heather?" asked Shepherd. Heather just shrugged and walked out. This was not like her and the policeman noted it.

Shepherd had collected a few of the letters already from people who had gone direct to the police. There was a clean-up operation in the village for the posters. There was though, Shepherd informed Paul, another load pasted up around Nottingham city centre and many buses had been targeted. They were looking at CCTV but so far all they had learned was that the culprits seemed to be young kids with their faces covered dressed in common regular clothes with no distinguishing features.

"It just gets better," was Paul's detached comment.

After half an hour of circular discussion it was decided that there was nothing that the police could do. They would keep watching the CCTV and ask around for witnesses but it seemed that tracks had been well covered.

There was no point going back to Muxlowe because he was still inside. "Anybody else that springs to mind that may have a grudge?" asked Shepherd.

"Not that I know of," Paul lied again. He was bored now and wanted the police to go.

It was decided to leave it, and hope that it was just a one-off malicious prank. The police were stretched to breaking point already and the last thing they wanted was to re-open the Muxlowe case. They just wanted to sweep it under the carpet and hope it went away.

"Well, Paul, Heather, if you get any more letters or contact from anybody, give me a call straight away. OK?"

"Yes, certainly." Confirmed Paul as he showed the policemen out. Heather just frowned.

Shepherd was suspicious as he left. He knew that they were both acting very strangely as he'd come to know them quite well during the past investigation. The trouble was that if he picked and picked, he might expose something he didn't want to. A big investigation was the last thing he wanted at this point in time. If there was something, Heather and Paul were obviously reluctant to seek help. No, he would leave it, visualising the proverbial can of worms. "Fuck 'em!" He thought.

The phone calls slowed down over the next few days, thankfully. All that Paul wanted to do now was to pay Myra the £35,000 and get it all over with.

The following Wednesday the letter arrived. Paul had been expecting it.

"Hello, Paul, I hope you enjoyed my little prank and you now realise how serious I am. I also hope that you managed to convince the police not to get too involved. I am quite crazy and am getting really excited putting you through all this pain.

"At the end of this letter I will give you the details of my numbered account in which you need to pay the £35,000. If it is not in there by four p.m. on Friday, stage 3 will start. Once the money has hit that account you must forget it. It will disappear overnight and you or anybody will have no chance of tracing it.

"Do the right thing, ferret man.

"I do so look forward to spending your money. Have a nice weekend, all my love, Myra XXXXX"

"Come on, Heather, we're off to the bank." Paul grabbed his coat.

The money was paid that morning from Paul's scratch card winning account. He wasn't sure if he'd done the right thing or not but, whatever, he felt relieved. He knew he'd been targeted by a big fish and he hoped that they would now just swim away and pick on somebody else. He never wanted to hear the name 'Myra' again.

Chapter 25

The downing of the Snakesbelly

Friday, 5th August was a warm sunny day, ideal for sitting outside a quaint little country pub downing a few cold lagers, maybe accompanied by a tasty steak and chips with extra mushrooms and onion rings.

Ernest Gerrity had been in The George and Dragon since four p.m.; it was now nine p.m. He'd indulged in the cold lagers but passed on the steak and chips. He'd been off solids lately, particularly when drinking. 'Eating is cheating' was his mantra. He was blissfully unaware of all the shit that had gone on in the village with the posters a couple of weeks ago. George had mentioned something a few days ago but Gerrity hadn't taken much notice. These days he was usually too pissed to converse at any intelligible level.

Five hours constant drinking at a good pace had done him. A lot of the time he'd been on his own although an odd friend would drift in and out. Gerrity had a few 'odd friends'. The 'early doors' set were by now sat at home with their wives watching the TV, or in the back garden with the barbeque. Although pissed, Gerrity was aware that he was likely to fall over and make a scene if he had any more to drink. He decided to leave.

Paul Milford had not been in, noted Gerrity. In fact he'd not been in for weeks. Initially he thought he'd been away on holiday, but he'd never said, and it had been quite a while now. "Fuck him!"

Thought Gerrity, believing that he'd probably found another pub to buy some friends at. He laughed out loud at the idea attracting attention from some other drinkers and diners. Yes, it was definitely time to fuck off.

"That's me, Paula." He shouted to the barmaid. "I'll probably see you tomorrow."

"See you tomorrow, Mr Gerrity." Paula was very young and new to bar work, she still felt uncomfortable calling anybody over thirty by their first name.

"Ernest, please." He was slurring now.

"OK, Ernest," she smiled, "see you."

Ernest had no coat. He was wearing beige canvas trousers and a tight yellow 'T' shirt – so tight as to show off his now ample beer belly. He felt good seeing the reflection of himself in the mirror behind the bar but fuck knows how he managed to leave the house sober looking like that.

He staggered out of the pub with a dilemma. He'd come in the car, a red Audi A4, thinking that he was just in for a couple of 'sharpeners', knowing that if he did have any more he could leave the car and walk home. The problem was that he had gone beyond that point and was struggling to walk properly at all. A taxi would take ages at this time on a Friday and wouldn't want to be pissing around taking him a mile down the road. Most would be down in the city centre ferrying around pissed-up twenty-somethings while they still had some money in their pockets.

Of course the beer had its effect also and the 'fuck it' factor kicked in. He headed towards the Audi. His same reasoning for the taxi drivers being in the city centre on a Friday night also held true for the police.

His car was parked in the far corner. He'd put it there just in case he had to leave it. Also people would not see it, and then see him pissed up in the bar and think he was drunk driving. He smiled at himself as he thought how clever he was. The car park was virtually empty as most customers were local people who had walked as it was such a nice evening.

As pissed as Gerrity was, he didn't notice the figure waiting for him crouched behind a van parked a few spaces away from his car. As he fumbled for his keys his legs were taken from under him in one fell swoop. The cricket bat smashed into his calf muscles just below and behind his knees. He didn't see his assailant. As his limp body hit the floor a hard fist crashed into his face again and again. Gerrity's vision became blurred and he could taste the blood on his lips. It had a sort of metallic flavour. He was rolled onto his face and his arms were harshly forced behind his back. He felt his wrists being fastened together, the sharp edges of the tie-wrap cutting into his skin as it was pulled tight. Within seconds he was dragged along the car park face down, lifted and slung unceremoniously into the back of the van that was parked close by. The powerful attacker then took a few seconds to pull a thick cloth bag over Gerrity's head so that he couldn't see a thing. He then pulled out a larger, industrial type tie-wrap and secured his throbbing legs together. As he started to shout in protest after the initial shock, the van's rear door was slammed shut. The thug then got into the driver's seat and set off. He never said a word.

"Stop! Stop!" Screamed Gerrity as the van moved out of the car park onto the main road. "I'm dying for a piss!" With his arms fastened up behind his back there was no point in the driver stopping the van unless he was going to unzip Gerrity himself and hold his pecker while he relieved himself. The man remained silent.

"Mate. Mate." Pleaded Gerrity. "What do you want? I've got money – loads of it. Please stop, mate – I've had eight pints and I'm busting!" Still silence. As the van travelled along the country lane a stab of pain hit Gerrity at every bump.

After twenty minutes driving and Gerrity squawking, he eventually pissed himself. The warm sensation down his legs and groin combined with the relief of an empty bladder soon left him to be replaced by the coldness and wetness. He fell silent. The driver turned on Radio 2.

Another twenty minutes and the van slowed down and turned off the main road onto some rough, bumpy ground, maybe a poorly maintained farm track. A couple of minutes later, after a slow drive, it came to a halt. The driver cut the engine and got out.

"Where are we?" asked Gerrity, talking now not shouting, not really expecting an answer. He didn't get one. The only thing he knew was that it was a bloke that had abducted him and he was fucking strong.

The guy opened the back door and dragged Gerrity out, dumping him on the ground. He landed hard, a sharp pain firing through his shoulder. He cried out in pain thinking that it had broken. He was right. He thought he heard the man mutter under his breath "dirty bastard." Then a sharp kick in the back – obviously he was upset at the prospect of having to clean the piss out of his van.

The light was just starting to fade, not that Gerrity could tell. He was drifting in and out of consciousness at this point. The man dragged his twisting body over the rough, uneven ground eventually through a wooden five-bar gate. He dumped him at the bottom of a hedge. He then went back to the van to fetch the cricket bat. When he got back, he at last spoke. He had an upper class English accent, not smooth and practiced, rather mimicked and false.

"Well, well, old boy, who's been a bad little Ernest?"

"What are you talking about?" Gerrity was confused and very dizzy; the thick cloth bag was still over his head making it difficult to breath. He could now taste salty snot along with the blood.

"Have you no shame, man? No guilt?"

"Who are you? What do you mean?"

"Tut, tut." He smashed Gerrity's right kneecap with the cricket bat. Gerrity screamed out in sickening pain. "Have a think," the voice suggested. It took a good minute for Gerrity to realise the ability to speak.

"I don't know what you're on about." Gerrity thought he could hear the 'fizz' of a camera taking photographs.

BANG! The other kneecap was smashed. Again a long wail of pain. Gerrity was on the verge of passing out. The noise didn't matter; the van man had taken him up into the hills of Derbyshire, not far from Matlock, to a deserted little farm track. Gerrity pissed himself again. He was shaking with terror. One of his kneecaps was definitely broken, the other had been knocked down his leg and was three inches lower than it should be. He lay there whimpering knowing full well that he wouldn't be able to stand. The attacker laughed, but not an upper class English laugh.

"You've upset a lot of people, Gerrity old bean. This is just one of them giving you a little bit of pay-back." With that the guy lifted the bat above his head and brought it down, full force, on Gerrity's back. Gerrity eventually passed out with the pain as he felt and heard a sickening 'crack' down his spine.

That same night, after a horrific day, Paul Milford and Heather sat at home drinking. They'd watched the soaps until nine p.m., and then opened the wine. They didn't feel comfortable or safe going out – they knew somebody that was close to them had stitched them up and they were vulnerable. Paul's mobile had run out of juice with all the incoming calls, but he had just let it die and slung it in a drawer until tomorrow. The wine helped them relax a little and by eleven p.m. they were sitting having an Indian meal that had just been delivered. They'd arranged it on the kitchen table – there was far too much but they'd eat the leftovers cold in the morning.

They had a lot to talk about with the obvious hate campaign as Paul Fairchild, the guy that ran Milford Park, was now sixty-five and although didn't want to retire, had been diagnosed that day with cancer of the prostate. It may give him a different outlook on life, thought Paul. Apparently prostate cancer is a slow moving disease that is relatively common. In older men, around seventy and upwards, it is not treated as a norm because usually the victim dies of something else before the cancer finishes them off. In Fairchild's case though, the condition was quite advanced as he'd been ignoring the symptoms for years. This meant that he would have to undergo delicate surgery and be out of action for months. Milford would have to get off his little ferret arse and run the business himself. He was not relishing the prospect as he didn't have good leadership qualities. He knew his staff would take the piss and laugh behind his back – he was a bit of a David Brent from 'The Office'.

Fairchild didn't believe in him either – he didn't trust his competency, reputation or intelligence, and certainly not his ability to run a business. He thought that Milford would be more at home in the boardroom of Reginald Perrin's Mickey Mouse company, 'Grot', in the famed TV comedy series.

After a bottle and a half of wine though, Paul's confidence in himself had built up a little; he was giving it large to Heather. How glad he would be to at last 'play with his train set,' what plans he had to exact change and move the business forward. Expansion plans, new areas of development. Heather sat smiling, swallowing it all up. Suddenly she heard a noise.

"What's that?" She interrupted Paul's flow.

"What?" Paul had heard nothing; he was too busy spouting shit and troughing poppadums.

"I heard a noise through the front room." They both listened but could hear nothing. "I'm sure I did." Heather was adamant. She stood up and walked through to the front room. Paul kept troughing.

Heather walked back into the kitchen looking horrified. In her hand she held a half brick with a sheet of paper attached to it by a rubber band. She took the paper off.

"What the fuck is that?" questioned Paul.

"I don't know," replied Heather, "but it's just come through the fucking front window."

"Fucking bastards!" Paul jumped up and ran to the front door, hoping not to find anything or anyone. Nothing. Phew! He walked a little way up the street as an act of bravery, once he was sure nobody was lurking. As he got back to the house, Heather was standing outside. "What is it?" he asked. "What did the paper have written on it?"

"It says…" Heather looked puzzled. "Have a look at your car, ferret man." They both looked over to his white Land Rover. It was parked on the street as normal. It looked OK. They had full sight of the back end. Heather's car was always parked on the drive. Paul, out of laziness, left his on the street.

"What's up with it?" He started to walk towards the car. Heather caught up. The car looked fine until they saw the bonnet. On it was writing in black permanent marker pen. The two of them read the message.

Who has had your 35 large?
Who's had your pants down, Mr Ferrity?
He's bought you drinks; he's sucked your cock
Look no further it's Ernest…

211

"Gerrity?" they both said at once, looking each other in the eye. A crude accusation, but to the point.

"Shall I ring the police?" said Heather.

"No," insisted Paul. Let's go inside and talk about it. It's obviously a malicious prank putting Ernest in the frame. He probably doesn't know a thing. I've not told anyone about the £35,000 I paid and the police, if we tell them, will go up the wall."

"True," agreed Heather, realising that she was as much to blame for not telling the police in the first place.

Paul tried to remove the writing from the bonnet but to no avail, he would probably have to have it painted. He'd sort it tomorrow; meanwhile he swapped the position of his car with Heather's so that the neighbours wouldn't see the bonnet and ask questions.

They then went inside to finish the meal and wine. Heather taped up the hole in the front room window. They'd claim it was an accident when they put a claim into the insurance company, that way they wouldn't need a crime number from the police.

They discussed the possibility of Gerrity's guilt until the early hours. They decided that the best plan was to ring him in the morning, meet him at The George and Dragon to see what, if anything, he knew. They also decided to keep the bonnet of the Freelander as it was for a while in case they did call in the police; it was evidence and they would want to analyse the writing and fingerprint the paint. So that was the plan. They left the rest of the food and crawled up to bed at two a.m.

Chapter 26
Wake up Snakesbelly

It was around two a.m. on the Saturday morning that Ernest Gerrity began to wake. His head was throbbing, his eyes felt pain as they slowly opened, but he was warm and in a comfortable bed.

At around eleven p.m. he had been picked up by an ambulance from a farmer's field just outside Matlock, Derbyshire, after someone had called the police on 999 to report his whereabouts. Had they not, it could have been days before he had been discovered. He may have died. The call was made by an anonymous male from a public phone box in a small village just down the road from where he lay.

Remembering the van and the pain, he looked around to see his hospital bed, the tubes into the back of his hands, the monitors and the drips. Stella was at his bedside, her face a picture of anxiety. She seemed to burst with joy when his eyes opened.

"Ernest! Ernest! Thank God you're OK." Gerrity could not talk. Stella called for help. "Doctor! Doctor! Come quick, he's awake."

They were joined by a small, wiry little male nurse: five feet two, very skinny, pock-marked weasely face with short cropped greasy hair. Very camp. "Hello, Mr Gerrity," he chirped. "Thanks for joining us." He'd obviously tried that line before to lighten the mood. "Can you hear me?" Gerrity just nodded slowly and slightly, in case his throbbing head fell off.

"Mr Gerrity?" Little nurse man said. Stella was sick with fear, anticipating the next question. Ernest looked up at wee boy. He continued. "Can you feel your legs?" The question had to be asked. Ernest looked blank. He could vaguely remember the pain of the cricket bat smashing into his knee caps but realised that he could not now feel anything. He tried to wiggle his toes. He couldn't. A panic started to build, his heart quickened and a look of frustration crossed his face as he tried to move. A quick concerned glance was exchanged between the nurse and Stella as they realised that the answer to the question was the wrong one.

"OK, Mr Gerrity, just rest. You've had a bit of a shake-up and you're full of all sorts of things to help you. I'm going to get a doctor to come and have a look at you, and then we'll do a few more tests to see what's wrong."

"You'll be fine, don't worry," added Stella, her expression completely contradicting what she was saying. Gerrity was worrying. He was fucking panicking. The gay nurse smiled down at him.

"I'm going to leave you now, Mr Gerrity. The important thing is that you try and relax a little and rest. Stella will be staying with you for a while." Ernest nodded as the nurse left the room, nodding and smiling to Stella. It didn't comfort her as it obviously was meant to.

Gerrity closed his eyes and fell asleep in the hope that when he woke up everything would be back to normal and he was just having a bad dream. Stella, even though it was the middle of the night, made a few phone calls. She was convinced that Ernest would never walk again.

The following morning, Saturday, Paul Milford tried to call Gerrity's mobile. It was switched off. "Idle little bastard, still in bed at eleven a.m.," he thought. He kept trying.

At one p.m. the phone was still off, so Paul decided to take Heather for her lunch at The George and Dragon. They may even bump into Gerrity. Maybe he was guilty and was trying to avoid them.

The bar was quiet. George, the landlord was serving. "Hi, George, a pint of lager, a medium white wine, a three bean chilli and a gammon steak with egg, please."

"Hi, Paul, certainly. How's it going?" replied George.

"Fine. Just off into town."

"Rather you than me on a Saturday morning. We've not seen you for a while."

"No, we've not been out at all. Can't be bothered; I think it's an age thing," he laughed.

"Right," George didn't pry, placing the drinks on the bar. "£19.75p, please. I'll bring the grub over when it's ready."

"Thanks," smiled Paul. "We'll be over in the corner." He picked up the two drinks then added; "Have you seen anything of Ernest Gerrity lately?"

"He's always in, regular as clockwork. Haven't you heard though?"

"Heard what?"

"Last night?"

"What about last night?" Paul put the drinks back on the bar.

"Well." George was now excited like the little old woman spilling the gossip to those that didn't know. "He was in here last night and had a skin full, which is not that unusual in itself, but when he left he got a right kicking. Somebody obviously caught up with him who he'd upset, or rather ripped-off."

"Ernest? Are you sure?" Paul was shocked, more of the co-incidence than the fact that Gerrity had had a kicking.

"Yes," George continued. "Sprocket came in earlier and told me. He was supposed to be helping him deliver a car this morning but Stella rang him and told him the news. In quite a bad way apparently – legs not working. Stella sounded very upset." 'Sprocket' was one of Gerrity's mates that helped him out now and again if a driving job came up. He paid him a little cash to supplement his benefits and allowed him to buy a bit of weed.

"Well, well, well." Paul picked the drinks back up, turned and walked over to join Heather. He told her of the news whilst they were waiting for lunch.

Heather listened with interest. "Shit," she frowned. "Well we still don't know whether he stitched us or not. If we do report it now the police will bollock us first for not getting in touch in the first place, and they may even think we paid someone to have him hit."

"Especially as we've just had the £35,000 go out of my bank without explanation."

"Well, we tell the police that that was the blackmail money," argued Heather.

"And hopefully they'll believe us." Paul was not convinced.

"What a fucking mess. Why didn't you just tell the police in the first place?" Heather was now directing the blame towards Paul.

"Fuck knows," he replied." I'll go and see him."

Meanwhile on that bright Saturday morning, Molly Muxlowe was making breakfast for her brother, Derek. She was getting happier by the day as Dean's release date approached. He could be potentially let out on a HDC (Home Detention Curfew) or 'tag' as it was affectionately known. Only six weeks to go if he qualified, as Molly was sure he would.

Derek sat down and tucked in to his full English breakfast. "Thanks, Molly, much appreciated."

"No problem." She was about to go to work – she was on the nine am-one p.m. Saturday morning shift.

"Molly?" Derek sounded sheepish.

"Yes, what is it? I'm just away to work."

"Shit, I didn't realise. Listen; something has come up at home and I'm going to have to go back up for a bit. When is Dean back?"

"Hopefully six weeks." Disappointment could be heard in her voice. "Why, what's happened?"

"Nothing serious," he continued. "I've got a few things that have piled up and I need to sort with the police. I'm not going back and I need to tell them. I've also maybe got a chance of a full time job."

"Oh, really? Good!" She didn't like him being in the police and what with what had happened to Dean, she hated the bastards anyway. "When are you going away?"

"This morning." He paused. "The catalogue job has finished now and the sooner I get sorted the better. I'll have a better chance at this job as well if I don't hang about."

"Oh, right." Molly was a little bit taken aback. She had expected this conversation at some point and, if truth be known, had not expected him to still be there then. He seemed to be getting on OK with his part-time job he had; out most afternoons and evenings. It was only part-time however and he was better than driving a van around for a living, fetching and delivering parcels. And, it was only six weeks until Dean was back. "Well, thanks for looking after me for these last few months." And she was genuinely grateful. She gave him a kiss on the head. "Will you be gone when I get back at a quarter past one?"

217

"Yes, I will," he replied. "I want to get back early evening, so I'll set off in about an hour."

"Fine." She had now had time to come to terms with it. "Well, you drive carefully, not too fast, and come back to see us soon. Make sure that you've washed, dried and put away all the pots before you go, and lock the door – put the key through the letter box."

"Yes, sis. Have a good day and I'll see you soon." He shovelled another fork full of sausage into his mouth.

"Yes." She gave him another kiss on the head. "I'll see you soon." With that she left for work.

Derek finished his breakfast and washed his pots before setting off, back up North. He'd enjoyed his time in England but wouldn't want to live there.

"What a state!" Paul Milford stood by Ernest Gerrity's hospital bed on the Monday afternoon. Visiting was two p.m. – nine p.m. It was two p.m. Gerrity's eyes opened and he looked up.

His face was a right sight; his eyes were black and blue, scratch and scuff marks etched with dry blood down his cheeks and chin, stitches across his forehead and one of his ears. He groaned as he recognised Milford.

"What have you been up to?" He placed the traditional brown bag of grapes on the bedside cabinet. No answer from Gerrity. He was still in pain when he tried to talk, let alone answer stupid fucking questions. Milford got the idea after a series of silences after similar inane questions. He was on his own. Stella arrived to sit by the bedside.

"Hi, Paul."

"Hi, Stella. What's the news?"

"Well." She took a deep breath to try and stop her eyes from filling up. "He had a bad kicking on Friday night. We don't know who did it, but he was found near Matlock in a farmer's field."

"Who found him?"

"The police. Someone rang them from a phone box; probably the guy, or one of the guys that did it to him."

"Really?"

"Yes." Another deep breath. "He has no feeling in his legs…" Her eyes started to water. She stopped and tried again. "It may be a bruised nerve that will repair or it may be that the nerve is permanently damaged and he won't ever walk again." The tears flowed and Paul put his arm around her to comfort her.

Paul stayed for an hour before he left Stella to sit alone. Gerrity didn't talk once and spent most of his time with his eyes shut.

Paul met Heather at The George and Dragon. She wanted to know what was what. They sat at the usual table in the corner with their usual drinks – it was four p.m.

"Well, someone has really given him a proper kicking," explained Paul. "And the chances are that he won't walk again. He'll be stuck in a wheelchair for the rest of his life."

"What did he say?" asked Heather. "Did he have any ideas who did it?"

"He didn't say fuck all. He couldn't speak."

"Was Stella there?"

"Yes."

"And what did she say?"

"Not a lot really. No idea who did it. She's just in bits."

"I'll bet." A frown crossed Heather's face. "Do you think he's had our thirty five grand?"

"I don't know." Paul was in two minds. "Everything fits in one way, but to be honest, I don't think so. I think someone else is trying to fit him up. Let's leave it for a while until he's recovered a bit. I'm sure it'll all come out in the wash."

"Mmm..." Heather wasn't convinced; she'd never really trusted Gerrity. He always looked like he was taking the piss out of somebody; she'd never seen him genuine and serious. Still, she'd leave it with Paul. There was nothing that could be done now. It was such a complicated mess. Things had gone too far in different directions.

The next few weeks passed without too much incident. Paul Milford and Heather continued to talk and try to solve the mystery of the blackmailer, the £35,000 and the attack on Gerrity.

Gerrity lay in bed recovering. His face got markedly better but his legs just would not respond. He started to give up hope of walking again.

Molly got more excited every day at the prospect of Dean coming home. She was relying on this 'tag' business; she would die if he didn't get it – well maybe not 'die, but she certainly wouldn't be very happy.

Mike and Bernie continued with MHB Finance Ltd and continued to tick over; not making massive profits, just enough to pay the bills.

James Hunter-Browne managed to get into even more debt. The money he had stolen from MHB had run out and the banks had stopped lending him more, but he'd found a guy in the property business, that was quiet at the time, who agreed to back him. It went without saying that some of the funds found their way to servicing his huge mortgage interest – the proverbial time bomb waiting to go off.

Derek Rafferty finally ended his career in the police. The job he had gone for hadn't materialised so he'd decided to follow his dream of a seafood bar. He even spoke to Molly about a joint venture – an Anglo-Scottish amalgamation. She told him she'd speak to Dean when he was out.

Dean kept his nose clean in the open prison, North Sea Camp, in Boston. He had several unaccompanied town visits, a home visit, which thrilled Molly, and completed a painting and decorating course. There was no reason for them to knock back his application for a HDC tag so that he could get out and get back to business; fingers crossed.

Chapter 27

Freedom

Wednesday 7th September 2011, 6.10 p.m.

"How do you mean you don't fucking know!" Molly was past the point of frustration. Dean had told her that the HDC tag for the following day had not been finalised yet.

"I don't fucking know." He'd lost count of how many times he'd told her not to get her hopes too far up.

"Well you don't seem to be too fucking unhappy about it," she squealed.

"Look, I'll call you tomorrow, right. I'll know by then I promise. My credit's running low so I'm off."

"Your credit always runs low when you don't want to fucking talk to me." She was by now, well bent out of shape.

"Look, Molly," he was pleading, "I promise I'll know one hundred per cent tomorrow. I'll ring you. I miss you and I love you. OK?"

"OK." She gave a frustrated sigh. "I love you." They both hung up.

Dean's tag had been approved and he was due to leave for home at eight a.m. the following morning and meet his 'tag people' after three p.m. to have it fitted. Bernie was picking him up from the prison and taking him home. The reason he hadn't told Molly was that the prison service was by no means an exact science. Nothing was ever done until it was done. He'd waited hours around for things that had never happened. It took him three weeks once to get a £1.10 prison alarm clock transferred from the stores to his property in reception so that he could actually get it out and use it. The stores were 400 yards away from reception. He had seen all sorts of cock-ups. Once there was a prisoner transferred into North Sea Camp, settled into his cell, before the authoritative twats that organised it realised that he was too young to be there – he should have been in a young offenders institution so had to be immediately 'shipped out'.

No, he wanted it to be cut and dry before Molly was told for definite. It would kill her to be stood waiting at the window all morning to get the phone call to say something had happened to delay things, or rather something not happened – some lazy screw not filling in the right paperwork, or some administrator not clearing his 'in' tray because it was time for lunch.

North Sea Camp

The smell of shit and rubber
Seeping through the halls
Tells the certain story
Of throbbing arse and aching balls

The place is full of monsters
With minds so cold and sour
They piss all up the toilet walls
And curl one in the shower

The real world does not exist
When they've been inside so long
You cannot let the beast go free
Out where it does not belong

What should become of all these ghouls?
Line them up and have them shot?
Better still, pile 'em high
Add some unleaded, burn the lot

Paedos, murderers, rapists
Death to them would be more kind
But years they spend inside a cell
Out of sight, out of mind

There must be a better way
To put these souls back on the rail
The Government spends billions
But always seems to fucking fail

Boys, as you walk free from the camp
Believe, I really feel for you
But it could be a whole lot worse
You could have been a fucking screw

The following morning all went to plan. Bernie dropped Dean off outside the house at eleven a.m. and drove straight off. "I'm sure you don't want me hanging around," he said. "And even if you do, Molly won't."

Dean had a sudden horrible thought; he'd not rung Molly as he thought he'd surprise her, but he'd not checked that she wasn't working.

Molly answered the door; she had been stood at the window all morning just in case. She stared at Dean, her mouth dropped, then suddenly formed into a smile. "You bastard!" she screamed, throwing her arms around her man, bouncing up and down. They moved inside and kicked the door shut before the dogs came ploughing through, leaping and barking, licking and clawing; Dean thought that their hearts might pack in.

Dean rolled around with them for a few minutes before kicking them into the utility room, very much under protest. As much as he loved the dogs, he and Molly had plenty of time to make up together, alone.

At four p.m. Dean's tag was fitted and he was given his instructions regarding restrictions. The guy that came to fit it was extremely nice. He came dressed casually with all the equipment in a ruck-sack over his shoulder, parking his car around the corner – very discreet. He set the little black box and telephone up in the spare bedroom and attached the electronic tag to Dean's left ankle. Dean then had three minutes to walk around the house, getting into all the extremities to set the boundaries of the device. The fitter then explained the rules; no going outside the limits between seven p.m. and seven am; if the phone rings you have to answer it, or at least be available to confirm your identity; you cannot take the tag off; you cannot move the black box (he put a security tag on the plug so it would be known if Dean had tried to move it – apparently the boundary limit moved with the black box); you can have a bath and it can get wet. The guy then shook Dean's hand and left, informing him that he would be back before midnight on the 21st January 2012 to remove the device.

Dean was so relieved to be out. He could now get back to work. He needed to. Whilst in prison he had had no income, so as a plan he had borrowed heavily just in case he had been sent down. It's a good job he had. The money had paid the mortgage and all bills whilst away, but it had now all gone and all that was left was debt. The situation was, if nothing else, great motivation.

To Molly

I'm sorry you were left alone
I realise I made you sad
I know I should regret the jail
But strange it seems, I feel quite glad

I know you think I'm crazy when
I say prison was good for me
It has made me realise
Just what it's like, to be free

I'm ready now to carry on
And squeeze the last drop out of life
No-one will stop me, clip my wings
I feel so sharp, a surgeon's knife

So come on Molly, buckle up
Get ready for a thrilling ride
There are no limits we can reach
Unleashed, with you right by my side

Chapter 28

Derek Rafferty's Story

Derek Rafferty travelled down the A1 on Friday 7th January 2011 from Fife, to look after his 'wee sister' in Nottingham. That was perfectly true, but he also needed to do something else; escape.

After a long period in the police force he was tired. He'd joined up fifteen years ago, spending a lot of his time in Fraud, but was now in Serious Crime. His seven hour journey time gave him plenty of thinking time, especially as he was in a hired Citroen van and the radio was pretty crap. He'd rather switch it off completely than have it fading in and out every time he went into a dip.

"How could it be," he thought, "that my brother-in-law, aged nearly forty-eight, with no previous criminal history, married for twenty-five years with a family and own business, could be jailed for blackmail when a senior consultant psychiatrist had categorically stated that the reason for his uncharacteristic behaviour in committing the crime was in most part to having a clinically depressive illness? How would banging him up in a prison cell help anybody? Public interest? Cost? Fairness? Treatment for the depression?

"What about all the career criminals that he had caught? They seemed to be immune to the system – or rather they knew the solicitors and barristers that could frighten and bamboozle the judges, play the system, act and lie to schmooze the juries, build sympathy, create empathy, rake through the process to expose discrepancies and loopholes, turn the perpetrator into the victim, the victim into the bad guy. What sort of fucking system was this? What sort of fucking wankers could play this God awful game every day and just treat it as bad luck if they lost, even when their player was odds-on to win. Had they no moral conscience for the obvious miscarriages of justice? Was there no place for common sense? Or was it purely down to money? If you could afford the best jockey to ride your horse, then the odds were dramatically reduced. Put a novice jockey on the favourite and it would probably fall at the first."

Derek ran over in his mind some of his recent cases. The sleepless nights he'd had preparing and reviewing, how he thought that the court would see things. Cases that had been 'watertight'. Criminals that he had caught 'red-handed'. Bad guys that needed to be off the streets, needed to be punished, that were a danger to the public. Many of these walked away, smiling. His blood had boiled. What had been achieved? It had put these wankers back on the streets to carry-on where they left off. It had also given them knowledge and experience. It had taught them useful techniques and introduced them to valuable contacts so they could ply their trade more efficiently and profitably. It was a sort of training course with on-the-job experience. There should probably be some sort of certificate or diploma awarded to recognise their level of expertise and achievement.

The barristers would just smile and say that the system demanded that everyone had a right to a fair defence. Fair! Derek could think of a few words to describe some of the defences that he had seen – 'inconsistent', price-driven', 'unfair', 'morally corrupt', blatant untruth', 'bullshit'…the list could go on and on.

No, Derek did not want to be part of this bullshit system anymore. Now was the time, at thirty-eight, to make the break and start something new. Another twenty-five years or so before retirement should give him sufficient time to do something constructive. This time away in Nottingham would give him plenty of time to decide what to do; security? Pub? Shop?

Disillusioned

I am a copper true and blue
Enforcing law; my work, my life
I know the facts, it's cost me dear
I miss my kids, I've lost my wife

They say this job's a 'calling'
We catch the thieves and stop the drugs
They say we are 'invaluable'
To jail the rapists, paedos, thugs

Without us what would it be like?
Everyone doing as they please
The gangsters rule with pain and fear
They'd fill our world with crime and sleaze

But when we catch them doing wrong
The work then starts, believe you me
The barristers and legal teams
Do all they must to set them free

They lie, deceive and bend the rules
"Admit fuck all", "do not confess"
Guilt is not enough no more
It's down to loopholes and process

Do I want this anymore?
Busting balls all night and day
I stick the bastards in the cells
Then watch them smile and walk away

My appetite for policing's gone
The justice system's so unfair
If some twat wants to break the law
Then I no longer fucking care!

Molly was obviously delighted to see him and needed the company and support. Derek was a bit handy around the house and soon got round to doing a few of the little jobs that Dean had neglected over the last couple of years.

One of these jobs was to clear out the garage, which was attached to the house and had its own attic. The rubbish they would either bang in a skip or put on eBay. It was Tuesday 22nd February; Derek had been down for about six weeks and had put this job off and off as he didn't know where to start.

He was getting on OK with it, piling the eBay stuff in one corner nice and neat ready for Rose to take the photos and get them on-line. All the rubbish was outside in the skip.

Molly was getting the tea as Derek had decided to finish off, up in the attic. There was a corner with a few bits and bobs; old 45 rpm records; books and tapes that needed straightening up. They wouldn't eBay those – sentimental value. (Plus, nobody would want them.)

As he was up in the dark with his torch Derek came across a small pile of letters addressed to Dean. Being a copper, and hence a nosey fucker, he slid one of the letters out to have a read. He justified this to himself by claiming he needed to see if they were important and needed keeping. In reality he wanted to see if they were love letters or something – just as I say, a nosey fucker.

He read the letters in dis-belief – "Dear, Deano…" It was the letters from Myra that Dean had hidden secretly and never mentioned to anybody. They were written in green felt-tipped pen using a child's stencil kit so that the handwriting could not be recognised or analysed.

Derek wondered why Dean had never told anyone. He had put them up there on purpose as he knew Molly had no head for heights and wouldn't dare venture up there. Strange.

What should he do? Blow the whistle? Re-open the case? Why did Dean cover it up? – No! He needed to think things through as to what road to take and the implications to everybody. What would be the point of re-opening the case? Dean had done some 'bird' and by the time the police pulled their fingers out he would probably have been released anyway. What would be the point? Should he talk to Dean? If so, now, or when he gets out? If now it would be on the phone and his calls would be monitored and recorded so complications may arise. No, he'd wait.

"Your tea is ready," shouted Molly from the kitchen.

"Aye, hen," Derek shouted back. He shoved the letters in another hiding place, a little more secure, and went down to have some stovies, just like home.

March 1st 2011 and Valerie's phone call came through to give the bad news about Andrew Foster and the fact that his funeral was the following Thursday. Derek had spent the last week thinking of the letters that he'd found and was frustrated and guilty that he'd done nothing. He must do something.

The funeral came and Derek escorted his sister, helping her cope with the strange looks, silences, probing questions – she couldn't have done it on her own. For Derek it had provided a bit of relief from the routine he'd gotten himself into; his days just lately had revolved around taking Guinness and Gilbert for a long walk whilst constantly going over in his head the secret knowledge he had and what he should do with it.

At The Peacock, after the service, Derek met Valerie Forsyth, Penelope Foster (Andrew's wife), and many others who he instantly forgot.

One of the characters though, he didn't forget. "Molly, how are you?" It was Ernest Gerrity. Molly obviously didn't know the guy, but muggled through and he eventually introduced himself.

Gerrity was obviously pissed and asked about 'Deano' and how the 'old lag' was doing. He then went on to talk about Rose and the dogs. Derek listened with interest, the old copper's nose starting to twitch, mind starting to turn things over – 'Deano', Rose, the dogs. Mmm…

Molly couldn't stand Gerrity for too long so she made an excuse to mingle a little over at the bar. Derek stayed on to talk to Gerrity, much to Molly's surprise.

"Well, Ernest." Time for a few little 'fact finders' he thought. "How well do you know Dean?"

"Oh, fuck, Dekkers, we go back years. I've known Deano since the early '90s when we used to sell Citroens together."

"Oh, really!"

"Yes, we lost touch a bit, but you do don't you? I feel sorry that he's inside – it should never have happened."

"No?" prompted Derek.

"Definitely not," Gerrity went on. "He's not a prison sort of guy. The judge was an absolute fucking arsehole. He probably didn't get a shag that morning. It was probably early morning choir practice so the twat didn't get his pick of little boys," Derek laughed.

The next hour or so saw Derek practicing his covert interrogation technique. He'd spent a lot of time in this role going undercover whilst in the Fraud squad in Edinburgh. His task was to find out as much information as possible –build up trust, create empathy – the sympathetic vibration between two human beings – form a relationship. He was not sure where he was going with it or why he was doing it, just a feeling. He suspected Gerrity of something. He couldn't quite put his finger on it but things just didn't add up with this guy. But Derek would get to the bottom of it. He knew now that Dean and Molly had been the victims of a scam and he had an idea that Gerrity had had something to do with it. He would not let it go.

"Derek?" It was Molly shouting from the bar. "Are you ready?" Gerrity immediately started to protest trying to force another drink upon Derek. Derek resisted.

"Yes, that's me." He stood up to go. Gerrity shook his hand firmly, wishing him all the best, sending his regards to Guinness and Gilbert, then went on to give him an open invitation to join him for a pint at The George and Dragon sometime soon. Derek promised that he would, although Gerrity would probably not recognise him from Adam once the booze had worn off.

Derek and Molly said their 'goodbyes' and left. As they drove back Derek was filing, sorting and analysing the information he had gleaned from the slime ball. It seemed strange that the guy knew Guinness, Gilbert and Rose. What about this 'Deano' business? He would certainly pay a visit to The George and Dragon – try and unpick some loose end that may lead to something more interesting.

When they got back it was six-thirty p.m. and Molly had missed Dean's six p.m. phone call. She was not very happy but nipped over to Tesco to get a carton of milk. Two minutes after she left the phone rang. Derek answered – it was Dean. He explained that he'd left it until later as he didn't know what time they'd be back. He told Derek to tell Molly that he'd call again the same time tomorrow.

"Will do," Derek confirmed. "While you are on though, mate…Ernest Gerrity?"

"Oh, yes."

"How well do you know the twat?"

"Not that well," laughed Dean. "Just that you are right – he is a twat."

"You don't speak or meet up regularly?"

"No, not at all." A slight pause as Dean wondered why the questions. "Probably one phone call every month or so when he's got a customer. I never hold out much hope with his punters though as most of them are uncreditworthy, and those that qualify for a loan

237

usually end up not paying. Why, was he at the funeral? I know he worked with Andrew for a bit."

"Yes, he was. Did he know you had dogs?"

"I'm not sure." Dean thought it an odd question.

"If he did," continued Derek. "Do you think he would have known that they were called Guinness and Gilbert?"

"I don't think so." Dean paused to think. "No, I can't remember talking to him about the dogs, but I may be wrong."

"What about Rose?"

"What about her?" Dean was even more puzzled.

"Does he know her?"

"No, he's never met her." He explained. "Rose was born after I'd left Citroen. I lost touch with Ernest at that point for a number of years. He may well know I've got a daughter but I can't ever recall a conversation about her. Again, though, I may be wrong. When you talk to Ernest Gerrity the conversation usually revolves around Ernest Gerrity."

"I gathered that earlier," laughed Derek. "He seems a bit of a shark."

"Yes," confirmed Dean. "He's a bit of a crook really, always looking for a scam, a quick easy way to make money, legal or otherwise. I know of a few dodgy tricks that he's been up to, but other people always seem to be around to take the fall."

"Really?" Derek was really thinking now.

"Yes," replied Dean – he didn't realise the gravity of what he was saying.

"Well, cheers then, pal. I'll tell Molly you'll bell her tomorrow." Derek hung up.

Chapter 29

The Investigation

Derek had come to a decision. He had a theory that Ernest Gerrity was in some way involved in Dean's stitch-up. He was going to investigate. He had told the police in Edinburgh that he was no way ready to go back to work yet. He needed more rest and his doctor confirmed this. He actually had no intention of ever returning to duty.

His first port of call was The George and Dragon. Gerrity had told him he was a regular and had even invited him over at any time.

The Friday morning after the funeral, Derek had a drive over to Nottingham. He didn't want to go to The George and Dragon straight away in case Gerrity was there and recognised him. He wanted to gather a few props for the task in hand first – sunglasses, a dark wig, a tube of fake tan, a woolly hat and a light jacket with a pull up collar. It was still March and temperatures were just about low enough to get away with it. He also purchased a large mirror and a battery operated lamp so that he could adopt the disguise in the back of his Citroen van.

At four p.m. Derek walked into The George and Dragon at Fenton all dressed up. He ordered a pint of lager and went to sit in the window with a 'Sun'. He looked like a ground worker or gardener possibly – just dropped in for a 'quickie' before going home.

He didn't have to wait long before the beast known as Ernest Gerrity swaggered through the door, sat down and ordered a pint, talking very loudly to the bar staff. Great, Derek had got the right place. He didn't feel confident to approach Gerrity for fear of recognition, so he just waited and observed for a while.

Fifteen minutes passed and Gerrity ordered another pint. Then something happened that Derek had not expected.

"Ernest!" came a call from the door. "How the devil?" It was Paul Milford.

"Hi, Paul." Replied Gerrity. "Is Heather with you? What are you having?"

"Yes she is." Heather walked through the door. "The usual, please," she chirped.

Derek nearly choked on his drink. He knew that face from the photo that Molly had shown him in the paper – the lottery winner photo – he was also Dean's blackmail victim. Very distinctive ferret-like features – Paul Milford and yes, his wife, or whatever she was, was called Heather. How very interesting!

They got their drinks and took a seat on the table next to Derek. He hoped that the smell of fake tan wasn't too noticeable. Most of the conversation was about the usual bollocks, but even after six months, Dean's name was mentioned a couple of times.

Derek wondered if they had hatched a plot together to stitch up Dean, or whether Gerrity had operated on his own and formed a relationship with the couple to get information. Or, was Gerrity taking advantage of a long term relationship? Derek knew one thing for certain – he was going to find out the truth and act accordingly. His appetite had been whetted, and he was free from the restrictions that an official police investigation would involve.

He decided not to get Molly involved at all. To stop her getting suspicious of his investigations and asking difficult questions, he told her he'd taken a part time job collecting and delivering catalogue orders. He'd seen the job advertised somewhere and it seemed like the perfect cover. Molly swallowed it hook, line and sinker.

What he actually did was a lot of surveillance. He spent time at The George and Dragon in the same disguise, sometimes sitting on his own for hours without Gerrity or Milford turning up. He became a regular – he would keep himself to himself and always have a paper to read so that other unwanted regulars wouldn't try and join him. He would follow Milford, Gerrity, even Heather in the hope of discovering something to add to his 'file'. He was watching and waiting for a breakthrough.

Derek spent a lot of time at the library on the internet. He discovered about Gerrity's 'loose' and 'alleged' connections to the disabled VAT scam. He found out about the allegations that Milford had stolen a scratch card worth £250,000 from a painter and decorator that lived locally. This had never been proven but the alleged victim, Rocco Solatti, was most insistent that he had been robbed. What a fantastic source of information the internet was, especially as Derek was well practiced in its use and had access to sites not generally available to the public. Derek was convinced that Gerrity was involved and needed to be punished for his crime. His conscience, however, would not let him do anything until he had conclusive proof. The investigation continued.

June 3rd 2011, Friday night. For weeks Derek had been waiting for the right opportunity. He had heard Gerrity arrange a long weekend in Newcastle-upon-Tyne, his home city, with Milford, Heather and Stella. It was one of those cheap weekend breaks at a special rate for Friday and Saturday night, check out Sunday, with a free meal on the first night – all in for £89 per couple – bargain!

Derek basically needed to break into Stella and Ernest's house to try and find some evidence linking Gerrity to the letters. He had

241

picked up lots of co-incidental and circumstantial evidence but nothing conclusive.

The four left for Newcastle at four p.m., they would arrive at the hotel around seven p.m., plenty of VDT left. (Valuable Drinking Time.)

Derek left it until around eleven p.m., just in case they had to return for some unplanned reason. It was fully dark then and many of the neighbours were still out drinking. He'd told Molly he would be late as he was going out with one of the other couriers he had met in the Derbyshire area.

Being a copper he knew the dance when it came to security. You know the old 'set a thief to catch a thief' phrase. There was an alarm box the house above the bedroom window but no alarm. The double glazing was still the original wood that the house had had since 1996 when it was built by Barrett's Homes. This made it easy to enter. The back garden was enclosed and surrounded mainly by Lleylandi conifers that gave a fine shield from prying neighbours.

Derek parked around the corner and walked around to the front door of the house. Nobody was in housesitting. There was access to the rear garden via a path between the side of the house and next door's fence. He opened the gate, and closed it behind him. The only lock was a door bolt fixed close to the top of the six foot high wooden gate that just slid open. Derek had collected his information over the last couple of weeks.

He reached the rear of the house and stood in front of the original wooden French doors. It took a matter of seconds to insert the twelve inch screwdriver and prise the doors open, breaking the tiny lock without a problem. No alarm, nothing. Derek entered the house to have a rummage around.

After a couple of hours intensive searching he had not had much success downstairs. At around twelve-thirty a.m., he entered Stella and Ernest's bedroom. It was in the bedside cabinet that he hit the jackpot. In Gerrity's drawers, under the several Jack Higgins books, he found it; a stencil. It looked like the exact template of the writing on the letters he'd found and yes, upon close inspection, there was dried green felt tip pen around the edges of most letters – or at least it looked green in the dim light of his torch. He'd check that later. Further delving into the drawer revealed a note pad; the paper seemed to match that of the blackmailer's. Derek's heart was pumping, he felt ecstatic; at last something concrete. He would have his revenge, justice, and no fucking barristers or judges to stop him.

Derek removed the stencil and a sheet of paper and took great care to leave everything as he found it. He left back through the French doors, pulling them together. You could hardly notice the damage. He'd not left any fingerprints as he'd worn gloves, and had been careful not to dirty the carpets with his shoes. He wasn't sure how often Stella and Gerrity used the doors but he thought that they'd probably not notice the damage for days, if not weeks. He'd noticed a thin coat of dust around the seals that had collected over the past few weeks at least.

Derek left through the gate, locking it as he went, over the moon with his success. He felt like a celebration; thank God that the new licencing laws meant that he could get a half bottle from the 24 hour Tesco. He'd check the stencil and the paper more closely when he got back and if all matched, he would have a wee swallow and congratulate himself on a job well done.

Yes it was green felt tip pen on the stencil that matched the letters and yes it was an exact match on the paper. Splendid, he didn't have to even save it as evidence; he didn't have to prove anything to anybody to exact justice. He was the Judge, the jury and the executioner and he was perfectly happy who was the guilty party – the verdict had been ascertained. Now the questions were firstly the punishment of Gerrity and secondly, what should he do with Milford? Yes he was the victim but he was also an arsehole who'd laid it on thick with the Judge to get Dean the longest sentence he could, and he had robbed some poor fucker of £250,000. Alright, there was no absolute proof of this but still, fuck it, the guy is a prick, he'd put contractors out of business by refusing to pay bills on time. Surely there was enough circumstantial evidence to prove that the guy needed to be taught a lesson. Of course there was. 'Judge' Derek Rafferty decided 'guilty' was the verdict; he would decide the sentence whilst partaking of his half bottle of scotch. One hour later the plans had been set, Derek chuckled to himself as he looked forward to carrying out the punishment.

Chapter 30

Sentencing and Punishment

Over the next few weeks the plans were made and the sentencing date set; Saturday 6th August, Derek would be heading back up to Scotland, mission accomplished.

Firstly Paul Milford; Derek had decided to carry out Myra's 'stage 2'. Dean was still in prison and so no possible suspicion could fall on him. Molly was totally unaware at what Derek was up to. He was certain that Milford would not be keen to get the police involved both through fear and not wanting to get the old case brought up and the verdict put into question with no other suspects.

Derek bought an old second-hand laptop and a cheap printer. Whilst Molly was at work he printed off 2,000 posters, created by his own hand. He also used the Post Office post code finder to collect several hundred addresses of neighbours and local businesses close to Paul Milford's home. He spent hours driving around for street names near the house.

The letters and posters gave Milford's name, address, phone numbers, business details, and car details. There was the same accusations of sexual deviation and membership of paedophile and homosexual organisations as Myra had highlighted. All false but so what? That didn't matter. Once the letters and posters had been printed off the laptop and printer were dumped in the River Trent at midnight.

A week before the shit hit the fan, Derek visited a few pubs in the St. Anne's and Sneinton areas of Nottingham. Eventually he found a guy that could get a team of lads together, no questions asked, to put the posters through letter boxes and paste some onto walls, lamp posts and buses etc. He paid the guy £500, with a bit more due on completion. If any of the lads got caught they had no link to Derek – they didn't even know him – and they certainly wouldn't squeal on the guy who recruited them for fear of death. The stamps for the letters cost him £420. Everything was due to happen on the morning of Friday 22nd July.

During Derek's years in the Fraud Squad he had learnt a lot. It was quite easy for him to set up a numbered account, no names, at one of the secretive banks on an island in the Caribbean. He would get Milford to transfer £35,000 there and then move it through several other accounts leaving an extremely difficult track to follow. Accounts in the Caribbean and Switzerland were notoriously difficult to gain any information on, by anybody.

He set a limit of forty-eight hours after the letter hit, with a promise of 'stage 3' if Milford didn't play ball. Of course Derek wouldn't harm any of Milford's relatives and friends, but Milford didn't know that.

The letters were all posted and the posters distributed. The ball was now well and truly in Paul Milford's court.

Derek stayed at home for a couple of days to let things develop. He wasn't one hundred percent sure whether Milford would cough or not. He thought he may even go to the police, so he'd covered his tracks as much as he could.

Derek told Molly that he was not very well and sat at her house watching back episodes of 'Wire in the Blood', 'Waking the Dead', and 'A touch of Frost'. This lasted two days, he didn't move out of the house.

On the Tuesday 26th July he went out to post the letter giving the details of the account that Milford had to send the money to, with the presumption that it would arrive the following day.

On the Friday, the 29th July, Derek left the house once again. He needed to make a phone call from a public phone box to an overseas Caribbean number. The Caribbean was six hours behind so he left it until around four p.m. to call his bank for a balance enquiry on the numbered account. He gave the relevant passwords and account details required and was told that the balance in his account was £36,000 sterling. (He'd put £1,000 in to set up the account a couple of weeks ago.) "Thank you," he hung up.

For a few moments Derek stood in silence shocked and slightly stunned that the guy had done as he'd been told. As the reality settled in, 'stunned' was replaced gradually by 'overjoyed'. He was £35,000 richer. He could fulfil his dream. He'd planned, 'pie in the sky', what he was going to do with the money. He could now turn it into reality. Justice at last. The only thing he had to do now was to use his Fraud Squad knowledge to make the money 'disappear', just in case. Then it was Gerrity's turn.

Chapter 31

Gerrity's Turn

The following week, Friday 5th August, around eight p.m., Derek pulled into the car park of The George and Dragon. He noticed Gerrity's car at the back of the almost deserted car park, and put the van a few spaces away.

Derek waited. At his side, on the passenger seat, lay a brand new cricket bat. Derek put on his black leather gloves and gave the bat a final rub down with a jay cloth to remove any stray prints. He was very careful in everything he did. He knew, better than most, the power of forensic science.

Nine p.m. came, and shortly after Derek noticed a familiar figure staggering from the door of the lounge bar. It was Gerrity. Nobody else was around. He jumped out of the van and squatted down out of Gerrity's sight, behind the van. He had the cricket bat in hand.

As Gerrity approached the car, rummaging for his keys, Derek saw his opportunity. Still nobody about; perfect.

He took Gerrity's legs away just below the knee; he hit the floor like a felled tree. Derek punched him a couple of times then forced his face into the gravel and hog tied him with some industrial size tie-wraps, shoved a bag over his head and after dragging him across to the van, slung him in the back. He was squealing about wanting a piss. "Fuck that," Derek thought, "that's the least of your problems, pal."

Derek drove Gerrity up to the Derbyshire Dales; it took him about forty-five minutes to find a nice, quiet deserted spot. About half way his prisoner stopped bleating about wanting a piss. That was the point, Derek found out later, that he'd pissed himself and he would have to clean it up.

When he stopped it was Derek's plan to give him a good hiding, Scottish style. He dragged Gerrity through a farmer's gate and threw him into the bottom of a hedge, returning to the van to fetch the cricket bat.

Derek's body was pumped full of adrenaline. He was in a bit of a haze. He'd never really done anything like this before; this was not his side of the law. He thought about what he was about to do. How wrong was it? Then he thought of the letters, Dean in prison, Molly at home on her own. The guilty feelings subsided and hatred took over. The red mist returned. He smashed the bat into Gerrity; first one kneecap, then the other, screams pouring from his dribbling mouth, tears flowing down his cheeks. He pissed himself again. Derek was talking to him in a false upper class English accent. He couldn't remember afterwards what he'd said to him, but he knew he'd basically told him what a wanker he was and how he deserved everything he was getting. He'd lost control. He brought the bat down again and again until Gerrity passed out with pain, he only stopped briefly to take a photograph of him on his mobile phone. Derek then had a panic attack as the world stopped spinning and the red mist subsided – he realised that he'd brought the bat down on his back and may have caused a serious injury.

Derek ran back to the van, throwing the bat in the back – he'd have to clean the blood and piss out later. He drove off, not looking as the van raced off pulling out onto the main road. Fortunately for him, there was nothing coming.

Half a mile down the road he pulled over at a phone box. He was sweating and shaking as he called '999' from the public phone. He gave his name as Mr Smith and told the operator his location and that an ambulance was needed urgently. He then hung up the phone and drove on.

When he felt a safe distance away he stopped by a river. He hauled out the rubber mat in the back of the van and washed it thoroughly in the river water. The next part of the plan involved Paul Milford, or rather his car.

Derek drove into Fenton and parked about half a mile from Milford's house. It was now approaching midnight. He had stopped again on the way to have a coffee, calm down, and relax a little.

He walked to Milford's house. The car was parked on the road and he saw a light on in one of the back rooms. Paul and Heather were in.

Derek had a quick scan around. The guy walking the dog took a long look at him but soon lost interest as his dog had a shit and he had to scoop it up. When he'd gone Derek set to work with his permanent black marker on the Land Rover's nice shiny white bonnet. The message was a little ditty pointing out Ernest Gerrity as the receiver of Milford's £35,000 blackmail money. To make sure that they got the message Derek fastened a note to a half-brick with a rubber band. The note said 'have a look at your car ferret man' or words to that effect. He couldn't resist it.

Derek then slung the brick through Milford's front window – direct hit. He then sloped away back to his van and then home. All in all a successful evening. All had been done that needed to be done. All justice administered accordingly and efficiently with not one spillage of tax payers money. Time to go home. He did have a pang of guilt about hitting Gerrity so hard in his back. "Fuck it!" He thought. "You live by the sword; you die by the fucking sword, Mr Gerrity."

Derek went home to get some sleep – he had a long journey tomorrow.

Revenge

I am not an angry man
I'd even say I'm quite laid back
I live my life with too and fro
People fuck up, I give them slack

But if my friends or family
Get hurt by someone cruel
My temper snaps, my rage will build
My hatred boils like rocket fuel

I have to balance up the books
They must forever feel the pain
An eye for an eye, the Bible says
Don't fuck with me or mine again

Snakesbelly is a putrid scum
Evil and greed beyond compare
He's hit my family very hard
He's heading for a wheelchair

Was the Ferret part of it?
Does it really matter?
Many businesses went bust
Whilst he was getting fatter

He nicked some poor guy's ticket
And cost him quarter mill
He must not go unpunished
He needs a bitter pill

So fuck it, they will both get theirs
The police will do no good
They both must pay for their dark deeds
In money, pain or blood

The following morning Derek got up to give the news to Molly that he was going back up to Scotland. He apologised for the short notice but explained that there were things he needed to sort and Dean would be home soon anyway.

Molly made him some breakfast before going out to work. She'd loved having him down but had always known it was only short term. He'd decided never to go back to the police force and would keep in touch, letting her know what was going on in his life. She gave him a kiss on the forehead as she went off to work.

Derek finished his breakfast, washed, dried and put away the pots, and set off home in his little van. He wanted to be back before it got dark and you could never predict the traffic, there was always some road works or an overturned lorry. He'd enjoyed his time in England, he felt he'd served a purpose, fulfilled a role, and put a few wrongs, right.

He now had a plan for the future. In a few weeks he would call Molly, when Dean was out, to see if she wanted to be part of these plans. Six weeks should be long enough for all the fuss with Gerrity and Milford to die down. Perfect.

Six weeks flew. Derek and Molly were in weekly contact. Molly was getting more and more excited as Dean was closer to being released on a 'tag'. Derek told her of his plans for a mobile seafood bar. He got very passionate about it at times. "It'll be great!' He enthused. "Picture it, Molly. The posh bars around Edinburgh centre, late at night. Not like a burger van for the young pissed up scrotes, more for your better class of sophisticated reveller, our sort of age. Cockles, muscles, shrimp, lobster, crab. The healthy option, hen. Smoked trout salad rolls with horseradish, tuna fish, mackerel, it'll be great."

"I'm sure it will." Molly was happy for him. He seemed to have a new energy about him. And she hated the police force. "How much will it cost you to set up?"

"Not too much, hen. I've got a few quid savings and I might borrow a bit – I'm old enough to have a decent credit rating. Why don't you join me?" Derek was fishing.

"How do you mean?"

"Well, how would you like to do it in Nottingham? Plenty of rich Gliterazzi around the city centre late at night. I can see it, hen, I can see it. We would have a van in Edinburgh and one in Nottingham to start with. We could even expand and meet in the middle of the country."

"Yeah, right!" Molly didn't have much ambition, she was just interested in one thing at that moment; Dean getting out of prison.

"Well, hen, the offer is there. I'd help with the financing at the start."

"We'll see."

"Yes, hen, we'll see. Bear it in mind though. Eh?"

"Yes." Molly was happy working at Tesco but Derek had completed his objective – to sow the seed. After a little watering, feeding and general nurturing, who knows how well it would grow? Of course the funding was quite straightforward; with his savings, his small police pay-off and the £35,000 contribution by Paul Milford, he didn't have to borrow much to fully set up and stock two mobile seafood vans.

The following week Dean was out. Molly was ecstatic. Nothing could put a damper on this. Nothing, that is, but an internal memo from Tesco informing the staff that the Express store was moving location to two miles away, apparently something to do with the new tram system that was being put down in a couple of years. This meant that Molly would have to fuck about with buses every day. More

255

money and more time. Still, Dean was out and that made everything OK.

Dean started back to work and tried to get back into a routine. Molly was due to start in the new store in a few weeks and as the time approached she was getting less comfortable with it.

"The offer's still there, hen," said Derek. "I've done all the research. The licences and permits and stuff, I can sort easily. I've just started in Edinburgh and we're holding our own. Once word gets around things will start to rock."

"I'll talk to Dean."

"Fuck that, hen. Put the old git on; I'll fucking talk to Dean."

Molly put Dean on the phone. After an hour of conversation Dean put the phone down. To Molly's surprise, Dean was all for it. "You and Rose could work it," was one idea. "Rose's boyfriend could help – he's not got a proper job and can drive."

They talked and talked and the little seed started to grow and flourish. Molly began to get excited at the thought; she had never had her own business.

"Let's do it," she finally agreed. "Fuck the shop job, let's do it. I'll talk to Rose and Simon, see if they're up for it too." They were.

Chapter 32

The next year

What happened to all the players over the next year or so?

When Dean Muxlowe was released from prison in September 2011, Gerrity was in hospital recovering from his nasty 'kicking', Milford was fearing for his Director's health or more rather what effect it would have on him, and Hunter-Browne was operating as 'Hunter-Browne Specialist Cars,' having transferred all the shares in MHB to Molly and walking away, taking all of the company funds with him – he effectively 'raped' MHB Finance limited and left it for Mike and Bernie to pick up the pieces.

Molly had supported Dean one hundred percent of the way whilst he was in prison. She had made regular visits at massive inconvenience and lived on a shoestring to preserve the money reserve. When Dean came out and her job at Tesco changed location, she launched herself into business with Derek, her brother, and between them now they have four mobile seafood bars. Molly ran one in Nottingham and one in Derby. Derek ran one in Edinburgh and one in Kirkcaldy, in Fife. Ideas had blossomed and there were definite possibilities that the business would grow further.

Molly had the help of Rose and Simon to run one of the vans, and one of Simon's mates, Gash, with his girlfriend Sash, ran the other. Molly would supervise and do the odd shift once in a while.

The basic idea was to place the seafood bars in the city centres on a Thursday, Friday and Saturday night, later on to cater for the hungry pub-goers. This proved very successful. The menu included the small nibble-size snacks such as cockles, mussels, shrimps, crabsticks, seafood cocktail, crab and lobster pots. For people wanting a bit more than that a selection of tasty rolls were offered – smoked trout and horseradish, Tuna and garlic mayonnaise, crab salad, pilchard and tomato, tinned red salmon and cucumber. The odd 'special' was tried and tested and one of Molly's vans tried a small fryer to cook haddock and plaice in a very light batter, to be served on a buttered roll with mayonnaise or whatever. The bar was loved by the older drinkers who may have been taken back to their youth when the old 'shellfish man' came round to most pubs late at night.

As the potential was realised Derek and Molly started placing their bars alongside burger vans at open-air markets, country fairs, shows and even football grounds. It was marketed as healthy food and could be priced at a premium to a certain extent, so profit margins were huge. All the takings were cash also and so any extra casual staff could be paid out of that, illegally of course, to save tax and national insurance. It soon became the norm for most of the vans to be run most of the day, most days of the week.

Molly ran the operation from Nottingham, buying the seafood, ensuring that the vans were staffed and that the staff were honest (apart from skanking the taxman and benefits agency), controlling the hygiene standards and all the permits and licences were relevant. Again, with time she could see the need to start doing things properly and employing more people through the books. In short, Molly's Seafood Bars were booming.

Dean, when not seconded into a seafood bar, ran MHB Finance. James Hunter-Browne had obviously gone, never to be seen again, and given Dean his shares – although in actual fact they were all in Molly's name as he didn't want the ownership of a finance company having a recent blackmail conviction. He was employed by the company as a Sales Manager, Mike and Bernie being the Directors. What would he do if Molly fucked off? At a later date Dean found out that when Hunter-Browne had done his 'Lord Lucan' impression, he had also relieved MHB Finance Ltd of virtually all of its money – paying it to Hunter-Browne Specialist Cars as some sort of consultancy fee.

All of Dean's old customers, bar none, had returned and Mike and Bernie were working wonders on picking up new business.

In June 2012, the company bought a run-down old terraced house in Long Eaton at auction for £60,000. Dean, using his new found plumbing, carpentry and plastering skills from prison, helped Mike and Bernie refurbish it. They spent £15,000 in total and in August they sold it for £105,000 – a profit of £30,000. MHB Finance Ltd (Property Division) was born.

In general all was going well for the Muxlowe's; after such a traumatic spell they seemed to have turned a corner. There were the obvious problems that they had not considered whilst he was inside; problems like getting car insurance or household insurance as a criminal – the insurance companies use the fact to really hoist up the premiums.

James Hunter-Browne, after turning his back on Muxlowe and MHB Finance, pocketing a rather large pay-off, didn't fair too well. His business, Hunter-Browne Specialist Cars eventually went under after the stolen MHB money had run out.

The business itself was quite profitable whilst it lasted. Hunter-Browne himself was a very good salesman and would work hard in the search for cheap cars that he could make a good margin on.

The problem with the Hunter-Brownes was that they weren't shy of spending a few quid – as much and as quickly as possible, before they had it if they could. They even spent the taxman's bit. Their house was huge; A £545,000 barn conversion in the countryside, fully mortgaged. They'd bought the house just after the business had started (MHB) and Hunter-Browne had self-assessed his income at £150,000 per year – at that time you didn't need accounts and things to prove anything. The house was now worth about £350,000 and his mortgage was still £2,000 per month, interest only, so he still owed what he borrowed back in the 'boom'.

Michelle demanded a Land Rover Discovery or Range Rover to fit in with the neighbours. They also 'needed' the accessories – in-keeping décor, ride-on lawnmower, quad bike, ponies for the daughters, the list went on and on. James also bought a second-hand tractor to help regularly repair the mile long driveway from the road to the courtyard.

All of this was OK when the money was rolling in but all of a sudden if you have a slack month or, God forbid, the tax man might want a contribution to help run the country, or one of the ponies might need a vet, the pressure was turned up. As bills mounted up and Hunter-Browne ignored them for fear of having to tell his wife 'NO!' the end very soon became inevitable.

The conversation happened mid-June 2012. It was a typical sunny early evening when James arrived home. Michelle had been a little bit worried about him recently as he'd been a bit out of sorts. Distracted. Distant. Not wanting to talk. He'd even started snapping at Michelle, which was strange because he was usually too frightened.

She was in the back garden with the girls and the horses… sorry, the paddock.

"We need to talk," called James – no smile, no 'hello', just 'we need to talk.'

"What's up?" Michelle was worried.

"Basically, we are fucked." He couldn't look Michelle in the eyes.

"Fucked?" She looked puzzled.

"Yes, fucked."

"Oh?" Michelle fell silent waiting for clarification and explanation.

"Basically," James continued as a lump was forming in his throat and his eyes started to water, "basically I've tried everywhere and I can't borrow any more money."

"What do you need to borrow more money for?" Michelle was oblivious to the real situation here.

"We owe the tax man £10,000 and have got to pay it now. I've not paid instalments on our cars for the past three months and the finance companies are threatening to take them back. The mortgage is due and I've not got the money to pay it. Work is shit – I've got more people screaming that their cars have problems and I need to sort it or they're going to trading standards, which if they do I'll be fucked because I've set finance up for them and don't have a Consumer Credit Licence – I've told everybody I have, but I haven't. I'm at a loss." He burst into tears.

Rather than put her arm around her husband and comfort him, she stood still, silent and stunned. Eventually she woke up and spoke up. "Why don't you sell our cars?"

"Because they're not worth anywhere near what we owe on them," he bawled. Basically he'd originally over-financed the cars, borrowing more on them than they were worth – lying about the model and mileage to make them look, on paper, worth more. This gave him extra money to pay his mortgage. As a result they were in massive negative equity so even if he could sell them he wouldn't be able to settle off the loans and the cars would still show on the HPI register as having outstanding finance. Michelle had not known and didn't understand.

"What about the house?" Michelle's voice was starting to fill with panic.

"We borrowed £500,000 on it, interest only, when the house prices were high, hence we still owe £500,000 on it. The fucking thing is now worth about £350,000 if anybody wants it. We are fucked. Do you understand yet?"

Michelle remained silent. James sat with his head in his hands. The girls stopped playing and ran over to mummy to see what was happening.

"Come and get ready, girls," said Michelle. "We are off to see your gran."

"What!" James looked up, his eyes now bright red.

"We're going to my mother's. I'm not having all this stress. I can't cope with this – you'll have to sort it. Come on, girls." She grabbed their hands and led them to the house to pack their things. The girls sensed that something bad was happening and started to cry.

Thirty minutes later they were pulling out of the courtyard onto the mile long drive to the main road. James did not move. He did not protest or argue. He sat there for what seemed like hours in a deep depression, contemplating suicide. It sounded good. Fortunately he was strong; he was going to have to be.

Over the next few months the house was re-possessed, the cars went, the ponies, everything went. Michelle stayed with her mother and filed for divorce.

James went to his mother's. He was originally from Fulwood, a tiny village near Oxford, and his mother still lived down there. She managed to get him a job with the local farm – £150 per week – slave labour really but the benefits were incomparable; working in the open air, being told what to do, no responsibility, no mortgage, no ride-on lawnmower or quad bike, no ponies to feed, no taxman breathing down your neck and no fucking wife and kids squawking at you all day – bliss!. For the first time in years he could sit down at night, after a hard day's work, with a can or two of beer and relax. 'Relax' – he'd almost forgotten the meaning of the word. There's a lot to be said for bankruptcy.

Ernest Gerrity was in hospital until November 2011 – three and a half months in total. The doctors had finally come to the conclusion that he would never walk again and had fitted him out with an electric wheelchair – an all-singing, all-dancing model that some victims of crime charity had helped pay for. He could still move his upper body, arms and head.

Initially he was very bitter and twisted out of shape about the beating. Nobody had been caught. He had one or two suspicions but nothing concrete. To be honest it could have been one of many people he'd upset in the past.

On the good side, Stella had stuck by him and was prepared to nurse him for the rest of his life. He was the first to admit that he'd never really appreciated what a fantastic, devoted person she was. He'd often thought of her as merely a place to live. He now looked upon her quite differently. In seeing the love that she showed him, he realised how much he truly had come to love her. They eventually married.

When he left hospital he got a visit from an old acquaintance. He'd met Joe Conliffe when he was operating his VAT scam on cars for the disabled. Joe had a business that fitted hand controls and accessories for the disabled drivers – wheelchair ramps and lifts and the like. His business was completely legitimate and quite a good earner. He'd branched into selling these little scooters that disabled people used, and needed someone to front his selling operation. It was only a small shop front that he'd got but he was sure that Gerrity would do well as he was a fantastic salesman and could now fully relate to the punters.

Gerrity appreciated and accepted the generous offer, starting just before Christmas 2011. He was an immediate success. He employed a junior; a nineteen-year-old able bodied lad to do any running around, but he would deal with nearly all of the customers and did put the hours in.

When the customer came in for a look they would generally end up buying. He sold them into lifts and ramps and trailers to transport the scooters he supplied. He had a deal with the local motor dealers to refer his customers to them to buy new cars on the Motability three year contract hire scheme. He even got a line of specialist clothing and accessories for the scooter drivers – convincing them that leather jackets, expensive boots, rear view mirrors and iPod music systems were essential for the safety and enjoyment of the mobility scooter rider.

As the range of scooters increased and the customers flooded in, more staff were added and new, bigger premises found. The new shop layout was designed by Gerrity and all staff trained by him. All this in a period of nine months.

Gerrity himself felt fantastic. He'd found true love and devotion in Stella, and true peace in himself doing something worthwhile, challenging and legal. He almost forgot he was disabled at times and sometimes thought that his condition had saved him, given him a new lease of life, a new energy. Who knows, in time he might even become a partner with Joe Conliffe in the business.

Gerrity's Salvation

I hate myself for what I've done
I've always taken things I need
I've ruined people, wrecked their lives
Through thoughtlessness, selfishness and greed

Someone decided, I need taught
Just how the heartache feels
With cricket bat and steel cap boots
He swapped my legs for wheels

Now I can't walk, I think much more
I've learnt to live as what you see
Appreciate the things I have
Try to forget what used to be

My future's bright, I've been reborn,
My knackered legs have proved a gift
I've even Stella by my side
To stop me if I start to drift

Paul Milford, the Ferret, became the Managing Director, and in fact sole Director, of Milford Park when Fairchild gave up in September 2011. He died shortly after of his cancer. If truth be known Milford should have set on a replacement but, with the backing of Heather, decided to do it himself. He very quickly realised that the job wasn't going to be an easy one.

Milford Park had succeeded by under-paying, or refusing to pay completely, sub-contractors. They would find fault in their job, implement big penalty clauses and generally fuck over the 'little man' with the help of their lawyers. Fairchild was impervious to the threats from these 'little men' as he had friends in the 'security business' that would, if necessary, persuade them not to use such threats. These 'security' guys were basically the local thugs who would put fear into the hearts of the victims. Many small businesses had gone bust in such a way. If they were found to be bad-mouthing Milford Park, Fairchild would arrange a visit to make them stop.

These thugs were no friends of Paul Milford and didn't really want anything to do with him. They thought of him as a bit of a joke figure. Very soon sub-contractors were turning up to confront Milford at his premises and invariably getting their just pay. In fact word soon got round and even the ones that were doing a shit job were getting paid by threatening to do Milford personal damage if they didn't.

Business dried up because Milford Park became unreliable as both a contractor and an employer. Every month losses started to mount up, the banks arses started to twitch like a rabbit's nose, and Paul Milford had to rely on what was left of his lottery scratch card fund to help keep the company afloat. He should have just ditched it but pride would not allow it. What would he tell his 'friends' down at The George and Dragon.

By January 2012 the company had gone into liquidation. The staff had been laid off and the premises put up for sale. Milford had to sell his house. After having re-mortgaged it several times he had very little equity left. Just enough, in fact, to get a small two-bedroomed ex-council house on the 'dark-side' of Fenton – the side that the George and Dragon crew would never even admit as being part of Fenton.

Through one of his company's old contacts he was given a job laying bricks for a wage. He got the impression that the job was given not out of friendship or loyalty, not even pity, but more a perverted sense of satisfaction that the owner had, to employ the once mighty Paul Milford. "Go and put the kettle on, Paul. Two sugars, duck."

All the big flash cars had long gone. No more Land Rovers and a Mercedes-Benz for the Mrs. No, an old Transit 200 Connect. No need for a car for Heather; she fucked off once the money ran out. The last Paul heard was that she'd shacked up with one of the old crew from The George and Dragon – she'd probably been shagging the guy while she was with Paul. Paul didn't find much out – he didn't go there anymore.

Gone

I've lost it all, the life I had
I thought forever, good times last
I cannot fully understand
How things all changed so very fast.

No Range Rover, No Rolex watch
No meals at Chateau Martin
My girlfriend Heather soon fucked off
I even miss her farting

It's not fair, what went so wrong
I'm sitting here alone and cold
There's nothing in my world no more
I feel so grey and very old

Do I want to hang around?
Is there something left for me?
No friends, no family, no light, no love
Death, at least, would set me free.

Chapter 33

The George and Dragon Meeting

The 6th November 2012, a miserable Tuesday morning. It was cold, wet and windy. At eight a.m. Paul Milford got the call that he wouldn't be working today as the weather was too bad. He couldn't decide in his head whether he was angry because he wouldn't be earning any money, or happy because he didn't have to get off his arse and go to work. He started analysing himself. He wondered if he was turning into a lazy bastard. He was arguing with himself about the fact, trying to justify not getting another job that didn't need good weather. At over sixty years of age what the fuck could he do?

He thought he was going mad – arguing with himself! Loneliness was affecting Paul Milford in a big way. He didn't go out anymore, he had no partner after Heather left, no business, and when he did go to work he didn't mix very well, kept himself to himself. All the other workers on site knew who he was and where he'd come from, so looked upon him with a lot of contempt. A lot of piss taking and animosity surrounded Paul Milford. Some of his colleagues had even worked for companies that Milford Park had sent under. Paul was not a happy person. Maybe another reason, in his mind, for feeling happy at not having to go to work – a bit like when little kids are bullied at school pretending to be sick.

Mind arguments over, the consensus of the parties was always the same in such situations. Something that he could agree with himself on. After getting washed and dressed he'd clean around the toilet and shower, make the bed, wash the pots from the night before and generally tidy up the living room. That's Mr Guilt satisfied. What a feeling of well-being. He then decided that he deserved a sit down and relax. He would even subconsciously wipe away non-existent sweat from his forehead.

The TV would go on – a full day of Jeremy Kyle, home buying and selling and repairing programs, old Batman, Minder, The Fall Guy and The Sweeney. Fantastic! It was nine-thirty a.m., time for a little drinkies. He thought he should really have something to eat before drinking so to keep Mr Guilt happy again, he chewed on a Tesco own brand cereal bar and a half eaten bag of pork scratchings.

Paul's fridge was always well stocked with cheap booze. For such occasions he had a large plastic beaker – you know, the sort that you get Coca Cola in at a theme park, the ones that hold about three quarters of a litre of fluid with a secure top and a straw. He'd try to convince himself that if he didn't drink spirits but stuck to beer, he was not an alcoholic, even though it was still early morning.

Into the beaker would go a fifty-fifty mix cocktail of White Lightning strong white cider (eight percent abv) and Kestrel Super Strength lager (nine and a half percent abv). This was Paul's version of 'Snakebite', something he used to drink as a youngster at the local pubs. This particular concoction though, looked like thick syrupy fuel topped with some sort of industrial effluent. The flavour was a unique acquired taste. The strong alcohol was obvious as it slipped down his throat. The sweet sharpness of the apples in the cider mingled beautifully with the fiery strength of the Kestrel. The taste stuck to his mouth and teeth. The effect was instant – he could feel the escape warming through his body as the drink hit the spot. He would usually put the top on the beaker and drink it through the bendy straw. As he sat down in his favourite chair, Jeremy Kyle was just starting. In less than a couple of hours he would be completely comatose. Oblivion for less than seven quid.

He'd have put all his problems right, made all sorts of plans, figured out how to regain his status in life and earn a million pounds – he would have also chosen the colour and spec of his new Lamborghini. He would then fall asleep, drop what was left of his drink (hopefully the lid would minimise the amount that escaped onto his lap), and forget everything. By mid-afternoon, he would wake up in a fuzzy haze and wonder where the day had gone. Jeremy Kyle would still be on the TV and his (Paul's not Jeremy's) pants would be wet.

Ding Dong. It was the doorbell. Paul had only taken one sip. "Shit," he sighed under his breath. He lifted himself out of the chair and ambled to the door with all the effort of someone who'd just finished a twelve hour shift, and was annoyed at not being allowed to take a well-deserved rest.

"Good morning." It was the 'oh so cheerful' postman. "Just a letter for you, whoever sent it didn't put a stamp on it so you'll have to pay the postage – sorry."

"Wankers," said Paul. "Still, I'd better pay it; it does say 'urgent' on the front." The postman just smiled. Paul handed him some change and shut the door. Back to the booze and 'Jezza.'

After a couple more swallows he sat back and opened the letter. He had no idea who it could be from. He read it with confusion and a little fear as the alcohol was coursing through his blood stream.

"Dear, Paul, you don't know me but I know you. I have some information that I know you will be very interested in.

"I would like you to go to The George and Dragon pub in Fenton, I know that you know it; I've seen you there in the past.

"Please be there on Friday night, the 9th of November 2012 at eight p.m. Please come on your own – you will be quite safe. Don't be late and don't be early.

"You will not be disappointed. A lot of questions about past events will be answered.

"When you see George, the landlord as you know, he will have something for you to look at. He will also get you a pint of lager – don't worry it will be paid for. Your old table in the corner will be available, go over and take a seat.

"All the best, A Friend."

Paul took another pull on the straw, a frown across his face. Did he want to delve into the past? What would turn up? Was he interested? Intrigued, maybe? Was it to do with Milford Park? Or Heather? The stolen scratch card? Myra? Something else?

Yes. Of course he would go; you don't get a carrot like that dangled and keep it hanging. He had no risk; George would be there and at eight p.m. on a Friday night there would be quite a few people knocking about, even at this time of year. And a free pint; yes he would go. He took another pull on the straw.

Paul put the letter down and concentrated on the TV; 'Jezza' was just about to read out the DNA results.

November 2012 was shaping up to be a good month for Ernest Gerrity. He'd got some good staff that were learning fast and sales were going from strength to strength. Every morning he would look forward to the new day. He felt better now than he ever had, even better than when he was making big money out of the VAT scam on the new disability cars. He always knew that would end, but this new business had no limits.

Even the cold, wind and rain on the first Tuesday morning in November 2012 could not dampen his spirits. He never opened the shop too early as the punters typically didn't get out of bed until mid-morning. He'd rather open up at eleven a.m. and stay open until eight p.m.

This particular morning at nine-forty-five a.m. he was sitting at the kitchen table having his breakfast as the doorbell went. Stella had already gone to work so Gerrity had to manoeuvre chair along the hallway to answer the door. He was just in time; the postman was turning to walk away. He looked back and seeing Gerrity in a wheelchair, apologised. "Sorry, mate, just a letter for you, the sender hasn't put a stamp on it." Had Gerrity not been in a wheelchair the postman would probably have come out with some acidic little comment for being kept waiting.

"That's good of them." Gerrity smiled, surprising the postman. Most customers would be annoyed at being put out; not this one. He counted out the required fee and took the letter.

"Cheers, mate," the postman called as he left, "and have a nice day."

"And, you," replied Gerrity. He closed the door and took the letter through to the kitchen so he could finish his breakfast. He'd made himself a couple of sausage and egg cobs as a treat. Stella would dis-approve as she had put him on a strict lifestyle regime – good food, regular exercise and less alcohol. She was convinced that this was helping him succeed in his life by giving him much more energy. He didn't argue, something was working well.

Stella let him have the odd glass of wine and pint of lager, but not too much. He didn't miss it and it was a pain for him to scoot off for a piss every five minutes anyway.

Gerrity opened the kitchen window to try and get rid of the smell of the cooking before he left for work. He washed the pots and wiped the cooker to remove as much evidence as possible, and put the opened box of porridge on the worktop. He was risking a bollocking for leaving the porridge out but it may make her think he'd had something a little more healthy for his breakfast. It was a long shot but it just might work.

Whilst waiting for the smell of the cooking to dissipate he opened the letter.

"Dear, Ernest," it began. "I hope that you and Stella are well and business is good.

"You do not know who I am but I have something that you will be very interested in. I would like you to go to The George and Dragon at eight p.m. on Friday 9th November. Please do not be late, but don't be too early, and come on your own.

"When you get there get a drink off George, it will be paid for, and take a seat at the table in the corner. George will have reserved it for you and all will become clear.

"Don't go in and quiz George before this date as he won't know anything and it'd only ruin the surprise. I can assure you you'll be completely safe.

"All the best, Ernest, my regards to Stella, A Friend."

"Mmm…" Ernest was puzzled. He couldn't not go because he might benefit. And there was no chance of getting battered like once when he went to The George and Dragon. He would be parked bang outside the front door in the disabled parking spaces, and at eight p.m. it should be quite busy. And of course, George would be there. Yes he would go.

But now he had to get to work. The house had been furnished with all sorts of disability aids and gadgets; his car was state of the art. He could lock the front door and set the alarm by remote control (Stella had insisted on an alarm when Ernest had got out of hospital last year as she'd found one of the French doors looking like someone had forced it open. Nothing seemed to be missing and nothing was disturbed, but it was better to be safe than sorry, especially now that Ernest was in a wheelchair. Recently though, it was usually left off as the novelty value had gone.)

The driver's door of his Vauxhall Astra swung open and he pulled himself in. The seats were leather that helped him slide into position. It was fitted with full hand controls to operate the brakes and accelerator. On the roof of the car he had a box for his chair.

Ernest had three wheelchairs. The first was a top of the range electric model that he used at home and, if going out with Stella, could be transported on a trailer. He would climb in the car and Stella would load it up. When he was going to work on his own he used a manual fold up chair that was lifted, when collapsed, by an electric hoist up to the box on the roof of his Astra. All very neat. The chair would fold and unfold very easily with the use of a small clasp. When he got to work he would unload the chair electrically, unfold the chair with the use of the same clasp, and roll off the leather seat into the chair. After getting into the showroom he would have his third chair waiting. Again electric, this one had all the gadgets available to show to the punters, a little like a car salesman would have a company demonstrator.

Gerrity felt terrific as he entered the building. It was large, clean and modern with the unmistakeable aroma of real coffee. On show was a huge display of scooters, wheelchairs, trailers, aids and accessories. He never ceased to feel proud as he surveyed his own work. The staff all greeted him with a smile, and he always smiled back.

The only difference today was a niggling little irritation at the back of his mind. "What the fuck can this meeting at The George and Dragon be about?"

That same miserable Tuesday morning, Dean Muxlowe had put some time aside to renew some copper piping in a run-down old semi-detached in Sandiacre that MHB had bought to either sell or rent out.

At nine-thirty a.m. he was on his front drive, loading the hired van up with tools and materials he had been storing in the garage, attached to the front of his house.

"Morning," called the postman, as Dean was searching for the blow lamp.

"Morning," Dean walked out to greet him.

"Just one today," he said, handing Dean the letter. "And I'm afraid you owe me £1.46 because the sender hasn't put a stamp on it."

"How much? A stamp is only 46p."

"Yes indeed," countered the postman. "But there is a one pound handling charge." The postman was obviously embarrassed.

"No problem," Dean smiled and handed him the fee, tucking the letter in his pocket. Relieved, the postman smiled and left.

Thirty minutes later Dean had finished the loading and went back into the kitchen to collect the new house keys. He dried his rain wet hair and remembered the letter he had tucked away. There was no rush so, being quite curios, he decided to have a look now.

Dear, Dean, I hope you and Molly are well and business is good." Dean's curiosity grew.

"I want you to go on Friday 9th November at eight-fifteen p.m. to the George and Dragon in Fenton. Come on your own and don't be late, but also don't be early.

"The landlord is called George, he will give you a drink, an envelope and show you to a table in the corner that I have reserved. He knows nothing of the business that I have with you.

"There is absolutely no need to fear anything. You will only be in there for a short period of time and I know that you will find it very interesting and beneficial.

"All the best, A Friend."

Again puzzlement and curiosity crossed Dean's mind, but didn't want to lose too much time; he wanted to get the job done by four p.m. as there was no electricity supply to the house and that is when it would be too dark to work. He put the letter back in the envelope, folded it and put it in the cupboard. He'd have another look that night. He'd have to think about whether he'd show it to Molly or not. He stopped on his way out, went back to the cupboard and retrieved the letter, put it in his pocket and left, locking the door as he did so.

As he cut and bent the pipes, fluxed and soldered the joints, he kept turning over in his mind what the mysterious letter could be all about. He really didn't have a clue. He really did want to go and find out but what would he tell Molly? How would he explain going out on his own on a Friday night for a couple of hours on his own? She may be working on one of her seafood bars, or she may not. Either way, she'd want to know what he was up to and she always knew when he was lying. And if she thought he was lying, she would automatically think that he was meeting some other woman. He'd have to come up with something because the more he thought, the more he needed to know what was going on.

That afternoon, after he'd finished the plumbing, he got home at four-thirty p.m. It was dark. Molly was in making Mexican chicken fillets, new potatoes, olives, sun-kissed tomatoes, jalapeno peppers, sour cream and salsa. "Hi, sugar puff," she giggled as he walked in. She was allowed to use that nick name in private but never in public.

"Ayup, babe," he smiled, gave her a kiss. "That looks good."

"Yes, and its ready so go and get changed and wash your hands, they are filthy." The copper and flux had turned his fingers black and there was that strong metallic smell."

"OK." He started to wash his hands with Fairy Liquid.

"Don't fucking splash that salad," she squawked as Dean scrubbed his hands.

"No, of course not." He thought he'd strike whilst the iron was hot. "Babe, Friday the ninth, this Friday, have you got any plans?" Molly thought for a few seconds.

"Yes, I'm going to Rachel's." Rachel was one of her mates from the old shop work. "She's having some sort of underwear party. I won't buy anything, just an excuse for a bevvy really."

"Oh, aren't you working?"

"No," she replied. "Rose and Simon have got the van covered. Gash is helping them as the other one is in for service; it's the only time we could get it in so we'll have to do it, it's overdue and the next available spot is not for three weeks. It means a lost night of sales but that can't be helped. It's got to be there Friday night so that he can do it first thing Saturday morning, so we've got it back for a show on Sunday.

"Oh."

"Why?" she asked.

"Oh, I was just wondering. I was going to nip out for a swift pint with Eddie who I used to work with. I've not seen him for ages." Dean then cupped his hands, filled them with water and covered his face as if washing it. A hope that it would cover up his lying eyes."

"No problem," chirped Molly. "Just watch that fucking salad. Look, you've splashed it, now dry your hands and fuck off while I put it out on a plate." Dean did what he was told, scurrying into the living room to switch on the TV and await further instructions.

"That was easy," he thought, a satisfied grin on his face as the TV warmed up. "Fuck, me! Not Jeremy Kyle again!"

Chapter 34

Friday 9th November

Seven-fifty-five p.m.; George Popodopolis stood at the bar of The George and Dragon, making himself busy drying and polishing some glasses. He hadn't named the pub, the 'George' bit being entirely co-incidental (so was the 'Dragon' bit, he would tell his wife.) He was the manager employed by the brewery and had been resident now for four years.

It was surprisingly quiet tonight, especially being a Friday, just a few kids meeting up before getting a taxi or bus into town, or the odd older couple grabbing a quick scampi and chips before getting a bottle of wine from Tesco Express to take home and watch TV.

The pub trade was not as it used to be, George reflected. The smoking ban and high prices coupled with the recession, had hit hard. Even the pensioners were suffering from low interest rates on their savings; it made them even more careful, watching every penny. George couldn't remember the last time he'd heard the old 'one for yourself, mate'. Many people didn't even eat out now. By staying in they could get drunk on cheap wine and supermarket spirits, have a take-away delivered, smoke when they want, drop to sleep if they want and watch what they want on TV. No rip-off taxis or queuing in the rain at a bus stop. All this and still have change from £20. Yes, the pub trade was hard at the moment. Many of George's fellow landlords had fallen by the wayside, and many traditionally busy pubs were lying empty, boarded up; once happy and warm, now cold and lonely. Sad really – what would they become?

As George gazed out of the front window he noticed the Astra pull up with the fancy, but rather ugly, battleship grey glass fibre roof box. He watched as the box opened and the clever electronically operated automatic hoist lowered down a folded wheelchair, positioning it perfectly beside the now opened driver's door. A hand emerged to push a button on the chair and it popped open. George, of course, knew that this was the arrival of Ernest Gerrity. Even he and his cronies didn't come in much these days. There was a time when four or five of them would sit around from four p.m. until eight or nine p.m. nearly every night, the old 'five and drive crew'. George should probably not have served them as he knew their cars sat outside, but without them the place would have probably gone under before now.

He didn't know if it had been Gerrity's beating that had put paid to it or what? He had seemed to be the 'leader', the 'life and soul', certainly the loudest. After he was condemned to a wheelchair everybody seemed to lose interest.

George was expecting Gerrity. Earlier that day he had received a special delivery parcel – one of these 'guaranteed' things that needed signing for. It contained three large sealed envelopes with a set of instructions. The envelopes each had a name stencilled on the front; 'Ernest Gerrity', 'Paul Milford' and 'Dean Muxlowe'. He obviously knew Gerrity and Milford, and Muxlowe's name seemed familiar but he couldn't place the face.

Also in the package, attached to the implicit instructions, was a new £50 note, as part payment to carry out the said instructions. There was a promise of another £50 if the task was carried out to the sender's satisfaction. It was meant to be a night off for George but the £100 incentive and the added bonus of not having to pay a member of staff on a Friday night, and of course the pure curiosity of the situation, forced him to be there.

Ernest Gerrity struggled up the disabled access ramp to the pub lounge in the manual wheelchair. "Evening, George," he called as he approached the bar.

"Hi, Ernest, how are you? You're looking well."

"Yes, fine," Ernest lied. "I understand that you have something for me."

"Yes, mate," replied George. "All very mysterious, any ideas?"

"Not a fucking clue."

"Well, I have strict instructions from a mystery man...... or woman of course – the letter that I got this morning was not signed.

"Mmm..." Gerrity frowned.

"Firstly a drink though; the usual pint of lager?"

"Yes, fine," answered Gerrity.

George poured the pint, remaining silent. Part of the instructions was not to tell the three of them who else would be in attendance. It would all become clear though.

"OK, Ernest. Let's have a table over here." George picked up the pint and envelope walking over to the reserved table in the corner. Gerrity followed.

"What's this?" Gerrity was referring to the envelope.

"Fuck knows," answered George. "I've been told that you can't open it until the others arrive or everything will be ruined." He was also thinking of his extra fifty quid.

"What others?" Gerrity had thought it was going to be a lone meeting with a mystery man.

"Can't say," said George. "But they'll be here very soon, so not long to wait. Should I hold on to this until the others get here?"

"No, no." Gerrity snatched up the envelope and pulled it close to his chest. "I'll not open it, I promise."

"Fine, Ernest, I'll see you shortly." George sauntered back to the bar to take up his original position. As he did so a white Transit Connect pulled up beside Gerrity's Astra and Paul Milford climbed out. "For fuck's sake," thought George. "It's a Friday night and he's still in his works clothes, hair all flat to his head where he'd obviously had a tight fitting hat on through the day, and no shave for probably three days." George also noticed a slight stumble as he walked through the lounge door. The slightly glazed eyes and vacant smile gave a suspicion that Milford had already had a swift libation, probably to give himself a bit of 'Dutch courage'.

"Long time, no see," chirped George as he leaned on the bar. Gerrity looked across, a frown still on his face

"Yes," grunted Milford. "I've been quite busy recently – no time for socialising."

"Heather still comes in quite a lot." George couldn't resist the dig, remembering the good old days when everybody took the piss out of Paul Milford. Was that a hint of a smile briefly crossing his face as he poured Milford a pint?

"Yes, I know. I don't see much of her these days – her loss. You got something for me, George?"

"Indeed, I have." George finished pouring the pint and picked up the large brown envelope with his name on it. "Follow me." And headed over to the table in the corner that Gerrity was sitting at. Milford looked surprised and shocked. He'd never officially fallen out with Gerrity, but after his beating and period of time in hospital, and the message scribbled on his Lamd Rover's bonnet, they had never really talked. There were a lot of unanswered questions between the two of them. It was a rather uncomfortable situation.

"Hi, Ernest." Milford tried to smile as warmly as his panic would allow.

"Paul, how are you?" Gerrity didn't return the smile – he was still frowning. Thinking.

"Fine." The look on Gerrity's face didn't really prompt any further comment from Milford.

"Have a seat, Paul." George pulled up a chair for him to sit on. "Here's your envelope – don't open it until the other guy arrives." He put the lager down and turned to walk to the bar.

"Who…?" Milford began.

"Don't ask, I can't tell you," George called over his shoulder. "He won't be long."

"Any ideas?" Milford turned to Gerrity.

"No," replied Gerrity. "We'll soon find out though. What have you been up to then? I heard that Milford Park went 'bang' and that you're back on the bricks."

The estranged friends spent the next ten minutes catching up with the last year or so. Gerrity couldn't help gloating about his success and achievements, Milford lying about his. They were both very cagey, not mentioning the events of the summer of 2010. The 'big elephant' in the room. They weren't really listening to what each other were saying, they were both too busy concentrating on what they were saying and what was about to happen. Who was the third man? How did everything fit?

Eight-ten p.m. and Dean Muxlowe strode into the lounge of The George and Dragon. He surveyed the room for someone that he maybe recognised. His heart did a flip as he saw, sitting in the corner, an old work colleague, Ernest Gerrity, who he'd heard was in a wheelchair now, and with him, would you believe it, the unmistakable ferret-like features of Paul Milford, his blackmail victim.

Milford was looking directly at Muxlowe, face of stone. Muxlowe was close to turning around and walking out. Gerrity's frown had grown and his look of puzzlement was even deeper.

"Mr Muxlowe?" The landlord was calling Dean from behind the bar. He snapped out of his trance.

"Yes?"

"I have something for you." He looked down as he started to pour a pint of lager. "Lager OK?"

"Yes, fine."

"Are you gentlemen ready for another yet?" George called over to the table in the corner.

"No, not yet," replied Gerrity, not bothering to ask Milford's opinion.

Muxlowe approached the bar, he could feel Milford's hateful glare stabbing into his back. George smiled as he approached. "Evening, mate. OK?"

"Yes, fine." Muxlowe seemed in another world, his mind racing, wondering what the fuck was going on. He didn't even think that he was still on licence and that part of the licence conditions were that he could have no contact directly, or indirectly with Paul Milford. Breach of licence could mean going back to prison for a few months.

"This way, Mr Muxlowe." George was off, clutching the drink and a brown envelope, heading towards the table in the corner. "Have a seat."

Dean reluctantly walked over to the table where George was offering him a chair. Every step was a trauma, as the three pairs of eyes scrutinised his every moment. He sat down at the table. "This is for you." He put the pint down and handed the envelope over. "You are all now present and can open your packs." George left them to it. He didn't want to as he was bursting with curiosity, but if he didn't follow instructions he wouldn't get his fifty quid extra.

Paul Milford remained silent, only now did his ferret eyes move from Muxlowe to the envelope. Gerrity felt like the forced mediator. "Well, chaps, let's put past events behind us for a while until we find out what this is all about." He started to break the seal of his own pack. Milford grunted and did the same. Muxlowe, still in a bit of a daze, followed suit. George stood behind the bar looking on with interest.

Gerrity was the first to get his envelope opened. It was an A4, about a quarter of an inch thick, sealed with Sellotape. The envelope contained a number of things. He turned away from the other two so they couldn't see what he was taking out, not that they were looking; they were too busy with their own envelopes.

The first thing he took out was a stencil, many of the letters of which were stained around the edges with green marker pen. When he realised what it was he shoved it straight back in. His heart was in his mouth – he'd traversed from intrigue to fear. He needed another sip of his lager.

The next thing he removed was a list of names. He read the title at the top of the sheet. 'VAT FRAUD.' On it were the names of many of the people that had been in trouble, some serious, through Gerrity's performance of the VAT free disabled cars scam some years before. Some had been arrested by the police, most had been sacked from their jobs, one had tried to commit suicide because of it and as a result of taking too many paracetamol, had ended up with serious kidney problems. Gerrity had managed to walk away under the radar and disappeared without any punishment. He'd actually 'grassed-up' a number of these people to divert attention and blame from himself. Gerrity slid the sheet back into the envelope and pulled out the next.

This was a list of sales managers and salesmen who had lost their jobs in the past due to being bribed by Gerrity. Once their jobs were gone, so was their use, so Gerrity had dropped them like hot potatoes, again trying to divert blame from himself. He took a sneaky look at the others, wondering what could be in their envelopes.

Next he pulled out one of the stencilled letters that he had sent to Dean Muxlowe from 'Myra'. He felt physically sick. The frown on his face had long since departed and a look of terror had taken over. Who could know all of this? Did the other two know that he was responsible? They obviously didn't know yet because they were still engrossed in their own little worlds. If they did, was it one of them who had had him battered or was it someone off one of the lists? Attached to the letter was a photograph of himself, lying battered at the bottom of a hedge in a farmer's field.

The final thing he removed from the pack was a letter – written using the stencil that was still in the envelope.

"Dear, Snakesbelly," it started. Who the fuck called him 'Snakesbelly'? "Thank you for attending tonight, I hope you like my little gifts.

"I wanted to give you something to reflect upon. An insight for you. Something to help you realise just what negative effect on people's lives you have had. People have lost their jobs, their marriages, their houses…all because of your greed. The VAT scam, the back-handers, and yes, I know that you are indeed 'Myra'. I know you said nothing when Dean Muxlowe was sent to prison for a year. Do you realise the harm that Paul Milford and Heather suffered? The fear that they felt? And all after you took the time to befriend them whilst driving the knives into their backs whilst they were not watching. Yes, Ernest Gerrity, you can indeed get lower than a snake's belly.

"Is there any wonder that you got beaten? Is there any wonder that you were left in a field near Matlock covered in mud, blood, sweat and piss, waiting for the ambulance? Yes, old chap, you'll never know who was responsible – too many candidates.

"How can Stella still be with you? All I can say is that you are a very lucky chap to have found your perfect partner, despite being such an arse. Either that or you've got a particularly big dick and can still use it.

"Ernest, there are questions that you will die not really knowing the answers to. I understand that you are now quite successful – you don't deserve it. I just hope that you can do good for the rest of time with us. I will be watching you, but I will not be contacting you.

"Be good, be careful, be lucky and you just might, as a result, be happy." The letter was not signed. He popped the letter back in the envelope. The others were just doing the same.

Paul Milford reached into his pack; the first thing that he drew out was a copy of an early letter he'd received from 'Myra'. Of course he'd seen it before; he'd even kept copies of the letters. But, who the fuck else would have a copy apart from the police? … 'Myra', himself? He looked up at Muxlowe who, of course, he knew was 'Myra' – he'd been convicted of it. Muxlowe had his head down in his own envelope.

Secondly Milford pulled out ten sheets of letter-headed business paper. All different, they had been stapled together. The front sheet was plain A4, and was headed 'Companies that Milford Park sent bust!' It was just that; the headed paper from companies, small operators, that had in the last few years gone into liquidation allegedly due to, or at least partly due to being unpaid by Milford

Park. Fairchild was ultimately the one to blame but he was dead now so Milford had to shoulder it. Anyway, Milford hadn't complained at the time when he was spending the money and was completely aware of where it was coming from and how it was being earned. Milford recognised many of the letterheads – it was only a small selection – the front sheet had a list of fifteen others.

The next thing to come out of the pack was a copy of the poster that had been plastered all over the village with Milford's personal details on, claiming that he was a paedophile. The one just before he handed over £35,000 to 'Myra' who was, apparently sat at the table with him at this very moment in time, but at the time it all happened was banged up in prison? Or was it the other one that sent it, the one that someone had implicated on the shiny white bonnet of his Land Rover? Fucking hell, this was starting to get confusing.

There was one sheet left in. It was an A4 sized letter written in stencil, Milford took it out. Oh, no – there was something else inside, something small that he'd nearly missed. He reached in to retrieve an old number 3 lottery scratch card. It had already been checked, it was not a winner.

Paul started to read the letter.

"Hello, ferret man." It began. His face flushed red with anger and fear at the anticipation of what he was about to read. It was obviously not going to be a friendly letter. He hated being likened to a ferret.

"I see that you have finally arrived at the level in life on which you belong. You never did deserve the nice house, big bank balance and prestige car. Oh, I hope that Land Rover scrubbed up OK; it would break my little heart if I thought I'd ruined such a fine vehicle.

"I know about the stolen lottery ticket, Paul. You stole all that money from a guy who really needed and deserved it. I know about the way Milford Park, your company, sent many other businesses under. You ruined many people, destroyed many marriages and lost many families their homes. Does that please you, Paul?

"I know about the £35,000 you paid 'Myra' but who is 'Myra'? You will probably never know. You think that you know, but you are wrong – you don't know the real 'Myra'. Why didn't you involve the police when you were asked for the £35k, Paul? Were you afraid they'd got the wrong man? Didn't you want to know the truth? Didn't you want true justice?

"You are an old man, Paul. Too old to be on a cold, wet building site laying bricks for a pittance. But at least you are no longer living a lie. No longer living off the dis-honest earnings of a morally corrupt company run, on your behalf, by a fucking crook, providing you with an over-inflated income, picked from the pockets of good honest tradesmen. I am glad Fairchild's dead and I have no sympathy for you and I hope my words have given you something to think about.

"As for Heather, I see she's fucked off and left you. Good for her. She was only with you for your money – now it's gone so has she.

"I'll be watching you, ferret man – stay in your ferret hole and live the rest of your insignificant little ferret life in peace and harmony with the rest of mankind." The letter was not signed. Paul gathered everything up and slid it back into the envelope. The others were just doing the same.

Dean Muxlowe didn't know what to expect in his pack. He was the last to get his open. The first thing that he pulled out was a letter to himself, from 'Myra'. It was a letter giving him instructions on how to blackmail Milford. Horrible memories flooded back, old feelings, the taste of bile as his stomach flipped and his heart raced. What did this mean? How was Gerrity involved? Was he the real

'Myra'? Was Milford an accomplice rather than the victim? He knew Milford and Gerrity knew each other. How well did they know each other?

The second sheet that he took out was a copy of one of the letters that he'd sent to Milford. Or rather it looked very much like a copy. Something was not quite right with it. Maybe it was a reproduction rather than a photocopy.

As he lifted the final A4 sheet from the pack he noticed a small card at the bottom of the envelope. It was a doctor's appointment card for Molly from June the previous year. What the fuck is this all about? Who could get hold of that?

The final sheet was a letter.

"Dear, Mr Muxlowe, you are nothing but a fucking stupid donkey. A fucking pack horse that everyone dumps their burden on and you, like a twat, willingly carry it for them up the steep hill.

"Why did you not tell the police about 'Myra', Dean? Why take the pill, Dean? Do you not realise the strain and pressure that you put Molly under whilst you were sitting in the joint with your own room, Freeview TV, three meals a day, no bills to pay, Dean. Your simple uncomplicated life, Dean. You didn't need to swallow it, Dean. Did you need a break? You selfish bastard, you left her all alone. She was in and out of the doctors all the time – sleeping pills and anti-depressants; you didn't know that did you? You don't know half of what she had to put up with. She nearly broke. She didn't tell you because she didn't want you to worry. She protected you out of loyalty and love." Dean then realised the significance of the appointment card. The letter went on.

"I hope that you've learned, donkey man. I hope you've got the message. Concentrate on the people that are important to you. Fuck the rest; let them sort their own problems out." Dean thought that this was a specific dig at how he'd let James Hunter-Browne walk all over him whilst he'd done all the work building and running MHB Finance. His frustrations he'd taken out on Molly with constant arguments and drinking. Whoever had written this letter knew a lot about his and Molly's lives. How did the other two fit in? The letter concluded.

"I'll be watching you closely, donkey. I will not tell the police who 'Myra' really is; I will let sleeping dogs lie. But if you start drifting again, you must expect a little nudge back onto the track. Let's call it a little carrot for the donkey, or I might even use a stick. Live long and prosper." The letter was not signed. Dean recognised the ending as a Vulcan farewell from the old Star Trek programs he used to watch as a kid. He put his pack back together and looked up, just as the others were doing the same.

The three stooges sat there looking at each other in silence. It was a strange situation. Nobody wanted to say anything, not knowing what the others knew or how they were all involved. Milford opened his mouth first. "What the fuck is all this about?"

"Your guess is as good as mine," answered Gerrity. "What does your letter say?"

"Nothing much," lied Milford. "Just some shit about Milford Park. What about yours?"

"Not a lot." Gerrity was fidgeting in his wheelchair; he did that when he was nervous, trying to hide something. "Just some beef about when I was a trader. Some arseholes obviously getting a bit upset about getting caught up in that old VAT scam for the disabled. What about you, Dean?"

"Just somebody bollocking me for getting sent to prison."

"What? How do you mean?" Milford was coming over all aggressive – obviously a nerve had been hit.

"Don't you talk to me like that you stupid looking idiot!" Muxlowe was trying to not be the donkey. Milford rose from his chair; Muxlowe did the same.

Gentlemen, gentlemen, please. Sit down, both of you." A small blonde Scottish woman had suddenly appeared next to the table. The three men stared at her.

"Molly? What the fuck are you doing here? I thought that you were at Rachel's." Dean was incredulous.

"I thought that you were with Eddie?" she replied smiling. There was a long silence. Molly continued. "No, I got a call from a mystery man to come and fetch you from here before eight-thirty p.m."

"Who?" asked Gerrity.

"A fucking mystery man, I said. If I knew who he was he wouldn't be a fucking mystery man, would he?" Gerrity shrank back into his wheelchair and looked away.

"Fair point," he mumbled.

"Come on," she grabbed Dean's shoulder. "We need to go. I got a taxi here – I'll drive you back." She turned and walked towards the door. George stood at the bar taking it all in. Molly turned to look at him. "Are you George?" She asked.

"Yes, duck," he replied.

"Well, George; firstly don't ever call me 'duck', and secondly I've been asked to give you this." She handed him a plain envelope with 'George' written on the front.

"Thank you," he took the envelope containing the £50 note. Molly and Dean left. "Another drink, gents… on me," he smiled as he finished opening the envelope to see the crisp reddish brown note.

"May as well," Gerrity looked at Milford. "You up for it, Paul?"

"I think I need it," replied Milford.

George brought them over. It would be the first of many. Gerrity sat on his envelope so that he wouldn't leave it unattended when he went for a piss. Milford shoved his down the back of his belt for the same reason. It was obvious to both that the envelopes held deep secrets.

There would be a lot of lies told that night, and there would remain many unanswered questions.

Molly took the keys off Dean and climbed into the driver's seat of their Subaru, as her mobile rang. "Hello." Dean got one half of the conversation as he put on his seat belt ready for the journey home.

"Yes, all OK."

"Stunned."

"Yes, I did."

"Yes, he is."

"Absolutely! I'll see you soon." Molly hung up and slid her phone into her bag on the back seat.

"Who was that?" asked Dean.

"Nobody," replied Molly.

"How do you mean 'nobody'? Who was it?" Dean looked irritated and angry, still confused about what had happened in the pub.

"Just fucking nobody, right! Now shut the fuck up as I need to concentrate." She turned to Dean; her face suddenly changed from angry and gave a huge warm smile. Then she gave Dean a little kiss on the lips.

"OK, then." He turned to face forward and Molly set off. He'd always be her donkey – do as you're told and follow that carrot. Nothing more was said.

Meanwhile, 350 miles north, somewhere in Fife, an old ex-copper sitting in a mobile seafood bar hung up his mobile phone. He had a smile on his face as he tucked in to his smoked trout and horseradish roll.

And finally…

Thanks for coming one and all
This past two years, it's been a blast
Many things we've all been through
Our lives have changed, and changed so fast

Snakesbelly, you can walk no more
Who stuck you in that chair?
Your past, it never goes away
There's always someone waiting there

Old donkey, will you ever learn?
To put the most important first
Discard the parasites of life
Or they'll put you in a hearse

Ferret, you stole a number three
Deprived a good man and his spouse
Now you're laying bricks all day
And coming home to empty house

Stella, you're one of life's true saints
You love your man through thick and thin
In this game of life you're playing
Against all odds, you're going to win

Molly, your man was sent away
You coped alone for all that time
I hope he's learnt his lesson well
To no more get involved with crime

And Heather, so you couldn't cope
It shows that you don't really care
The money went, big house, flash cars
You took your big fat arse elsewhere